ACID TEST

ACID TEST

A 'McCarthy Family' Mystery

Richard S. Wasley

iUniverse, Inc.

New York Lincoln Shanghai

Acid Test
A 'McCarthy Family' Mystery

iUniverse, Inc.

For information address:
iUniverse, Inc.
2021 Pine Lake Road, Suite 100
Lincoln, NE 68512
www.iuniverse.com

ISBN: 0-595-32982-9

This book is dedicated to;

My Mother who inspired me

My Daughter who helped me

And....

My wife...who believed in me

PROLOGUE

▼

Cambridge, Mass.
April 1968

Former Boston Homicide Detective Michael McCarthy, stopped in front of the seedy looking pizza/sub shop on Mass. Ave, in Cambridge's equally seedy looking, Central Square. He glanced at the likewise seedy reflection that stared back at him from the dirty steamed up window, of the almost deserted eatery. He wasn't crazy about what he saw in the reflection, but what the hell could he do about it? Thirty years of pounding a beat or manning a stakeout in all kinds of weather, had left his skin rubbed red and raw. Add to the list, a nose that had been smashed one too many times, while breaking up one too many bar fights.

That, along with a permanently pissed off expression, and you had, he smiled sadly to himself, the classic guy that, "you wouldn't want to meet in a dark alley."

"And speaking of alley's," he said to himself, "what I otta' do, is forget about getting another 'heartburn special' pizza, and just cut down the alley here over to Broadway and catch an Orange Line trolley car to home. Home," he thought bitterly, "yeah, as if you could call a roach infested third floor walk-up in Leachmere Square, home. Maybe, I should just move into my office," he mused. "Hell, even a one room detective agency office would be better than the shit hole I'm livin' in now. Besides," he thought, "at least the Harvard Square location has got a little class, and I could kinda' keep an eye on Mickey and Bronwyn."

He smiled as he thought about his two youngest kids.

Acid Test 2

Twenty-year-old Mickey was just like he'd been at that age. All full of piss and ready to take on anyone at the drop of at hat. "That's probably why they promoted him to Sergeant over in Vietnam." Michael senior shook his head as he remembered the row he and his middle son had after Mick had gotten kicked out of Harvard during his freshman year for fighting. In a fit of "McCarthy anger", 'Big Mike' had told his son, "if you like fightin' so damn much why don't you join the army?"

Mickey had.

That burst of temper had cost 'Big Mike' many sleepless nights, during 1966 when Mick joined up…along with the last cordial word that he'd ever gotten from his ex-wife.

He shook his head.

But now Mick was back. And in one piece, thank God. And he was even back at Harvard. And maybe he'd even become a lawyer like his older brother Frankie. And maybe…. "Yeah," he muttered to himself, "and maybe pigs would fly."

"But at least," he thought, continuing the dialog in his head, "if I do move into the office in Harvard Square, I could sorta' keep an eye on him and at the same time make sure that Bronwyn was ok too."

Bronwyn. And now he did actually smile, as he almost always did when he thought about his only daughter. By God, there was a beauty. Long dark hair that curled around her shoulders. Eyes as gray as the sky's over County Cork where the uncounted generations of McCarthy's had been born. And green as the mythical fields of Ireland in the stories that his own mother had told him in the small kitchen of the overcrowded triple-decker where he'd grown up in 'Southie' as a kid.

Now, he thought still with a tinge of disbelief, his beautiful and talented daughter was a freshman at Radcliffe College…friend and equal to the beautiful, talented and privileged daughters of the finest families of not just Boston and New England, but the entire country!

"How's that for dumb, Irish-mick, beat-cop from Southie," he laughed into the wet drizzle that had just started to blow through Central Square.

There was no answer and that was ok with Mike.

He turned towards the alley that would cut his walk to the trolley by half. Screw the pizza, he'd settle for a good shot of the Bushmills Irish Whiskey that was waiting for him back at the apartment.

Halfway down the dirty alley, he started to get that old, all too familiar itching feeling between his shoulder blades. Something wasn't right.

The wind blew a gust of drizzle and rancid pizza smell down the alley as a momentary shift in the dirty grey clouds covering the moon, allowed a sliver of light to trickle through and illuminated…something next to the overturned trash cans halfway down the dim, gloom shrouded, cut-through. The clouds came back again and scene was plunged back into darkness.

Mike pushed his hands back into the pockets of his raincoat and started towards the thin tunnel of light at the alley's end. And then…

Some leftover beat cop instinct caused him to pause just a half second before a beer bottle came whizzing past his head and shattered against the alley wall.

He whirled around in one smooth movement, flipping up the back of his suit coat. His hand reached for the butt of his snub nose .38 Smith and Wesson, that 30 years of habit would have placed, clipped to the back of his belt. Carefully placed with the gun's butt tilted towards his right hip, ready for a smooth, quick draw.

Except…It wasn't there!

"God damn!" he muttered, as he remembered a split second later, how that bastard Bannon, just this afternoon, had pulled his P.I. ticket.

It all flashed in front of his eyes. That former little schoolyard toady from St.

Bartholomew's, who Mike had helped and protected out of pity and neighborhood loyalty, had sucked his way up to become precinct captain.

And he had one brief, angry recollection of the newly made Cambridge Precinct Captain's smug, grinning face, as he'd swept McCarthy's holstered .38 across his desk and into a waiting drawer…before the second bottle hit him just below the left eye and shattered his cheek bone

CHAPTER 1

▼

Harvard University
April, 1968

"Therefore, would not one be correct in assuming that if a true existentialist in the model of Kant and Kierkegaard were to remain true to their own moral compass, then it must follow, that they would be equally morally opposed to an immoral war of aggression such as this current Vietnam conflict."

The professor paused to mop his profusely perspiring forehead with a purple and gold Paisley handkerchief (a gift from yet another admiring coed undergrad). His eyes gazed out over the sea of admiring young faces that packed the lecture hall just off the east end of the Harvard Yard quadrangle. They had all come to hear him speak, he thought with a self-satisfied smile, despite the unseasonable summer-like April weather that had sent the temperature inside the main venue of the much-heralded "Teach-in Against the War" soaring into the high 80s inside the room.

Stuffing the sopping wet handkerchief back into the pocket of his now almost unbearably hot tweed jacket, he surveyed the room of rapturously attentive upturned faces that were nodding their heads with murmurs of assent.

He beamed benevolently back at them until his swiveling gaze stopped at one face which was neither rapturously attentive nor even moderately interested. The professor's benign observance halted and the tolerant smile modified itself into a frown. The professor's eyes narrowed as they focused in on the young man slouched in a folding chair at the far side of the hall who was staring blankly out the window at the branches of a barely budding elm tree as they rustled in the warm wind.

"Do you not agree, Mr. McCarthy?" the professor called in his direction. "Or have you merely come to occupy space once again in another of your series of non-participatory classes, of your non-participatory, far too long, and unfortunately far too undistinguished, University career." There was a low murmur of potentially amused and partially embarrassed laughter from the lecture hall as the young man pulled his gaze away from the open window and focused it in on the professor.

The young man didn't say anything. He just stared with his blue and gray eyes back at the professor, with no expression at all. The hall fell still as the seconds ticked by and there was only the sound of chairs creaking and bodies shifting nervously. The professor seemed mesmerized, like a bird in front of a snake, as he looked into the young man's cold, old, hard eyes. He pulled out the damp handkerchief once again and ran it over the tip of his nose where a drop of sweat was about to join others on his lecture notes. Someone in the back of the hall coughed, and the spell was broken. The young man's icy, gray and blue eyes suddenly crinkled with mirth.

"Sorry, Professor Hibbert," he called back to the lectern at the front of the room, "I was just watching the squirrels gather nuts."

"Mr. McCarthy," the professor called back, his confidence returning, "Squirrels only gather nuts in the fall and in case you hadn't noticed," he paused for effect, "this is spring."

An appreciative titter filled the room. The young man pushed his long sandy, brown hair out of his eyes and grinned back. "Yeah, that's what I thought, too. I guess that's what makes 'em nuts."

CHAPTER 2

▼

Vietnam—1966—Somewhere
north of Firebase Bravo

The Colonel stopped short just at the southwest corner of the overgrown rice paddy. He said something to the lieutenant over his shoulder and the lieutenant pumped his arm up and down twice, signaling a halt. The non-coms relayed the message down the line with, "Hold up…Hey dickwad, get the wax out of your ears…I said hold up!"

Sergeant McCarthy (Mick when off duty) didn't yell back at his squad, he just repeated the signal with his right hand as he finished out his last step and stopped. He didn't have to look back to see if everyone had gotten the word. He knew they would. They had learned to watch him because they said he had almost E.S.P. when it came to sniffing out an ambush. So there was never any debate. When Sergeant "Mick" stopped, they all stopped.

"Okay, listen up," yelled the First Lieutenant from the head of the column, "the Colonel says we've got VC operating out of this area. That's why the local villagers are afraid to work these fields. They probably know that the VC have got them mined. So we're gonna' be proceeding in a single file. Mine sweeper and Demo Team take the point. Once they've gone through, make sure you step nowhere but in their footsteps. When we get to the eastern side of the rice paddy, regroup with your squad leaders. Squad leaders, line 'em up and then form up on the western perimeter of that village you can just about make out about three klicks from here. Questions? No? Okay ladies, let's move out, single file, and stay alert!"

Sergeant McCarthy watched the poor bastard with the minesweeper start tentatively across the southwest corner of the rice paddy, swinging the long arm of the sweeper in three-foot arcs back and forth in front of him. He was followed by two equally uncomfortable-looking 'Demo' men whose unpleasant, dangerous, and often short-lived job it was to disarm any mines the sweeper found, that it is if they didn't wind up getting their guts strewn all over the paddy.

As it came their turn for Mick's squad to step off, he said to the men listening behind him, "OK, guys, let's go and remember what the first Louie said, step in the footprints of the guy in front of you…that is, unless you don't plan doing anything with that dick of yours when you get home," and added almost to himself as the nervous laughter filtered down the line, "That is, if you get home."

Sergeant McCarthy's squad had finally reached the eastern edge of the rice paddy and were gratefully clambering up the side of the dirt track that would wind them around to the village when PFC Scagaliani, nicknamed Skaggs, whether for his last name or choice of women no one really knew, lost his grip on the tough but slippery long grass that he was using to pull himself up and out of the rice paddy with and slipped back into three-foot stagnant water with a loud, "Shit!" Which was followed by a much louder scream.

Everyone still in the rice paddy froze and some were just about to throw themselves down into the water to escape what they assumed was a now triggered land mine, but Mick knew that Skaggs' scream was not a scream of fear. It was a scream of pain.

"Skaggs," Mick said in what he hoped was his calmest voice, as he carefully made his way back to where PFC Scagaliani was now writhing in pain and screaming, "Ah shit, it hurts. Jesus Christ Mick, it hurts so much man. It really fuckin' hurts!"

"Pungee stick right?" Mick said in a low voice as he cautiously moved through the greenish, brown water and tried gently to lift Private Skaggs out of the spot in the water that had now been turned a murky, muddy, red.

"Oh, fuck. Son of a bitch, stop it, man…Shit, you're killing me. Oh Jesus!" he screamed and started thrashing the water with his hands, driving the 18-inch, needle-sharp bamboo pungee stick deeper through his combat-booted foot, making the murky water even redder.

"Smitty," Mick called to his mortar man and friend, "Shuck your gear and get down here and give me a hand."

"Sure, Mick," the Corporal said, dropping his pack and mortar tube on the dirt track and climbing down into the rice paddy and next to Mick.

"Here, hold his hands and arms," Mick said and then whispered as Smitty sidled past him. "Tight."

Smitty positioned himself behind the now feebly moaning Skaggs and took hold of his two arms while supporting his head with his chest. He nodded silently to Mick who bent down into the slimy water and, grabbing Skaggs' boot by the laces, gave up one quick upwards heave. Mick was almost thrown backwards into the rice paddy as the wounded PFC shrieked and kicked back with his good foot and then fell back limply into Smitty's arms.

"He's out cold," Mick said to Smitty, "Quick, let's get him up on the bank."

Mick and Smitty quickly passed the limp form to waiting hands on the rice paddy embankment and Private Scagaliani was laid out next to the dirt track where a medic was waiting who began quickly cutting off the bloodstained boot.

"Is it bad, Doc?" Sergeant McCarthy asked wiping the sweat, water and Skaggs' blood out of his eyes.

"Well," said the young blond medic from Ohio, "the pungee stick went right through his boot and out the top of his foot but that really isn't the big problem. The real nasty on this one is that the VC smear shit all over the sticks and even if they didn't, there's enough crap floating in that water to give him one hell of an infection. But," he added hopefully, "I'm gonna shoot him full of penicillin, so I think he'll have a fighting chance."

"Yeah, thanks, Doc," Mick said and smiled down at the white faced PFC. "Hey, Skaggs, you've got that golden ticket home, man. Hell, a couple of weeks from now you'll be banging every girl on the east side of Philly." Skaggs smiled back weakly as he was hoisted upon the stretcher to await the med-evac helicopter.

By now the rest of the column had made it up onto the dirt track and had formed up around their squad leaders in a semi-circle around the Colonel and the First Lieutenant who were squatting in the dirt drawing the village layout.

"OK," said the lieutenant," "listen up." The Colonel began to speak.

"Okay, men, here's the mission. It's got two major objectives: one, we know the VC are operating out of this area so part one is to surround this village so no one can get out and then move in quietly and clean out any VC and take them prisoners, if possible and if practical," he added. "And part two of the mission is the most important part. There is one very important person in this village who must be taken prisoner, alive, at all cost. Your noncoms are being passed a photo of him right now, so take a good look and study it well. I don't want any screw-ups on this. There'll be no shooting until we've got this guy. After that," the Colonel just shrugged his shoulders dismissively. "OK, any questions before we move out?"

"Yeah, Colonel," came the gravel voice of a big, beefy sergeant from Fox Company, "Just who the hell is this guy, sir? Ho Chi Min's brother-in-law?"

"Could be, Sgt.," the Colonel said as the laughter died away, "but all you need to know is that your mission is to bring him to me. Alive."

"Yes, sir," the sergeant grunted and then growled out, "Okay, you heard the Colonel. Let's mount up and move."

"One minute, Sgt.," the Colonel called as the men started struggling into their packs and hitching up ammo belts, "We've been on the march for five hours now and I've seen how you men are sweating out buckets, so HQ has given me a new kind of salt tablet to try out. It's supposed to be better at stopping water loss without making you feeling as thirsty. Take one as they come your way and pass them along."

Smitty looked at Mick and Mick just shrugged and popped the little white tablet into his mouth, swallowing it down with a swig from his canteen, but out of the corner of his eye he noticed Smitty palming his and slipping it into his flak jacket.

"What gives?" Mick asked as they formed up the squad into a column of twos and moved down the muddy dirt track to the village. "What, oh, the salt tablet?" Smitty looked over at Mick and shrugged, "they always give me the shits, man!" Mick laughed and shook his head.

CHAPTER 3

▼

Inman Square
Cambridge
April 1968

"Mickey," a soft female voice with more than just a hint of County Cork called from the top floor landing of the Inman Square triple-decker. Michael Prescott McCarthy looked up to the top of the stairwell and smiled.

"Hi, Bridge," he called back, pausing to fiddle with the chain of the big padlock that he always used to wrap through the front tire of his 750cc BSA motorcycle and loop around the railing of the sagging front porch.

"Hurry up, can't you," Bridget Connelly admonish him, "I've got the same buggery lawyer's office that's been calling for you all afternoon holding on the phone, for pity sake."

With a sigh, he gave up fiddling with the chain and started the long winding ascent up three flights of rickety stairs as the rundown heels of his cracked cowboy boots clattered on each stair tread.

"And by the by," Bridget said, arching her black eye brows at him as he drew even with the third floor landing, "They don't seem to know any Mickey McCarthy. It's a Mr. Michael Prescott they're wantin'. Now who do you suppose that could be?" she asked with a mischievous grin as she handed him the phone. Mick grinned back at her and tickled her in that 'guaranteed-to-make-her-jump-a mile' spot, just below her third rib, catching the outstretched phone just as she squealed, dropped it, and tried to hit him all at the same time.

"McCarthy here," he barked while simultaneously dodging, just barely, one of Bridget's well-aimed kicks at his rapidly retreating backside.

"Please hold for Mr. Prescott," came a nasal, clipped voice on the other end of the line. Mick rolled his eyes and winked at the now hysterically laughing

Bridget. Then a low, perfectly modulated and crisply professional voice, picked up and said, "Franklin Prescott, may I help you?"

"Hey, Frankie, Mick McCarthy here, and you called me, remember?"

"Yes, I remember," came the cold and well-modulated tone over the old, early 50's vintage phone's tinny little speaker. "I also remember, Michael," he paused to emphasize the name, "that it's been quite some time since anyone in your family has heard from you."

"So?"

"So, did you remember that your mother is going to be celebrating her fifty-fifth birthday next week?"

"Cool," Mick replied.

There was a pause on the other end of the line and then the voice resumed. "So we'll expect you at the Brattle Street house at 8 pm next Saturday."

"Groovy. Like, far out, man" Mick answered. He knew how much his straight-laced, corporate lawyer, older brother hated everything to do with 'hippies' and the free-wheeling youth culture around Harvard Square, so Mick never lost an opportunity to tease him with the silly college catch phrases. He could almost hear Frankie grinding his teeth and he grinned up at Bridget who was now hugging her elbows in a futile attempt to stop the hysterical giggles from becoming gasping laughter.

"Michael," came the disgusted and weary voice over the phone, "Why don't you grow up and stop acting like some hippie adolescent."

"Because I *am* a hippie adolescent!" Mick answered, making a clown face at the now laughing and hiccupping Bridget, while he arched his eyebrows up as high as they would go and crossed his eyes at the same time.

"Oh sweet Jesus, stop it will ya'", Bridget managed to gasp, her Cork accent becoming more pronounced as she began to giggle uncontrollably, "Yer gonna' make me pee me knickers, ya' horrible man."

Mick cradled the receiver between his left cheek and shoulder as he made wide, exaggerated clapping motions with both hands while Bridget swatted ineffectually at him as tears of laughter trickled out of her eyes.

"Well, are you quite finished being an immature idiot?" came the now icy voice of Franklin. He was born Frances McCarthy Prescott, eldest son of the unlikely and disastrous union of Felicity Parker Prescott and Michael Francis McCarthy, and the youngest vice president of Hayward, Elliott & Delbert; he took himself quite seriously. He continued, "you just might be interested to note that the other half of your parents that you never see is currently in the emergency room at Mount Auburn Hospital undergoing surgery for a ruptured spleen and broken cheekbone."

Mick stopped grinning as if some one had thrown a switch. "Shit," he said, now serious, "what has the old man gone and done now?"

"Chased one too many thugs down one too many alleys, I should imagine," responded the clipped voice on the other end of the line.

"Is it serious?" asked Mick quietly.

"I don't know," his brother answered. "I just found out and was hoping that you could get down there and tell me. You're closer," he added.

"Yeah, sure, OK," Mick said, "I'll leave right now. I haven't even locked up the bike and with it traffic will be no problem. So I should be down there in 10 to 15 minutes and I'll call you back in, say, an hour? Will you be in your office?

"Yes, I have a meeting with a new client at 3 pm, but I'll tell Margaret to interrupt me."

"Great," Mick answered and then added, "and Frankie, tell the 'Wicked Witch of the West' not to put me on hold, OK? I'm gonna' be calling from a pay phone and my current net worth only adds up to, let us see…oh, two dimes and three nickels."

*   *   *   *

"Can you give me a ride, Luv?" Bridget asked from the porch of the triple-decker. "Or maybe I should just bugger off work and come with you to see yer Da'."

"Na," Mick said as he opened the petcock to the motorcycle's gas tank,

"I'll be lucky if he doesn't go into cardiac arrest just from seeing me show up, let alone a beautiful lass from County Cork. Hell, darlin'; one glimpse of you would probably push him right over the edge. I know it sure does me," he grinned and added, "especially in that outfit."

"Get away wi' ya," she scoffed, but he could tell she was secretly pleased all the same.

"Climb on" he said as he pushed his right boot heel down on the BSA's kick-start for the third time. This time it caught and he slowly feathered the hand grip on the throttle until the cylinders warmed up and the sound of the engine through the twin pipes smoothed out. "Hop on, Bridge," Mick said as he pushed the bike off its kickstand, "and I think I'm gonna' have to buy you a set of 'Biker Leathers' or you're gonna' have to start riding side saddle."

"Oh, and why it is that, Mr. McCarthy?" Bridget said, arching her eyebrows again.

"Ahh, because," Mick said looking back at her and as she wrapped her arms around his waist and pressed her left cheek against his denim-jacketed back, "every horny guy from Inman Square to Mount Auburn street is gonna' be looking up that sexy little black dress!"

"Stop it," she said, freeing one hand from his waist and punching him lightly in the back.

"Hey, you know it's true," Mick shouted over the roar of the engine. "You look like one of those Playboy models in that thing."

"I do not!" she yelled, then added, "and how do you know what one of them Playboy models look like, ye' dirty old man!"

"What are you talking about," he grinned back at her, "what would I need with Playboy models with you around?"

She mumbled something like "umph" but pressed her cheek tighter against his back.

"But you gotta' admit, Babe," he called back to her as he downshifted opposite the Harvard Co-Op and leaned the bike right towards Mount Auburn Street, "that get-up kinda' looks like one of those 'French Maid' outfits in those magazines like Playboy that, of course, I don't read," he added laughing into the wind.

"It does not!" she shouted back. "It is a perfectly respectable waitress uniform for a poor workin' girl from County Cork who may have an academic scholarship to Radcliffe College, but doesn't have rich, blue-blood, Protestant parents to pay her room and board."

Mick jammed his boot down on the foot brake and pumped the hand brake at the same time, sending the BSA into a controlled skid and coming to rest next to an enormous old elm tree on the west side of Harvard Square. Putting both legs down on the pavement and turning back to look at her he said, "That was a really shitty thing to say, Bridge, you know I've never taken a friggin' dime from the Prescotts since I got kicked out of Harvard and went to 'Nam.

"I'm sorry, Mick," Bridget said in a small voice barely audible over the rumble of the idling engine. "You're right. I was being a little witch 'cause I hate playing serving girl to all of those snotty, condescending professors and their blond, milk and water, WASP-y wives."

"So quit," Mick said, "we 'otta get something out of that pissy little check the government sends me every month for..." he let his voice trailed off.

"No," Bridget replied, "You know it is part of the terms of my scholarship. Besides, I think it gives those 'Proddy' bastards a thrill to see a little Irish serving wench' waitin' their tables."

"Whoa," Mick commented sarcastically, "and I thought I was bitter."

"Sorry again," she mumbled. "I must be gettin' me period."

"Yeah, well I know all about that," Mick said as he gunned the bike back into traffic. "I think I've been on the rag most of my life, too".

"You're bloody impossible!" she yelled, hitting his back again as she re-gripped his waist.

$$* \qquad * \qquad * \qquad *$$

"I'll drop you off up near Fresh Pond and then loop around back to the hospital." Mick called back to her.

"No, Mick," she shouted into the back of his jacket. "You need to get to the hospital and see how your Da' is doing. Just let me off in front and I can take the bus right up to Fresh Pond. And, Jesus Mick, look out!"

Mick swiveled his head back to the street just in time to see a big 1956 Buick Roadmaster with a little white haired old lady peering over the steering wheel cross the center dividing line and head straight towards him.

"Sh—i-tt!" he screamed and as the big chrome grille of the Buick filled his field of vision.

He stamped his right foot down on the foot brake and gunned the throttle with his right hand, sending the bike desperately fishtailing between two parked cars and a newly flowered forsythia bush and into one of the cement and green 2x4 Bus Stop benches in front of the hospital.

A split second before the skidding cycle struck the bench, Mick stuck out his right boot and pushed the still moving bike away to the left and then locked up the foot and hand brake. He heard Bridget scream as the bike slid out from under him, and as the still spinning back wheel chewed up the thin grass behind the bench, he reached around with his left hand and pulled Bridget over his right shoulder and on top of him. A moment later she was gone and he and centrifugal force continued the cycle into a low scraggly hedge at the east end of the hospital.

Seconds or minutes later Mick was aware that his left hand was caught on something and there was a roaring in his ears. It was the engine. The throttle was stuck opened. He couldn't reach it. His right hand was tangled in his jacket, his left hand was pinned under his body, and the bike was pinning him to the spring-soft ground like a bug in an entomologist's display. Bridget. Where was Bridge?

"Bridget!" he called. "Babe, answer me. Where are you, are you OK?"

For a second there was nothing, and then he heard, "Mick, Mick I'm OK...I think.,Oh sweet mercy darlin' what about you?" And her face came into focus over his left shoulder. "Are you OK? Oh bleedin' hell, Mick can you move? I can't get the damn bike offa' you."

"It's OK, Bridge. I think I'm OK, I'm just pinned. Get some help. The hospital's just on the other side of the courtyard."

Bridget started to get up off her knees and then stopped short with horror and said in a terrified voice, "God all mighty Mick, I smell something burnin'. Oh merciful heaven Mick, your leg."

"What?" Shock and adrenaline were wearing off and all of a sudden Mick was aware of a terrible pain in his left leg that was pinned under the 500 lb. machine. Son of a bitch! The exhaust pipe was burning right through his dungarees and into his leg.

"Ah-h-hh, shit!" he hissed, drawing in his breath in a single pain-filled gasp and tried to pull his leg out, which only succeeded in dragging his boot down to expose a new spot on his calf for the stove-hot pipe to burn. "God damn!" he screamed as he tried to push the bike off with his right foot, but it was no use. His left leg was pinned too high and he couldn't get the leverage with his right.

He was aware of Bridget crying, pulling at his jacket and pushing ineffectually at the big motorcycle. The pain was making him nauseous and he felt like he was going to pass out or throw up or both.

"Bridge," he gasped from between clenched teeth, "get help. The hospital. Run...run." Then the pain washed over him like a thick red blanket and the world seemed to get frayed around the edges. Shit, he was passing out. "Got to get out from under this before...before..." He smelled something burning and he knew it was him.

The pain came next, a hundred times worse than before, and he screamed and kicked and kicked and kicked at the dead weight bike with his right foot. He kicked and kicked with a frenzied desperation but he was getting weaker and the pain was getting worse. As he was going to pass out again and gave one last kick and, miraculously, he felt the bike move. Then it was off him and he was free and hands were lifting him, putting him on to something soft that had wheels and was rolling. He looked up, puzzled and saw Bridget's sweet, little white face looking at him. She had tears streaming down her pale cheeks.

She grabbed his hand like an anchor cable and whispered, "Don't worry, dar-lin', you're gonna' be all right."

He tried to answer but nothing came out. The world went mushy around the edges. And then, nothing.

CHAPTER 4

▼

There was an angel. She was dressed in white robes all shimmering with silver and gold and diamonds. She was floating in a beautiful soft golden haze.

Mick looked up at her with pain filled eyes and she looked back at him.

"I, I hurt…So goddamn much. Oh, Sweet Jesus make it stop," he said from between pain clenched teeth.

"I know," the beautiful figure said. "I know everything, Michael. Everything."

"Ah-h, Mother Mary, it hurts. I'm sorry, I'm so sorry."

"I know you are, Michael," the apparition said. As the tears rolled down Michael's face, the achingly beautiful, impossibly spiritual, heavenly ethereal Angel began to weep. The tears poured down her cheeks and they were silver and gold just like her body.

"Oh, God," Michael sobbed, "please, please don't cry."

"Michael," the angel answered, "I weep for you. For what you were and what you did. But most of all for what you could become if you wanted to."

"What do you mean?" He cried, "What are you talking about? What can I do? What can I be, now, after that? Answer me…answer me. Please!"

He looked up again. She was so beautiful. So kind. So sweet. So forgiving, just like the angels he'd drawn every Sunday in the car coming back from 9 a.m. Mass in Southie with his father. He remembered how 'Big Mike' had driven him, stone-faced, the seven miles between 'Our Lady of the Sacred Heart' on D Street, and the First Parish Congregational Church of Cambridge where Felice (Felicity Parker Prescott), his mother, was waiting. She would sit impatiently on the front steps of the white-steepled, 200 year-old clapboard descendant of the Puritan church.

"Here he is," his father would grunt.

"Thank you, Michael," his mother would answer, barely looking in his father's direction. "I appreciate your being prompt." And she would turn her back to his Dad, but shone her beaming, loving face down on his. She was so pretty, all velvet and lavender and smelling of flowers and perfume. Just like one of the angels he drew in the back seat of his father's car. So, so pretty and sweet, and loving. Just like the angel.

He looked up again and through the pain he saw that the angel was still there. She looked just like his mother, just as sweet and loving like he'd always wanted to believe she was. And so sad like she really was.

The angel kept saying, "I know Michael, I know everything and I'm so, so sorry." And she started to cry again. Angel tears made of silver and gold and diamonds.

Now Michael was crying along with the angel. "I'm sorry, too. I'm so, so sorry. I never meant to…do you think I wanted that? I'm not like that. Do you think I could ever be like that? Do you?"

Mick and the Angel cried together. The silver and gold and diamond tears mixed with his own bloody, sweaty tears and Mick looked up at her and said,

"When will it stop?"

Her silver and gold and diamond tears turned to rubies, crystal red rubies. Now the angel looked down at him with a face so sad. So sad for him, for everything, and the blood red ruby tears became redder and redder and they ran down her beautiful angelic face and left red runnels on her cheeks like a bright red blood. The angel was crying blood. She wept blood. Wept blood as her face changed. The pale white faced changed and became a mixture of copper and gold. Her round blue eyes became brown and elongated little cat's eyes and the soft wavy golden hair became straight and jet black and still she wept. Harder and harder. Now she was screaming right along with Mick, "No, no, no!" and the bloody tears kept dripping from her eyes and running down her cheeks. All Mick could hear was the sound of her voice and her screams inside of his head, screaming and screaming over and over and over again.

"No, No. No!"

CHAPTER 5

▼

Vietnam—June 14,1966—A Village somewhere north of Firebase Bravo

Sergeant McCarthy put two fingers to his lips for silence and then motioned back to his squad, "Two men up ahead, probably VC pickets." He made the movement of going to either side of them, pulled out his double-edged Fairbairn-Sykes combat dagger and made a throat-cutting motion.

Privates Bell and Lubosky nodded back and moved out and around the two sentries. A few minutes later they came silently back and Lubosky reported with a big, bared-teeth grin, "All set, Sarge." Mick just nodded and motioned them forward.

Suddenly, there was a single shot from an old model 1911 Army issue Colt .45, the colonel's gun. Two hundred men stood up and came out of the jungle surrounding the village, closing in with a ragged line that contracted toward the beaten earth center of the village. Two or three obvious VCs darted out from the flimsy huts and tried to dodge through the tightening line but were brought down by thrown knives and rifle butts.

"Easy does it!" Mick called. "Keep your eye out for the 'Big Magoo'," as they had named the mysterious objective of the mission. They closed up on the center of the village and burst into each hut, M-16s at hip level and selectors on full automatic but fingers on the guard rather than the trigger. In each hut, however, all they saw were terrified dark eyes staring back at them. Mick smiled back at one woman's trembling, lined face as she clutched her young teenage daughter and a quietly crying three year-old.

"Hey, Mama," Mick said, "No worries, OK? We're not gonna' hurt you, Ok?" But the terrified expression never changed and Mick backed out of the hut.

He heard a commotion coming from the village square and moved towards it. The colonel and lieutenant were squatted down in front of a Vietnamese prisoner, who was sitting cross-legged on the ground with his hands tied behind his back. The colonel said something to the prisoner in halting Vietnamese and the prisoner responded in French. The colonel smiled and said, "tres bien." He smiled back at the lieutenant, who grinned back in return, and got up, brushing off his pant legs. He turned around to the assembled soldiers and called out, "Good job, men! Well done! A perfect operation. No shots fired and we've got our man," and added, "thanks to Sgt. Walzac, who I would not be surprised to hear just might be in line for a Silver Star!"

There were a few claps and, "Way to go, Sarge," from the troops.

"Okay, lieutenant, would you take the 'prisoner'" (he smiled again)

"to the rear while I give a few last minute 'suggestions' to the men?"

"There's a strange choice of words?" Mick thought idly, "Since when do colonels 'suggest' anything?"

"Okay, men" the colonel was calling, "at ease."

The men relaxed and looked towards the colonel. "You've all done a fine job today and I'm proud of each and every one of you. I know it's been almost eight hours since you've had any hot chow, so while I accompany the lieutenant and our prisoner back to the base, why don't you fall out and grab some rest and a hot food?" With that he stood up to go but then he turned back and added, "However, I think that there are still some VC in this village, so I want you all to be careful. Very, very careful. Keep your pieces ready and on full automatic and if you even think you see a VC...well, you boys know what to do, right?"

"Yes, sir!" came the crashing answer in unison from twohundred throats. Mick almost startled himself with how loud he'd yelled.

Then the colonel was gone and for a moment the men just stood there as if they didn't know what to do. They slowly drifted into little groups and started cook fires for food. There was very little talking. Everyone seemed very subdued, Mick thought.

Suddenly, there was a noise and movement from one of the huts. What looked like an old man in dirty white pants crawled out and smiled hesitantly. The big, burly Sgt Walzac started to smile back, but his smile changed to a frown and he suddenly snarled, "VC!" and raised his M-16 and emptied the full clip into the old man's body.

"Wait," cried Mick. "Walzac, what the fuck are you doing?" But as Mick looked back towards the old man he suddenly realized that the writhing body in front of him was not clad in dirty white pants but in VC black pajamas and he held an AK-47 in his hands. Suddenly there were other VC emerging from the huts all clad in black VC pajamas and all clutching AK-47's. Christ, they were surrounded.

"Open fire," he yelled, "Kill the VC motherfuckers before they kill us!" and the Square erupted as the 5.56mm M-16 slugs tore through huts and bodies. Mick fired blindly, head swiveling madly back and forth as he ran through the village.

Suddenly there appeared at the door of a hut, the old woman and her kids.

Three frightened faces, but when he looked again they weren't kids at all. They were fuckin' VC and they were just about to open up on him! Mick slapped a new thirty round clip in place, slid back the bolt, and pulled the trigger as the world turned red around him.

*　　　*　　　*　　　*

"No, no, no! Oh shit. Please, can't you just make it stop? Stop, please stop." His words trailed off into an incoherent mumble. "Just…make it…stop," and in a barely audible whisper at the end he said again, "please."

Then the angel heard him, and she came back. She took his face, his agony-filled face scorched by napalm and the sun, in her hands and kissed his eyelids and said, "Yes, I'll make it stop. It's all over. It's all better. Yes, please come back. It's all over now and I'm here and I want you to come back."

"Mick, Mick please. Come back to me."

Mick opened his eyes and looked up at the angel. Her face shimmered and wavered around the edges and settled into a beautiful tiny, white, elfin face with high cheekbones and green eyes framed by soft, feathery, jet-black hair.

"Hey, Mick," Bridget whispered.

"Hi, Bridge," he smiled as her wet, green eyes found and held his.

CHAPTER 6

▼

Mount Auburn Hospital
Cambridge Mass
April 1968

"So what the hell happened to you," Michael McCarthy (Big Mike) said to his youngest son by way of greeting.

"Glad to see you, too, Pop," Mick answered sarcastically, getting nothing but one raised eyebrow and a snort for his trouble.

"You feelin' OK, Dad?" Mick said, ignoring the question.

"I asked you first, hot shot," 'Big Mike' responded grimacing as the pain shot up through his taped and plastered cheekbone.

Mick just shrugged and then gritted his teeth as a pain shot through his own heavily bandaged left leg and his fractured left elbow. He looked back at the bigger, stouter and, if possible, more banged up and bruised foreshadow of his future self. He smiled up at his washed-out and wavy reflection in the dark gray eyes and said "Yeah, well I was kinda' stuck in a deep crap for a while but," and he put his one good arm around Bridget's little-girl waist and pulled her close, "but I think it's gonna' be OK."

*   *   *   *

Later, when the little Belmont High candy striper had delivered the partially coagulated and mostly inedible, industrial strength hospital Jell-O and rice pudding, Mick leaned back in the steel and the vinyl hospital chair and said,

"Okay, Pop, true confession time. I'll tell you mine if you tell me yours." They locked eyes for a split second and then said in unison, "You go first."

Bridget leaned over the back of Mick's chair and tried not to smile as she watched big bull dog and little bull dog try to stare each other down and finally break out into big grins. "Ok, Pop, you got me," Mick said, "I'll go first."

A half hour later he finished, with Bridget filling in the gaps of the last two hours when he'd been more unconscious than with it. Mick drew a deep breath and finished up with, "So that's it, Pop. At least, all I can remember until I woke up and saw this sweet, young colleen looking down at me," he added with a grin and surreptitious squeeze of Brigitte's tight little rump.

She gently removed his hand, looking for a place to whack him that wasn't bruised or bandaged, but gave it up, deciding suddenly that she was glad there still was some place on him left to whack. She smiled down at him, still standing behind him, and when she looked up she realized that Big Mike was grinning back at her with that same quirky, lopsided grin he had obviously bequeathed to his son. She thought, "What a flamin' fool Mrs. Felicity Parker Prescott McCarthy must of been for leavin' this pair."

"OK, Pop, no more stalling, it's your turn," said Mick as he slipped the second empty Carling Black Label Beer can into the tiny white plastic wastebasket next to Big Mike's hospital bed.

Bridget shook her head and said, "Yer both a pair of wicked Spalpeens fer makin' me go out and gettin' me to smuggle them rancid, dishwater American excuse fer beer into your hospital beds. God forgive me!"

Mick smiled back up at her where she perched on the left arm of the hospital chair he slouched in while he swallowed the last of the codeine painkillers and washed it down with it the remnants of his third Black Label.

"Brewed on the shores of friggin' Lake Cochituate." he belched and was rewarded with a sharp smack on the top of his head from Bridget.

"Owww. Damn it, babe. I am already like the proverbial penguin in a blender. You know, black and white and red all over!" he moaned piteously rolling his eyes.

"Oh, all right, ya' big baby, there," she said kissing him on the top of the head, "All better now."

"Just make it a little lower," he said with another grin, "and you've got a deal. Ok, OK," Mick added hastily and as Bridget raised her tiny but very sharp fist (he knew). "I surrender, King's X, I'll be a good boy, at least I'll try," he whispered and nuzzled her shoulder.

She sighed, smiled and shook her head as she smoothed the unruly hair from the back of his neck and gently pushed it out of his eyes as he settled back into the vinyl chair cushion and said, "Ok Pop. Who did you piss off this time?"

CHAPTER 7

▼

Boston
September 24th, 1937

Sgt. Michael Francis McCarthy felt good. Damn good! As his uncles and brothers and pals on D Street in Southie liked to remind him, it wasn't every day that a big, dumb 'mick' beat cop made detective grade. Well, goddamn it, it was something to be proud of. Something to celebrate, and by sweet St. Michael, his patron saint, they were going to celebrate tonight at Callaghan's. Hell, even Father Finneran had said it was a toss-up. He'd either wind up going to jail, or putting the rest of his friends there.

Well, he hadn't done either, although sometimes he did have to manage to be facing the other way when the boys from the old neighborhood got out of line, as long as it wasn't too far out of line.

Yes, he was really feeling good, and he even paused in front of the window of S.S. Pierce on Tremont Street and surreptitiously flipped open the jacket of his heavy wool suit coat to reveal the gold detective shield inside.

He grinned back at his reflection in the store window and winked, "Not bad, McCarthy. Not bad at all for a 'dumb bog trotter', as Mrs. Wentworth, his third grade teacher had called him when he got expelled for fighting...again. Well his parents had sent him off to St. Bartholomew's and the Brothers had sure beat some sense into him.

"Hell," he thought to himself and stopped grinning. It had probably taken all of Ma's sewing money that she made stitching slipcovers for rich ladies' sofas and chairs upstairs at Peck & Pecks' at night.

"Damn" he said to himself as he felt a sting at the corner of his eye, "I'm gonna' go see her tonight. I'll take her some of those English taffies from Bonwit Teller that she likes so much, and—"

"I said, no. Please leave me alone."

Mike heard a small breathy voice speaking in perfectly enunciated English, the kind you never heard on D Street, followed up by a now frightened, "I said stop. Please, don't!"

Mike turned slightly to his right so he could catch the reflection in the pane of glass that canted at a 45 degree angle out to lower Tremont Street and saw reflected a slight, wispy blond vision wrapped in a full-length red fox fur coat. A white cashmere scarf draped around a long aristocratic neck which supported a finely chiseled face with a pair of the bluest eyes he'd ever seen.

In that one moment he felt absolutely and hopelessly in love. But in the next moment he grabbed himself right back to Earth because this vision in red fox and white cashmere was being pulled into the darkened doorway of a shuttered luggage store by a weasel thin, pock-faced punk and his grinning fat, greasy friend.

Now the girl was becoming truly terrified as what had started out as a bored harassment was turning down that road that his old training sergeant at the academy had referred to as "a fate worse than death for a good girl."

Well, this sure as hell was a good girl. And as a matter of fact, probably the 'goodest' girl Mike had ever seen. He was bloody dammed if these two pieces of crud were gonna' put their slimy, greasy hands all over her.

He drew in a breath and felt behind his new suit coat where the butt of his brand new, department-issued .38 Police Special waited in his holster. "Not yet," he thought. "Let's try a little 'sweet reason' with them first," and instead his hand closed on the thick leather of a lead birdshot filled sap. Twelve ounces of bone-crushing stopping power. Six inches long with a strap that he looped around his wrist.

He took a half dozen seemingly casual looking steps towards the recessed entrance to the luggage store. With a flash of inspiration he gave two more lurching steps and straggled drunkenly into the doorway, banging into the fat guy with an "Oops, sorry. Sorry old buddy, pal of mine," in his best drunk imitation.

"Hey, watch it, Mac!" the skinny guy yelled.

"Yeah, sorry. Sorry I said. Ah, what ya' got there?" he asked in what he hoped was his most convincing drunken leer.

"A little 'rich bitch' who didn't want to be nice when all we wanted to do was to be nice and friendly and buy her a cuppa' coffee in Schrafts. So now, she's gonna' have to be nice. Real nice," Weasel Face said licking his lower lip and the fat one snorted and wiped the spittle off his mouth with the back of his hand.

The girl was now white-faced and shaking, like a rabbit in front of two junk-yard dogs. "Hey, Boyos," Mike said throwing his left arm companionably around the shoulders of the fat grinning thug.

"Fuck off!" snarled Weasel Face. "This one's ours. Go find your own, cause we're gonna'—Owwww!" This last word was delivered as Mike's size 11 thick, black shoes slammed into his balls and sent him crashing back against the luggage store door.

"Huh?" said the fat one as Mike's companionable arm around his neck turned into a head lock and he smashed the shot-weighted leather sap into his stupidly grinning face, shattering his nose like a ripe pumpkin.

"Oh, Jesus. O' mother of Christ. Son of a bitch, you broke my fuckin' nose, you bastard!" Blood streamed through his fat fingers as he staggered out of the doorway and down the street, both hands cupping his spurting nose.

"OK, fucker," came a snarl from the dark corner of the doorway. "You and this bitch are dead meat!"

Mike turned slowly back towards the doorway and saw Weasel Face with one arm around the white-faced blonds' neck and the other hand clutching a slender, Italian-made stiletto with a five-inch, spring-loaded blade pressed under her jaw, just where one blue-white vein pulsed with arterial blood.

"Back away, you piece of shit, or 'Miss White Face' here is gonna' get a big new red mouth right in the middle of her throat."

Mike looked at the knife and the girl's pleading eyes. He tried to reassure her with his. "Okay, okay, no trouble. I'm going," he said.

"Drop the sap," Weasel Face said. Mike threw the lead-shot leather down.

"Now empty your pockets," he snarled, thin mustache twitching.

"OK, Hey, you got it," Mike said backing up a step.

"Is that everything?" Weasel Face barked. "No money belt?" Mike quickly looked down towards his belt.

"Get it off, and quick, or…" he sneered and pushed the needle sharp stiletto a millimeter deeper into the alabaster white neck as two tiny twin tears of pain and fear ran down the girl's perfect pale white cheeks.

"Whoa, whoa, easy friend. Here it is," Mike said slowly as he undid the belt, pulling it from left to right through the fingers of his right hand until it came in contact with the butt of his .38 snub nose revolver. In one smooth movement, he drew the revolver, thumbed back the hammer and shot Weasel Face straight through the left kneecap.

Michael Francis McCarthy and Felicity Parker Prescott were married six months later.

CHAPTER 8

▼

Mount Auburn Hospital
Cambridge Mass

"Great story, Pop, and I love it every time I hear it," Mick turned and grinning, whispered to Bridget, "Which probably makes an even a hundred times by now," and was rewarded by another whack on his head to which he gave a loud, theatrical "Yow!"

"Hey, Bridge, lay off will you. I'm only two hours out of intensive care, for Christ sakes!"

"Well, that's what you get for being disrespectful of your Da'. And Lord help you, Mick McCarthy, if you ever take that tone with me own Da'." Then as she suddenly realized the implications of her statement, she blushed and looked down at the cracked linoleum tiles of the hospital floor.

Big Mike looked at Bridget and then back at his youngest son who now seemed to be studiously engaged in counting the number of holes in the ceiling panels of Mike's hospital room. Mike looked first at Bridget and then his son, and although his taped and plastered-up face still hurt like hell, he smiled.

After the Belmont High Candy Striper had cleared away the remnants of the left over Jell-O and custard from the McCarthy Junior and Senior's barely touched trays, Mick launched back into the question with, "Okay Pop. Well, thanks for the story and crappy Jell-O," which brought a "tish, tish" from the Candy Striper and a glare from Bridget, "But my question still stands, who did you piss off this time?"

＊   ＊   ＊   ＊

"Get me that pillow, Mick," Big Mike said pointing over to the small, pressed cardboard wardrobe.

"Huh, what Pop?" Mick said and as he looked up from Bridget's elbow which he had been contentedly nuzzling for the past five minutes.

"I said bring me the damn pillow, ya' fuckin' moron," Mike snapped, and then looking up at Bridget, looking back at him with a mother-like disapproval, blushed beet red and mumbled, "Sorry, sorry darlin'. It's them pills, they're makin' me wacko. But no excuses, yer' a nice girl Bridget and my Mickey's a lucky little bastard to—Sorry, sorry again, to, to...Have ya'."

He blushed again and then glared at his son. "And I hope you know that you bloody, sweet idiot!"

Mick didn't say anything for a minute but just squeezed Bridget's leg where it brushed against his shoulder in the formica and vinyl chair arm that she perched on. He finally responded simply, "Yeah, Pop. I know."

"So now in answer to your question," Big Mike said, swallowing his Percoset with a grimace and a swig of overly sweet hospital Kool Aid, "as to 'who I pissed off this time', the proper answer would be, who haven't I pissed off over the last thirty years between Cambridge and Station B?"

Both Mick and Bridget smiled, and Big Mike's angry, red bulldog face relaxed into something approaching a lopsided smile, or it would have been if the white hospital tape and sticking plaster had permitted it.

"Well, do you remember the little weasel-faced bastard with the mustache that I kneecaped back in 1937?" Big Mike asked as he settled back into the lumpy hospital pillows. Bridget nodded and Mick said nothing.

"Well," Mike continued, "It turns out that this little prick, sorry darlin'," he winked at Bridget "whose name was Dennis Shaughnessy, was the first cousin of none other than my dear friend and future boss (he spat the word), Patrick Bannon!"

"Whew," Mick whistled, "so that's why he's been crawling up your butt for the past two years!"

"Ya' catch on quick, Mickey," Big Mike snapped bitterly.

"Is that why he pulled your P.I. license, Pop?"

"Yeah," Big Mike concurred morosely and added, "but that's not what put me in this hospital bed."

Mick raised his eyebrows quizzically as his father said, "That miserable little piss-ant pulled my ticket and confiscated my piece today in the Cambridge precinct house!"

"Jesus, Pop," Mick commented, "You must feel naked without your old pal 'Mr. .38 Special'."

"Well, let me put it this way; do you think it's a fuckin', sorry again Bridget darlin', coincidence that ten minutes after that bastard Bannon takes my piece, not more than three blocks from his goddamn office, I get jumped by two punks and left for dead in that Central Square alley?" Big Mike stopped to draw a breath and the mottled red slowly started to fade from his cheeks and neck.

"Easy does it, Pop," Mick said. "They're gonna' keep you in here long enough as it is without adding apoplexy to your list of problems."

Big Mike glared and then breathed out heavily through his nostrils, and finally said "You're right Mickey, damn me, but yeah, you're right," and then added, "but there's still something that doesn't seem right to me. Forget about that little weasel piece of crap Bannon, I still think he has something to do with…Something else. That case I was working on," he yawned as the pain medications finally started to kick in, "for the Chinaman…" His voice trailed off into a snore.

"Poor old Pop," Mick shook his head. "He sees a deep, dark, plot and conspiracy on every corner." He looked up and noticed that Bridget wasn't smiling. "What?" he grinned and poked her, but her serious expression remained.

"I don't know Mick," she said quietly, "maybe he's not just a paranoid old cop."

"What do you mean?" Mick asked now troubled.

"Do you remember that little old lady in the big Buick who hit us?" Bridget asked.

"Yeah, why?" Mick responded.

"Well," Bridget replied, "she had a five o'clock shadow."

CHAPTER 9

▼

Radcliffe College
Cambridge Mass.
April 1968

"Miss Connelly?" the nondescript man in the nondescript, drab, leaf-mold brown suit said. "Miss Bridget Ann Connelly." The question wasn't there any more. It was just a verification of a known fact as he stared alternately at Bridget and back to a black-and-white photo of her that he held in the palm of his hand.

"And who wants to know?" Bridget asked warily, pausing but not stopping.

"We'd like to have a few words with you," drab brown suit said motioning to a mirror image of himself loitering in the shadow of the archway that separated the Radcliffe campus from the rest of Cambridge.

Drab suit #2 (this one was a dirty, dust-under-the-bed gray), fell in step on the other side of Bridget, but never even looked at her. He just kept pace with her determined but now nervous stride, matching it step for step.

They continued on like that marching down the springtime-soft street. They remained in unison over the uneven worn red brick sidewalk, until Bridget took two quick steps ahead and suddenly spun back towards the two men who stopped in unison, hands folded one upon the other in front of them, and stared back at her.

"What do you want?" Bridget spat at them. "If it is money yer after, I've none. And if it's companionship, I've sure none for the likes of you two, though God knows it looks like ye'd be happier with each other than a lady. Not that one would want to be seen walking out with the likes of you two!" she added almost, but not quite, under her breath.

"Miss Bridget Ann Connelly, you have a brother by the name of Collin Andrew Connelly and a father, Sean McManus Connelly." Again, this was not a question but just a statement of fact read out from a small, black spiral notebook.

"Sweet Christ, has something happened to them?" she asked still not knowing if she should be alarmed or suspicious, or both.

"I think you should come with us, Miss Connelly," Mr. Drab Brown Suit said, putting a pale white hand on her soft, wool-sweatered sleeve.

"Keep yer hand to yerself," Bridget snapped, pulling her arm away, "And just who the hell are you to be giving me orders, the bleedin' Black and Tans?"

They looked at one another and then back at Bridget.

"Not quite," Mr. Drab Brown Suit replied, "But I think we're going to have to insist," and he pulled out a worn wallet with a badge on one side and a photo ID on the other. "We're from the INS, and I think there may be a small problem."

*   *   *   *

"Mickey darlin'," came a very small and unusually frightened voice over the small, tinny ear piece of the Inman Square phone. "Oh, Jesus Luv. I'm so sorry to be botherin' you, and you not 24 hours out of the hospital, but I don't know who else to turn to." The lyrical County Cork lilt broke at the end of the sentence.

"Easy, Babe, it's OK. What's up?" Mick asked on the other end of the line, reaching for the jar of instant Maxwell House with one hand and the whistling tea kettle with the other as he tried to keep the phone wedged between his left cheek and shoulder.

"Oh, Mickey," she cried, her normally soft Irish lilt reverting to a heavy brogue under fear-induced stress. "The bastards. The bloody Black and Tans, they've took me! They say it's because of Colin and me Da', and they're gonna' take away me visa and the scholarship as goes with it, and…and…" Bridget's voice dissolved into sobs. "Oh Christ, Mickey darlin', they can't do that can they? This ain't like the ballocky 'Specials' at home is it? It can't be!"

"Whoa, easy does it, babe. Take a breath and let me take one, too. Where the hell are you?" Mick finally managed to get out, rubbing one rough hand over the back of his neck and trying desperately to bring things into focus.

"Down near the waterfront by the old City Hall. The one that me ancestors quarried and carted the granite for!" Bridget shouted indignantly at someone beyond the range of the cheap old Inman Square's tinny phone earpiece pickup.

"Shush," Mick soothed. "Don't say anything else; just hang on until I get there, ok? Ok?"

There was silence on the line and then finally, a very uncharacteristically subdued Bridget said quietly, "Yes, darlin'. And please, come soon."

CHAPTER 10

▼

Downtown Boston
Federal Building

Mick drew another deep breath and vowed for the tenth time in as many minutes to hold his temper as he looked back and forth to "brown suit and gray suit".

"I'm afraid there's very little we can do, Mr. McCarthy." Brown Suit smiled insincerely and pushed a grainy black-and-white photo across the stainless steel and formica tabletop that ran almost the full length of the INS interrogation room.

Mick picked up the photo warily with an already sinking feeling in the pit of his stomach.

Yes, it was Bridget all right, and Mick knew exactly where it was taken. It was the night they met in the Club 47 on Mount Auburn Street. How could he ever forget it?

*   *   *   *

It was a cool October night with the special, romantic smell of fall and leaves and hopes unburned. He'd ridden in on the BSA with Kevin and Danny, his 'ready-for-a-fight-anytime' cousins from Southie who were following two feet from his tail light in their '65 Mustang, roaring full out behind him with Kevin's newly installed 427 cubic inch engine.

They'd pulled up in front of the former Mount Auburn Street storefront, still tagged with the No. 47, and Danny said, "Hey Mick, what the hell is this? Is this where those hippie fags hang out? C'mon Kev, let's go in and kick their little commie faggy asses!"

"Hey, Danny," Mick said grabbing and holding onto Danny's sweatshirted shoulder, "Don't be a jerk, ok. Ok, You got it?"

"Yeah. Shit, fine, Mick," Danny grimaced. "But if I hear any of them faggots saying anything about Vietnam and 'baby killers,' there's gonna' be some serious ass kicking."

"Just listen to the music, Danny," Mick said quietly as he paused at the door to show the white worn square of cardboard that identified him as a member of the Club 47 Mount Auburn Street. It really didn't entitle him to much more than drinking watery cappuccino served by intense Radcliffe undergrads and occasionally getting to jam on 'Hoot' nights with the likes of Bob Dylan, Tom Rush, Joan Baez and James Taylor. But as far as Mick was concerned, that and a strong mug of Russian tea (made with strawberry preserves) made it all worthwhile.

"Hey Mickey, they got any Pabst Blue Ribbon beer here?" Kevin asked as he shouldered a rail-thin MIT student out of his way, pre-empting the small table that the MIT undergrad had been hoping to save for his friends. They sat down at the candle-wax scarred table and Danny tried in vain to get the attention of the beaded and bell-bottomed waitress with futile and unsuccessful calls of, "Hey sweetie, over here!"

Mick smiled and turned back towards the stage where a thin, wispy, shy, pale-eyed waif was trying to get through the multi verses of Dylan's 'Masters of War' without much success, Mick ruefully thought. She struggled on with more heat than light and more tenacity than technical talent. Though the little voice was soft, sweet and pure, for all of the good it did, the majority of the audience talked, drank their tea and coffee drinks and debated outside of her sphere of musical penetration.

Mick looked around and almost no one was watching the poor kid. And suddenly he was mad. It was starting with his two cousin who were "fuck this"-ing and "fuck that"-ing about everything and nothing. As Mick got madder and madder he looked over at Kevin with the "old McCarthy look."

"What the fuck are you looking at?" Kevin snarled back at him. And then Mick looked at him with eyes that had suddenly turned to an iceberg cold Arctic gray and Danny had just enough time to say, "Oh, oh" before Mick grabbed Kevin by his sweatshirted collar and slammed his face into the table top.

"You friggin' prick," Kevin shouted, holding his throbbing bleeding nose to the napkin filled with ice swiped from a passing pitcher of Sangria. How appropriate, Mick thought remembering the Latin he'd been taught before he'd flunked out of the class at Andover Prep School.

"Hush, Kevin," Mick said putting his fingers to his lips." Be a good Boy-o and listened to the nice young lady." Mick listened to the thin, crystal pure tones and thought, "I think I'm falling in love...Again." Then a dirty, tattered paper coffee cup with a label that read "Give a dime, buy a bullet and kill a British pig! Free Ireland—Up Sein Fein!" was plopped down in the middle of the tiny table by a slim, white, silver-ringed hand.

While his two bemused cousins looked at one another, shrugged and reached for their wallets, Mick looked up into the emerald green eyes of Eire and for the first time fell truly and hopelessly in love.

CHAPTER 11

▼

Downtown Boston—Near the Freedom trail

"What are you grinnin' at you great, bloody and totally sweet fool," Bridget sniffled, wiping her still red eyes and dabbing at her nose before stuffing the now sopping wet handkerchief back into the pocket of her cardigan.

"I was just remembering something," Mick smiled.

"What?" She asked still sniffling.

"The first time I ever saw you," Mick answered and kissed her ear.

Bridget stopped and looked at him. Then she smiled for the first time that day and said, "God bless you, Michael McCarthy," as she stood up on tiptoe and kissed him full on the lips in the middle of Congress Street. The taxicabs honked and a trio of teenie boppers from Westwood Junior High, walking the Freedom Trail with their bored and beleaguered history teacher, poked one another and giggled.

Mick smiled down at Bridget, but he was still seething inside that in the end he'd finally had to swallow his pride and call big brother Frankie to bring in the 'big legal guns' to get Bridget out.

He did have to admit that when Frank had showed up, in his blue pinstripe and handed Brown Suit and Gray Suit his elegantly gold-embossed card that proclaimed him a partner, albeit a junior one, of Hayward, Elliott and Delbert, there had been a definite change of attitude in the INS detention room.

It seemed like it had only taken Frankie ("or I guess I'd better get used to calling him 'Franklin' from now on," Mick thought ruefully) suggesting coldly that Brown Suit and Gray Suit call Bennett Cabot, his squash partner, and, by the way, the presiding judge on the INS Review Board, to "vouch for Miss Connelly's character." The drab duo then hastily agreed that Miss Connelly posed no risk of flight until her case could be investigated more thoroughly.

So now, thanks to Frankie and the 'establishment', he was walking Bridge back to where he'd parked the bike up on Washington Street. He looked down at her as she clutched onto his arm. "Kind of like the chick on the cover of Dylan's first album, 'Free-Wheeling'," he thought. "But prettier!"

His mind kept turning over everything that had happened in the past 24 hours. His old man getting the crap beat in out of him in a dirty Central Square alley. Him and Bridge getting squished by some old 'blue head', or what was it that Bridge had said about a five o'clock shadow? And now this bullshit with the INS's version of Beaver and Wally Cleaver.

Something didn't feel right. He was getting that creepy, itchy feeling between his shoulder blades just like in 'Nam when his intuition was working overtime. And just like in 'Nam, when he felt this way, suddenly he knew. It was time to go and see the lieutenant.

CHAPTER 12

▼

Commonwealth Avenue
Allston Mass—Near Boston University

"S'cuse me," Mick called to the probable B.U. coed who brushed by him so fast that he almost lost his grip on the wobbly banister of the first floor landing.

"Oops, sorry," she called back. "I'm late for Soc. class. But I didn't mean to run you over," she added with a giggle.

"Hey, no problem, babe," Mick laughed. "You're sure a hell of a lot prettier than the last female that ran in to me."

The brown-haired, button-nosed, coed paused and turned halfway back to him with an expectant smile and a quizzical cock of her head.

"She was about ninety years old, so I guess that's why she felt she had to get my attention with the front bumper of her 1957 Buick," Mick called back down with one hand cupped to his mouth in a fake stage whisper.

The brown haired girl's pretty amber eyes crinkled as she giggled again and said, "Well, I guess that's one way to meet guys," and added with a wink,

"But at least I've never had to run over them with a car to get their attention."

"And by the looks of things, you certainly won't have to for at least…mmmmh?" and Mick fingered his jaw with his right thumb and forefinger as if assessing weighty matters, "I'd say about 80 or 90 more years."

She gave him a smile and her freckled cheeks became tinged with pink as she said, "I don't know if that's sweet or a pick-up line, but I'm gonna' be at the student union tonight, so if you happen to be over there and happen to see me, maybe you can tell me which."

"Oh, shit," Mick thought, "now what have I done? I've gotta' start learning to keep my big mouth shut or one of these days Bridget is gonna' have my balls for breakfast."

The pretty little coed opened the big front door of the Commonwealth Avenue apartment and called back to Mick, "Bye. Gotta' go."

"Wait a second," Mick yelled back as she stood on the front stoop with one foot already out the door, "Do you know if Steve Benson lives in this building?"

"Gee, no I don't, but I only moved in last week 'cause Linda dropped out, so there was room in Sally's and Janie's apartment, and I just had to get out of the dorm, 'cause my roommate was really driving me crazy, 'cause she—Oh my God, now I really am late! "she gasped breathlessly and looked at her watch like she was hoping it was wrong. She took off down the stairs at a dead run, calling back over her shoulder, "Hope I see you again. Remember, The Union tonight!"

Mick smiled, shook his head and murmured to himself as he watched the cute blue-jeaned form dodge between two parked cars and hop onto the steps of one of the lumbering Green Line trolley cars, just as it gave a hiss and moved down Commonwealth Avenue.

"Man, how come stuff like that never happened to me when I was eighteen and lookin' for love?"

"A little young to be talking to yourself, ain't ya' Grandpa?" came a voice from behind Mick. "And with an ego like that, how do you know you won't be soon?"

Mick turned back around slowly and looked up the stairs toward a bell-bottomed form leaning against the wall of the first floor landing. His eyes traveled upwards past a beaded leather belt and Indian embroidered peasant blouse topped off by a mass of flaming red curls. He could barely make out her face because it was shrouded in a blue haze of, he sniffed twice, yep, marijuana smoke.

"Jesus, take a picture, Curly," an obvious reference to Mick's own unruly hair, she drawled still slouching against the wall, "It'll last longer. Or are you a 'Narc'?" she added suspiciously sauntering slowly down the stairs. As she moved into the slightly brighter sixty-watt light of the front foyer, and some of the pot smoke dissipated, Mick saw that while she has had a great-looking body, which she certainly knew how to accentuate with the skin-tight bellbottoms and low-cut peasant blouse, she was sure no undergrad. And, he thought cynically, definitely not the grad student type either.

"Whatcha' lookin' for, man?" She asked studying him through half-closed purple-painted eyelids, as she surreptitiously pinched out the glowing end of the joint and let it fall down between the stairwell and the wall.

"Well, first of all," Mick said, "you didn't have to deep-six that roach, cause I'm not a Narc. Tisk, tisk, tisk," he smiled up at her, "what a waste of good pot. Smells like Cambodian Red."

"How would you know?" She countered still suspicious, "Unless you are a Narc!"

"Cause it's the same shit we used to smoke in 'Nam," Mick drawled back.

"One of them, huh?" She asked raising her eyebrows.

"One of what?" Mick said back slowly, his gray-blue eyes going cold.

She looked at him for a minute and then shrugged and pushing her shoulders off the wall, finally responded, "Nothing."

Now that Mick could see her in the daylight shining through the glass door of the building, he could see that while the face surrounded by the bright red hair might have been pretty once, now it was just hard. "Too many years of booze, pot and parties," he thought.

Mick glanced at the row of apartment mailbox names embedded in the wall and said, "I am looking for someone though. A friend. A friend from 'Nam. This is the last address I had for him but I don't see his name here."

"What is it?" She asked.

"Steve," Mick said," Steve Benson."

"Sorry, General," she said sarcastically, "no 'Steve's' around here."

"It was Sergeant," Mick said.

"What was that Sunshine?" She asked.

"I said, it was Sergeant. Not a goddamn General"

She smiled for the first time and said, "What did this 'Steve' guy look like?"

"Tall, blond hair, blue eyes, crew cut."

"Whoa," she laughed, "what was he, a friggin' Nazi?"

"No," Mick smiled back sadly, "just a big, nice, idealistic Iowa farm boy. At least he was once," he added bitterly.

"Follow me, Sarge," she called back over her shoulder as she moved back up the stairs.

"Why not," Mick shrugged to himself and followed her bell-bottomed butt as she climbed up one, two, three and four flights of chipped tiled stairs until she finally turned down a hallway barely illuminated by a forty-watt bulb, and banged on a dented steel door at the end.

"Hey, Boomer," she yelled through the door, "Crawl outta' your rack, you got company."

There was silence for a moment and she winked at Mick mischievously and yelled, "Hey man, I think it's the MPs, they say you've got a tank hidden under your bed!"

The steel door flew open with a bang and a tall, skinny hippie with long, tangled, dirty blond hair, clad only in a pair of ratty old army issue boxer shorts, stared down at Mick, owlishly blinking as he tried to bring the world into focus.

Mick smiled up at the unshaven, scarecrow-thin form and said, "Hi Lieutenant."

CHAPTER 13

▼

**Vietnam—June 15, 1966—2:00 a.m.—A village,
somewhere north of Firebase Bravo**

The flames from a dozen smoldering charred clumps of bamboo that used to be huts gave the village square a Dante's Inferno type of nightmarish surrealism. But if this scene gave the semblance of hell, then the sweating, vacant eyed zombies who shuffled through the ruins were surely its demons. Wild-eyed, bloodstained demons without, but the demons within, had just barely begun for the men of C Company.

Mick stood in the flickering shadows of guttering, blackened mounds that had become a score of pitiful funeral pyres. He kept wiping his face with the same dripping red hands that had colored his face a dull clay red ochre and was now made brighter as he stepped back into the firelight and tried to make his lips form the words that would get his squad formed up and out of there.

"Listen up!", he thought he said, but in truth nothing must have come out because no one listened up. The men just kept walking zombie-like around and around the burning piles of destroyed huts looking back and forth at the smaller sad and shriveled blackened things that used to be something.

"What Mick?" He thought he heard sane, rational Mick ask the Mick in the jungle clearing in the middle of hell; that Mick who would never be sane or rational again. "What are those blackened things Mick, and how did they get here? And how did you get here, and why?"

Mick shook his head violently as if to drive the voice away and spat through bloodstained lips to clear his throat and finally shouted, "Okay, listen the fuck up, you miserable, motherless sons of bitches! Form up on me, now!" The white-faced, hollow eyed, automatons, began to shuffle towards Mick, M-16s trailing at their sides.

"Column of twos, and move out to the assembly point," Mick shouted as he heard the first beating of rotor blades of a helicopter gunship.

"Okay, let's move and—" His strained and cracking voice command was abruptly cut off by the sustained burst of an M-16 emptying a full 30 round clip in one short but savage stream of 5.56 mm steel jacketed slugs.

"Who the fuck?" Mick screamed, through teeth that were bared like a rabid wolf. He turned around, wildly searching until he saw private Mark Begley standing slack-jawed over a small, blackened lump that somehow almost seemed to be quivering.

Mick ran up to him, grabbed him by his bloodstained, sweat-soaked shirt and screamed in his face, "What are you doing? You miserable, fucking piece of shit. I'm gonna' fucking kill you!! "He slammed one fist into the left side of the dumbly staring private's head. When that produced no reaction, Mick followed it up with a backhanded slap across the unresisting soldier's face. And then another, and another, and another. And then, arms gripping him from behind and someone was shouting at in his ear. It was Smitty.

Smitty, who hadn't been there.

Smitty, who didn't seem to belong in this nightmare.

Smitty, who was still shouting in his ear, "Stop it Mick. For Christ sakes, you're fucked up, man. All of you…" and his voice started to trail off.

"You're all fucked up. Oh, Jesus Christ."

Mick shook his head to try to clear it, and private Begley who was still staring slack-jawed, said "Sarge, he was moving. He was getting up I swear. It was a VC. He had an AK, and he was coming at me just like all of them other VC, you know, the whole village full, that we just…" His voice trailed off into a mumble as his swollen, bruised jaw fell open again and blood and spittle dribbled down his chin.

Mick stood there, chest heaving, hands clenching and unclenching until Smitty relaxed his grip and pulled him back towards the sound of the choppers.

"Smitty, What happened man?" Mick finally asked in a bewildered voice.

"I dunno, man," Smitty said shaking his head as he led Mick and the dazed soldiers of C Company into the clearing where a tall, slim, straight-backed figure stood out-lined by the lights of the three waiting helicopter gunships.

Smitty guided Mick up to the figure and said "I got 'em, lieutenant, but there's something wrong. Like I told you, they're all…fucked up."

"McCarthy!" The lieutenant's voice crackled out, and then when there was no response he turned Mick around so that the lights from the chopper illuminated his Sergeant's face. "Jesus!" Was all he said.

"Sergeant, report!" It came almost as more of a plea than an order. And when there was still nothing, the lieutenant leaned close and whispered, "Mick, what the hell happened back there?"

"I don't know, lieutenant," Mick said woodenly. "I don't know."

"Corporal Smith," Lt. Benson said, "Take me into the village."

Fifteen minutes later an ashen-faced lieutenant climbed slowly into the chopper and slumped down next to Mick who was still staring comatosely at nothing. The lieutenant looked at the vacant-eyed men with an expression on his face that seem to indicate that it would be a long time before he would be able to smile, or even sleep through the night again, and hissed from between clenched teeth, "The Colonel. The motherfuckin' Colonel."

CHAPTER 14

▼

Boston Mass
Commonwealth Ave.
April 1968

"Hey 'Louie'," Mick smiled.

There was silence in the dim hallway. And it stretched to fill all the available space between comprehension and wishful thinking. The tall, painfully thin figure squinted down at Mick for another infinite minute until suddenly dawn broke through the fog of drug-induced haze and the ex-lieutenant, for the first time in almost three years, smiled.

*   *   *   *

"Hey, Starr, get us some coffee. Or herbal tea. Or maybe just some herbs, or tea. You know what I mean," ex-Lt. Benson laughed with a dry racking cough.

"Hey, lieutenant; Steve man, take it easy," Mick said, still smiling, but with concern for the bedraggled skeleton of the clean-cut, healthy Iowa farm boy that he knew in 'Nam.

"No problem, Mick my man," Steve coughed, "everything is just fine. Now. Starr, Baby, get us something. Ok, babe?"

The bell-bottomed, hard-looking girl stopped and stood beside the hollow-eyed, skeletal form and ran her long purple nailed fingers through his dirty hair and whispered, "Okay, Boomer, just take a breath, honey. Let Mama take care of it." She looked past the top of his uncomprehending head and gave Mick a look that was more of a challenge than an affirmation.

Steve, 'Boomer', smiled and slipped back onto the broken springs of the Salvation Army couch in the corner of the apartment and absently scratched his balls while "Miss Bell Bottoms" went off to make tea, or something.

"So lieutenant," Mick began.

"Don't call me that," the scarecrow said.

"Okay, lieutenant Steve," Mick rephrased. "I really need to—"

"Don't call me that either," Mick's former CO shook his head.

"Okay, man," Mick said, his patience wore paper-thin by now. "What the hell should I call you, you dumb, fuckin' son of a...sorry lieutenant, you don't deserve that. Especially from me. Especially for what you did for me and everyone else in the goddamned squad."

"No, Mick, no," the ex lieutenant shook his head. "Like the 'Stones' say, 'It's all over now'," and turning back to Starr, who had just re-entered the room, the ex-lieutenant, 'All-American', clean-cut Iowa farm boy, buried his face in the soft breasts of her embroidered peasant blouse and oh so quietly began to cry.

CHAPTER 15

▼

"Here, Sarge," Starr said. "Drink this," and she held out a cup of herbal tea.

"But I'm not thirsty," Mick countered and as she thrust the cracked yellow mug into his hands.

"Drink it," Starr said with an expression that said "I'm not screwing around, Dude," to Mick.

"Okay, okay," Mick said, and looked over the rim of his cracked mug as he downed the concoction.

"Come here, you poor, skinny, big dumb jerk," Starr said to the apparition who still sat on the ratty old, spring-sprung, stuffing-split couch. Lt. Steve had seemed genuinely glad to see Mick until the memory had caused a short circuit in the faulty fuses of his mind and he had blown a circuit breaker in the short hairs of what was left of his cerebellum.

"So why do they call you Starr?" Mick asked, as the tough-tender Janis Joplin look-alike wiped the former first lieutenant Steve Benson's eyes and smoothed the back of his dirty tangled hair tenderly, while constantly whispering, "hush baby, It's ok."

She looked back at Mick and pushed one handful of flaming red hair behind her right ear, and began, "Well, if you really need to get a life or are just terminally curious, I was born on Pease Airforce Base. An Army/Navy brat, depending how you want to look at it. And as I'm sure you can tell," she gave Mick a grin and a wink, "me and the military didn't get along too well. So I left home at fifteen and moved in with my boyfriend on Mission Hill, and became, well how did Elton John put it? Oh yeah, 'seamstress to the band'."

Mick sipped his now cooling herbal tea as Starr continued to spin out the story of her life. "Yeah, but the question still stands. Where did you pick up the name Starr?" Mick asked, to make conversation as much as anything else.

Her mouth twisted up at the side before she laughed again. "Hey man," she responded with a deep throaty chuckle, "it was the guys who picked it. Not me."

Mick raised his eyebrows and as if to say, "Hey, don't stop now!"

"Well," she began, "After they left the military, my parents became 'entertainers'. Or if you want to put it another way, the old lady was a stripper/hooker, and the old man was her manager and pimp." She snorted and shook her head. "Anyway, one of the old lady's favorite songs was 'Stella by Starlight', so they named me Stella."

Mick just looked at her and didn't say anything until she said, "Yeah, I thought it sucked, too. So when I ran away at fifteen me and the guys in the band changed it to just Starr. "Kinda' cute, huh?" Mick just smiled and shrugged his shoulders noncommittally.

"So, screw you, too. But Boomer, hey, he likes it." She finished defensively.

"One more question, Starr?" Mick said raising his hand like a kid in the third grade. "Why do you call him 'Boomer'?"

Starr's sad, hard eyes got harder still and she said, "Come here," as she led him into the bedroom.

Mick followed slowly as she passed down the long, narrow, dark hallway of the railroad style apartment into the back bedroom. As she closed the bedroom door and turned back towards him, Mick put up both hands and said, "Whoa, Starr. I mean, you're a very foxy chick, but Steve is a really good friend and I—"

"Don't flatter yourself, asshole," she cut him off. "You may be a cute little puppy, but I'd had enough of 'cute little puppies' by the time I was sixteen so stick it back in your jeans 'cause for better or for worse, I seem to be stuck on broken things. Like Boomer."

"Sorry, Starr," Mick said quietly. And then added, "Oh yeah, you were going to tell me why you called him Boomer?"

"That's why I brought you in here, Ace," she smiled sardonically and opened the top drawer of the Salvation Army, student-apartment style bureau. She reached down underneath a crumpled pile of worn boxer shorts and frayed bras.

"Ah," she said, "Here you go, Sarge." Her fingers closed on something cold, hard and heavy in the small top drawer, and with one nonchalant motion tossed him a Smith and Wesson .44 Magnum revolver.

Mick grabbed for it with his left hand and missed getting a full grip but managed to snag the barrel and catch the butt with his right. He quickly flipped the catch up with his thumb and was horrified but not surprised to see that it was fully loaded with hollow point slugs. "Jesus," Mick hissed, "what does the Louie need with this?"

"You wanted to know, chief," Starr shrugged. "When it gets really bad; when he starts wanting to talk about It: you, and the jungle and 'Nam and the village," and her eyes narrowed, "then he gets out this little 'play toy' and starts playing Russian roulette with it. So that's why we call him 'Boomer'. Get it? Yeah, you get it Sarge, don't you. Yeah," she said again, looking at him with her cold, hard, sad eyes. "I can tell you do."

CHAPTER 16

▼

**Inmann Square
Cambridge, Mass**

Mick sat on the front porch of the Inman Square triple-decker and idlely peeled the label off of the long necked bottle of a Miller High Life beer as he stared at the cars parked haphazardly along the slowly darkening street.

"So then, what are we celebrating, Luv?" came Bridget's soft lilt and as she moved quietly up behind him and put her cool, slim fingers on either side of his head.

"Celebrating?" Mick said, without turning around. "What do you mean?"

"You're drinking 'the champagne of bottled beers'. Or at least that's what they call that sad, sorry excuse for the lost art of brewin' in America on those silly commercials on the telly," Bridget sniffed.

Mick leaned his head back and looked upside down at Bridget, absently wondering if she was trying to make a statement about American culture or the lack of it, especially where beer was concerned, and then decided he really didn't care which, as long as those cool, slim fingers continued to gently massage the now, starting-to-hurt-less, throbbing veins on the sides of his temples.

"Mmmmm, that feels great, babe. Thanks," He murmured.

"So did you find your Mate then?" Bridget asked while continuing to rub his head and working her way down to his shoulders.

Mick sighed and stretched himself back into her talented hands. "Stop it. Sit still then," Bridget said with a gentle slap. "I swear, you're worse than a damn puppy dog, what with your squirming and all."

"Yeah, I found him," Mick finally answered.

"And...?" Bridget let the questioned trail off.

"And there wasn't much left of First Lieutenant Steve Benson from Company C; but what there was told me things. Finally told me what I was afraid I already knew. Told me the nightmares weren't just bad dreams. They were real. And he also told me who gave them to me and," Mick's eyes grew hard and cold, "and where to find him."

*   *   *   *

April 29th 1968
Prides Crossing
Boston's North Shore

Mick punched the faded, ivory looking button set in the antique corroded brass doorbell sconce for the third time and again heard the bells chimes echoing back through the bowels of the big house. But once again, as the chimes faded away, he was answered by only silence. He stepped back off the half-moon shaped red brick, pillared, porticoed entrance to 'Sea Mist House', as this mass of weathered clapboard and granite set at the end of Grape Vine Lane was called.

Mick thought back to his conversation with the first Louie, now a.k.a. 'Boomer', and he smiled thinking back to yesterday's conversation with his former officer in his new persona. They'd sat around the cheap Formica kitchen table in the fourth floor Commonwealth Avenue walk-up and Starr had rolled them both joints of Boomer's seemingly unlimited supply of Cambodian Red…Mick frowned thinking back and said softly to himself "What do you think are the chances that our boy, Lieutenant 'Boomer' is dealing, big time."

Mick shook his head to clear it and sat down on the warm bricks of the front steps of the imposing but bleak Gothic oceanfront house, and recalled his first and most important question for Lieutenant Steve 'Boomer' Benson;

"Just what the hell happened that stifling June night in that nameless Vietnamese village back in 1966?"

Steve…Boomer, had stared at the table top for what seemed like an hour before he looked up slowly and said, "Why do you want to know, man? I mean, I know it was a shitty, horrible nightmare. I mean hell, look what it's done to me and I wasn't even directly part of…" His voice trailed off into nothing as he took a lung-searing drag of the joint and stared off into space letting the smoke hiss out from between his teeth.

"Part of what, Steve?" Mick said quietly, putting one hand on his former lieutenant's arm.

"Mick. Mick, man," he shook his sorrowful, shaggy-haired head, "let it go. Please."

"No," said Mick flatly.

"Why?" Boomer asked still shaking his head.

"Because some really weird shit has been going on in my life very recently and somehow, I don't know how or why, I just have this feeling that it all connects back to that horrible night in the jungle two years ago."

"Stuff like what man?" Boomer said, trying to focus his eyes on Mick.

"Like getting run off the road two days ago by a little old lady who, according to my girl Bridget," he smiled and Steve and Starr almost smiled back, "was no little old lady. And my old man getting the crap kicked out of him in a Central Square alley. And then the next day, Bridget gets rousted by the INS on a very bullshit charge. Something smells, man," Mick finished harshly.

"Yeah, man, I hear you," said Boomer shaking his head again. "But I mean, like, how can I help you?"

"Like I said," Mick answered, "I think it all goes back to Nam. And ever since we all got 'discharged' real sudden before our hitches were up, I keep thinking that there have been people watching me, following me, you know like something you see out of the corner of your eye, but when you look again, it isn't there."

Boomer and Starr didn't say anything, but just exchanged a look.

Mick looked back and forth between them and said quietly, "You've seen it too, haven't you? Yeah, maybe the steel door and Starr's lookout on the stairs aren't just for narcs. Are they, lieutenant?"

*   *   *   *

In the end Mick had gotten very little. He could tell Boomer wanted to talk, but Starr had stepped in and shut the conversation down with, "Okay, Sarge, 'Lieutenant space cowboy' here has had enough of old time reminiscing for one day. Haven't you, baby," She smiled kissing the top of his greasy head. "So why don't you hit the bricks for now and come back another time. Maybe on 'open mike night'," she smiled with her hard smile.

"Whatever," Mick shrugged and started to get up from the table but Boomer grabbed his sleeve and said, "wait, if you really think you have to do this man, I think you know where you've got to start."

Mick nodded and said in a flat voice, "Colonel Chalmers, Right?"

"Yeah," said ex-lieutenant Steve 'Boomer' Benson, "The Colonel. The mother-fuckin' Colonel."

CHAPTER 17

▼

Prides Crossing
Boston's North Shore

Strangely enough, Boomer had known just where to find the colonel. "He's living in a big old pile up on the North Shore; Prides Crossing. You know, home of the 'Lowells who speak only to the Cabots, and the Cabots who speak only to God'," he smiled thinly.

In the end they'd slapped their hands together in the old 'Nam Brotherhood salute and under Starr's watchful eyes, he'd retraced his steps back down the stairwell, fired up the BSA and headed for the north shore.

＊　　　＊　　　＊　　　＊

Now he was sitting on the cooling bricks of the Prides Crossing address and soaking up the last rays of the setting sun as he wondered what he was going to do next.

"Hey, asshole, you're trespassing on private property."

Mick looked up at the voice of the lump that was silhouetted against the setting sun. Actually, it was one big lumpy voice attended by a smaller lump.

A cloud blew over the sun and the lumps of various sizes came into sharper focus for a minute.

Mick looked up and groaned to himself, "Aw, shit," as recognition swept over him with the clouds brief illumination, and unpleasant memories came flooding back from the last time he'd seen this unpleasant pair.

Actually the first time had been when he'd been a skinny Andover prep senior and he and his geeky, bespectacled roommate Wesley had made the mistake of showing up at a Ringe High School dance in Cambridge. Wesley, as always, had been unfailingly polite to the bevy of teased hair, tight skirted, over-sexed Somerville girls they'd tried to put the moves on while the pomenaded, tight pants band had run through "Who Wrote the Book of Love" for the third time. Mick, as he remembered, had his usual "thing" for petite, dark-eyed, little bombshells and had been flirting, quite successfully he thought, with a sexy little number with the ironic name of "Angelica" who was teasingly leading him on, as he only figured out later, and too late, to see the fun as 6 ft. 2 in. of 'already running to adult size beef', clamped down on Mick's shoulder and spun him around.

The last thing Mick remembered of that night was, "Hey, asshole. What are you doing talking to my girl?" Mick had gotten a black eye and a fractured rib, but the goons had put poor, innocent and unsuspecting Wesley in the school infirmary with a concussion.

The second time he'd run into this ghastly pair had been in the South Boston Army Base on the day of his induction. It was hard, he remembered, to be cool when you're standing in line in your underwear, holding a plastic bag with your worldly valuables looped around your wrist. So naturally the last thing he needed or expected was to hear a nasal North Somerville whine from behind him saying, "Hey Tony, isn't that the little prick we whaled the crap out of at the Cambridge Ringe Senior Class dance back in '64?"

"Yeah, Bingie. I think you're right," answered a larger gravel voice. Which was followed by "Hey, jerk off. Turn around, we're talking to you!"

Mick drew a deep breath and slowly turned to look behind him. They grinned back at him with bad toothed grins and the skinny, pimple faced specimen called 'Bingie' poked the bigger one and said, "Hey, Tony, I think the little shit needs another good ass kicking."

"Yeah, Bingie," the larger lump agreed, "I think you're right." As the line of inductees filed into the army debarkation centers locker room, Tony gave Bingie a nudge and they started to circle Mick.

He instinctively backed up until his naked shoulders came into contact with the cold steel of the bank of olive drab Army lockers. Mick knew what was coming. It had already come for him once. But at least this time, he swore to himself, they weren't gonna' sucker punch him again. He raised his left hand level with his eyes and set his right just to the right side of his jaw, just like Big Mike had taught him all those years ago. He remembered all of Big Mike's stories about low-life scumbags that had been stood up to, and put down by his Pop and he vowed to himself that he wasn't going to lie down this time without a fight.

And then it was almost over before it started. The rat-faced Bingie feinted towards his right and the beefy Tony caught him on the left ear. Mick's head rang off the lockers but he managed to lash out with his right hand and catch Bingie on his ferret-like lip before he could jerk his head back.

"God damn!" He squealed as his crooked, yellow teeth, gashed his lip and a small trickle of blood ran down his acne-scarred chin.

"Smash his face, Tony!" Bingie screamed and Tony moved in, pushing a huge meaty fist into Mick's solar plexus just below his ribcage. Mick felt his breath leave with an agonizing whoosh and he tried to respond with a short left jab to Tony's fat, thick gut. But he knew he didn't have enough force behind it. And then, while he was still fighting for breath, he felt Bingie's skinny arms loop through his elbows pinning them behind him and he smelled the stink of Bingie's accumulated years of bad dental hygiene breath in his face.

"I got 'em Tony, I got 'em! Hit 'em, man. Smash his goddamn face in." Bingie yelled and Mick strained his head back, waiting for the ham-like fist to crash into his face.

"What's the problem, friend?" Came a soft Southern drawl from just beyond Mick's limited vision.

Tony's fist paused as he growled back over his shoulder at the unseen voice, "Beat it, cracker, this ain't none of your business. And if you're smart, you'll make sure it isn't."

"Well, you see, friend," came the soft Kentucky drawl, "That's where your wrong, cuz I don't like gettin' blood all over this nice clean army locker room. Not even yours," he added and the deceptively gentle southern voice took on just the slightest tone of menace.

"You dumb fuckin' hillbilly!" Tony snarled. But Tony never got any further, because a cowboy boot attached to a pair of long, hairy legs, came out of nowhere and buried their scuffed, pointed toe right in the middle of Fat Tony's balls. As Tony fell backwards screaming onto the cold stone tiles, Mick jerked his head backwards and heard the satisfying crunch as he shattered the cartilage of Bingie's nose. The next second there was a shriek from behind him and he felt something warm as the spurting blood from Bingie's nose hit the back of his neck.

"Ow, ow. Crap," the pimple faced punk screamed, "You broke it. You son of a bitch! We'll kill you! Me and Tony, we're gonna' kill you. Ah, crap, you bastard."

"I don't think so, friend," came the soft drawl again. "I think your friend Tony is gonna' have ta' git himself a nut transplant before he can ever think about killin' someone, and then," the soft voice added, now harder again, as the long-legged hillbilly grabbed hold of Bingie's bloody T-shirt and looked at him with eyes as hard as the anthracite coal mines he'd grown up next to, "I'd suggest he don't. Friend."

The Kentucky coal miner's son let Bingie's head drop back to the tiled floor with a satisfying 'thunk' and straightening up, stuck his now bloodstained hand out to Mick and said, "How ya'll doin', friend, my name is Harlan'. Harland Beaufort Smith. My friends call me Smitty."

*   *   *   *

Mick looked up again at the sneering pair, and said fatalistically to himself, "Yep, it's them, all right, the 'gruesome twosome'. Oh, Smitty, man, where are you when I need you. Again."

CHAPTER 18

▼

Prides Crossing
Boston's North Shore

It was deja vu all over again, with Bingie sneering, "Get up asshole, or do you want us to kick your butt while you're sitting there."

"Well, Bingie," Mick said stretching his legs out and lifting up his face to catch the last feeble rays of the setting sun, "That would present a problem that must be obvious even to a whiz kid like you."

"What the hell are you talking about, jerk off," Bingie snapped back.

"Oops, sorry, Bingie. You're right, the question was way over your head. Hey, I know, why don't you ask 'Fat Tony'. I mean two half-wits oughtta make one whole."

"I said, what the hell are you talking about?" Bingie snarled, advancing on him.

"Well, Bingie," Mick drawled, "Just how are you and 'lard bucket' gonna' kick my ass, when I'm sitting on it." As he saw the red rage flush creep up Tony's neck, he added for good measure, "Oh yeah, but I was forgetting; you two guys have always been experts on the subject of asses. Must be all that 'quality time' you spend together." Yep, that did it. 'Fat Tony' went right over the edge and charged him straight on, with Bingie right beside him.

"Good!" Thought Mick as he kicked out with his right foot, catching Bingie in the kneecap and rolling to his right as Bingie went down, tripping Fat Tony.

The first move had worked. They'd charged him straight on instead of circling around to either side. He had a fighting chance now if he could roll clear and clip Tony before he could turn back around.

But apparently there was only one lucky move to a customer today, because just as he thought he'd rolled clear and was about to gather his feet under him, his head cracked against one of the large white rocks set in a pattern around the horseshoe driveway, and he was momentarily stunned as small black dots swam before his eyes. As Mick tried to get to his knees, shaking his head to clear it, Bingie limped over to him and kicked him in the stomach.

"How do you like that, smart ass," Bingie snarled.

"Jesus, there you go with the 'butt' references again, Bingie," Mick rasped out trying desperately to draw in enough breath. "You and Tony really gotta' start going out with girls soon. On the other hand," Mick said, painfully trying to grin as he inched backwards towards the stone steps, "maybe you've both just really gotten used to having your heads stuck up each other's assholes." But it didn't work this time.

Yep, they were pissed all right, but on a nod from Tony, Bingie went right and as Tony circled around from the left. Mick backed up until his back was against the old, black painted front door and he tried desperately to fill his lungs as he prepared for the rush.

Mick watched as Tony pulled a greasy bike chain out of the back pocket of his jeans and Bingie reached into his jacket pocket and fitted a pair of homemade brass knuckles, consisting of woven copper wire studded with one-inch electrical staples, to his right hand.

"Yeah," Mick thought, "this one is for keeps all right." The thick greasy motorcycle chain slashed in towards Mick's face from his left while Bingie's sneering, acne-scarred face filled Mick's vision on the right, while the final dabs of sunlight, twinkled off the points on the wickedly gleaming inch-long electrical staples, as they headed for his eye.

Mick threw up his left arm to be shattered by the chain and right hand to try to catch the wire and staple knuckles before they could take out his right eye. But neither blow ever came. As the chain came forward to complete its arc, it was stopped cold as a black, leather-gloved hand clamped around its end. With a sharp, smooth tug, Tony was pulled off balance to the right and crashed into Bingie sending him sprawling into the bushes.

Fat Tony landed heavily on his wrist, which gave a sickening crack and brought him up howling, "God damn, it's broken you bastard!"

Bingie came charging out of the bushes, screaming, "You son of a bitch, I'll kill you, you—" and stopped short as the small man dressed in a severe black suit, just folded his black gloved hands in front of him, and stared. "God damn it, 'Spook', I mean Mr. Sloan, what did you do that for? We were just taking care of this jerk like you told us to."

"Yeah," Fat Tony moaned still holding his fractured wrist, "he's a frigging trespasser, and you told us to get rid of him. Permanently."

"There's been a change of thinking," the slight figure said quietly.

"Change of thinking? Screw you, Spook!" Tony roared and charged Mick, yelling, "I'm gonna beat that mother's brains in." But before he managed two steps, Tony found himself sprawled face first in the gravel. As he looked up, the small pale form wrapped one black gloved hand through his hair, pulling his head back till the small bones in his neck were about to pop while the diminutive foot clad in immaculately polished black wingtips stepped deliberately on his broken wrist.

"Don't ever questioned my orders again," the soft voice said with an ice-cold menace that turned Tony's screams into quiet whimpers. "Is that clear, gentlemen?" He said expressionlessly, looking slowly from Tony's moaning, prone position, to where Bingie crawled sullenly out of the bushes.

"Yes sir, Mr. Sloan," they both said slowly.

The small neatly dressed man turned away from them as if they no longer existed. Mick looked at him. He couldn't have been more than 5 ft. 3 in. and maybe 110 lbs. soaking wet. He had slight, almost delicate features and hair so blond it was almost white with skin that looked like it had never been touched by the sun.

"Christ," thought Mick, "I wonder if Dracula has a twin, cause this must sure be it."

But the thing that Mick noticed most were the eyes. They were bone white with jet-black irises. So black that they reflected like two tiny mirrors. Mick could see himself reflected, but nothing else. Because there was nothing else there. Nothing shown from behind those eyes. No light, no warmth, no hopes, no fears. No life. It was like looking into two black dead reflecting pools with no bottom.

Mick shivered slightly and thought, "Christ, no wonder he scares the crap out of those two dimwits, I think I'd better get the hell out of here while I still can."

And he said, "Ah, thanks for your help, Mr.. .ah.. . Sloan, is it? Well I've gotta' get going so thanks again and—"

Mick was cut short as one black-gloved hand was held up and the soft voice said, "As I mentioned, there has been a change of thinking. You'll come with me." It was not an invitation. He opened the big black front door and said to Mick without turning around, "The Colonel wishes to see you."

CHAPTER 19

▼

Fort Benning Georgia
July 2, 1966

"So what is your 'professional assessment', Major?" The voices came through to Mick like the wrong end of a bad connection made by two tin cans and a string. They were fuzzy and echoed in his head.

"As a major," came another voice, "I'd say excellent. As a doctor, well, that's something different."

"Very well, then, we will consider your report accepted." The clipped voice paused and then emphasized "Major."

Mick tried to open his eyes but his vision was as fuzzy as his hearing. All he could see were silhouettes. Dark shadows outlined against a window and features made invisible by the blinding noonday sunlight streaming in behind them. Mick could just barely make out the high peaks of three officers' caps and at least one or two other forms standing beside them.

"He seems to be coming around," said the voice that had been identified as the Major. Or was it Doctor? Everything was swimming in his mind.

"Yes," said the voice, "he's definitely beginning to come around, but he's very confused."

"Alright then," came the clipped voice of command. "Captain?"

"Sir!" came another voice…this one different in timber. It sounded almost…feminine.

"Do you have everything you need then?" the voice in charge enquired.

"Yes, Sir, everything," came the terse but softer reply.

"Then I suggest that you catch that 0:100 plane to Camp David."

Mick heard a clipped "Sir!" and struggled again to open his eyes and just barely saw a figure in a uniform skirt, walking away. He couldn't keep his eyes open any more and the remaining backlit figures blurred as the room started swimming again and the bright Georgia sunlight blinked out.

*   *   *   *

Mick shook his head and pinched the bridge of nose to clear away the sharp momentary stab of déjà vu' that came without warning as he stared at the figure that was standing backlit against a roaring fire in the massive six-foot high granite fireplace.

Suddenly, the two images overlapped and clicked into place as the foggy memory and the figure standing back towards the crackling fireplace, merged into one, and Mick knew why he'd had to come. The Colonel.

CHAPTER 20

▼

April 28th 1968
Brattle Street—Cambridge Mass

"Michael dear, come and sit next to me," Felicity Parker Prescott (McCarthy) said to her youngest son, patting the worn cushion of one of the genteelly shabby antique Queen Ann chairs that circled the twelve foot long dining room table that ran almost the full length of the solarium of the Brattle Street house.

"It's okay, Mom," Mick said, trying to smile, "I really don't need to sit."

"Nonsense, Michael," the still beautiful, thin, patrician, country club archetype that was his mother, said in her quiet assured tone. A tone which also said there would be no room for dissenting opinions.

Michael looked around quickly, like a trapped rabbit, looking for a hole in the cage. All he saw were his sister, Bronwyn, a Radcliffe freshman, and his brother; Franklin, Francis, Frankie, holding court with two young Prescott cousins from Andover and Groton respectively, who wanted to know if they should just start right in on pre-law next year at Harvard or take a semester or two at Oxford or the Sorbonne before buckling down to their predestined path that would lead them eventually to their rightful place at Hayward, Elliott and Delbert.

"Arrogant little pricks," Mick thought. "Christ, give me three days with those little dickheads in my squad in 'Nam and I'd have had them eating the crests off their prissy little prep school blazers."

"My goodness, Michael darling," came a low, cool, cultured voice from behind him. "You look ready to chew the stem right off that Baccarat crystal."

Slim, soft fingers, lightly drifted along the back of his neck and a tiny, little hummingbird tongue darted into his ear for a millisecond, as the once familiar smell of Chanel perfume swirled around him and mixed with the smell of antiques and ancient traditions in the place where three centuries of Prescotts had sat and eaten and judged.

Mick looked up at his mother and saw the amused look on her face as she said, "Good evening, Paige. How nice it is to see you. Your father and mother are well, I trust?"

"Oh yes, Mrs. Prescott, and they send their very best wishes on your birthday. As do I. It's so awfully nice of you to let me come. And the house and everything look so lovely, as always. And especially you."

"Oh, Paige, thank you darling you're so sweet and charming, as you say, 'as always'," said Mick's former debutante mother. Turning her long aristocratic neck, she looked at her youngest son and added, "don't you agree Michael?"

Mick looked from one to the other and thought incongruously, "Christ, they could be mother and daughter," and wondered for a split second, "Shit, you don't suppose they are, do you? That would make Paige and I…good lord, no!" thought Mick, "that's one bit of speculation I'm gonna' stick back in that musty old trunk I keep locked up in the dark old attic part of my brain." Instead he forced a smile and said, "Hi Paige."

"Clink, Clink, Clink," came the sound of an antique silver shrimp fork being hit three times on a Baccarat crystal champagne glass. Everyone in the room turned to look at the impressive figure clad in a Brooks Brothers suit who stood at the head of the table and clanked a glass for silence.

"Attention everyone," Franklin Prescott called out in a well modulated but commanding tone, "Please join me in wishing the very happiest, and most affectionate of birthday wishes to my own dear mother and constant inspiration to all of my endeavors, Mrs. Felicity Parker Prescott."

Mick winced involuntarily at the deliberate snub of the poor old beat-up and still banged up figure slumped in a rickety old Hitchcock armchair in the corner.

"Oh, Pop," thought Mick sadly, "you poor old bastard. You were always the 'Bull' in the Prescott china shop', but Christ, you deserve better than this."

"Thank you so much, Franklin dear," Mick's mother was saying, "for that lovely, lovely sentiment. And now, if everyone would please be seated."

"You're right here, Michael darling, "Mrs. Felicity Prescott said to her son, "right next to me."

"Oh, where am I Mrs. Prescott?" Asked the Channel breathed voice behind Mick.

"Why let me see, dear," came the measured tones, and lifting up one of the cream-colored vellum place cards on the table, said in mock surprise, "Why right there. On the other side of Michael."

*   *   *   *

"So Michael," Paige smiled her cool unflappable smile. "How is Harvard this semester? Have you finally applied to law school?"

"The jury's still out and, no," Mick answered.

"Well, at least," Paige said lightly, "you're starting to use law terms."

Mick gave her a weak excuse for a smile and looked back down at his congealing slice of ice cream cake.

"What is the matter, Michael?" Page asked, using her very best, Wellesley College, Seven Sisters, expression of 'deep concern for a dear friend' voice. "I know we're not as 'close'," the slightest emphasis on the word, "as we once were, but you must know how very deeply I still care."

Mick slowly turned towards his left and looked at Paige where she sat next to him absently drawing delicate designs in the melted residue of her ice cream cake.

"Do you really?" He thought, and looked at her finely chiseled profile. Milk white skin, pale blue eyes and her hair so blond, it was almost white. Three hundred years of Back Bay inbreeding he thought bitterly, as a little voice inside his head said mockingly, "Yep, and you used to be in love with her, boy-o. And are you sure you're still not?"

As if to throw more contrary gasoline on his confusions fire, Paige, perhaps sensing the moment put a delicate, pale hand on top of his and said, "I would so like for us to be friends again. That is," and to Mick's amazement, she actually seemed to blush, "if you think you could ever forgive me. Do you think you ever could?" She paused, just barely looking at him with demurely downcast eyes.

"Christ," thought Mick "do you suppose she really means it, or is this just another B.S. scam like the last time. I know I'm a sucker, but damned if I almost don't think she's serious."

"Hell, Paige," he answered, "I never wanted us to be pissed off at one another. You know how I felt about you all the time we were going out during prep school. And then when you went off to Wellesley and I got booted out of Harvard my freshman year, well you remember what you told me. I mean about being a rebel and too wild and how you couldn't go steady with someone like me, cause you knew what kind of future you'd like. And you didn't even know if I'd have one."

"Oh Michael," she said holding his hand tighter as her lashes became wet with tears, "I was a silly, spoiled selfish little child then. And I am so, so very sorry for the rotten way I behaved. Do you think you could ever, ever forgive me?"

Mick finally smiled and said, "Hey, babe, stranger things have happened."

She gave him a soft, self-effacing smile and said, "You're still so sweet."

Mick looked back at Paige and smiled and she smiled back at him. From the other side of Mick, Felicity Parker Prescott shared a satisfied smile with Paige.

*   *   *   *

"Michael, darling," Paige said, continuing to smile her disingenuous smile. "Mummy and Daddy are having a few friends in tomorrow night from the Club. The Delberts and Haywards. And as a matter of fact your brother will be there too. So, I thought if you weren't busy perhaps," And she paused to motion one of the black bow tied, severely uniformed waitresses from the catering service to refill her cup with Earl Grey tea, "Then you could—Yow! You clumsy little bitch!"

Page's mouth twisted into rage as she frantically rubbed her left arm, which had just been doused with scalding hot water.

"Oh, and it's sorry I am, m'um," came a wildly exaggerated, but familiar lilt. "I'm just fresh off the boat and all and I ain't learned the proper way of behavin' around me betters. Maybe your fine gentleman can pour yer tea better than a clumsy Irish girl," And as the teapot slammed down onto the table top, Mick looked up into the angry, flashing and hurt, tear-filled eyes of Bridget Connelly.

CHAPTER 21

▼

April 29, 1968
Prides Crossing
Boston's North Shore

A log popped and threw a spark out of the wall-length fireplace onto the thread-bare Oriental rug. The colonel watched it burn for a moment and then quietly walked over to the smoldering spot on the carpet and very slowly and deliberately, ground the tip of his soft-toed moccasin into the glowing ember.

"So you've finally come, Sergeant," he said without looking up.

"What do you mean 'finally come' sir?" Mick asked, silently cursing himself for slipping so easily back into the ingrained deference that he'd once owed to this man.

"I knew that someday you would be here," the colonel said, still not looking up from the now burnt and dead blackened spot under his foot. The silence stretched out until only the sounds of the fire crackling in the massive wrought iron grate filled the room.

"What happened, colonel. I really need to know. It's screwing up my life. And everyone's around me."

The colonel still didn't speak. He just stared into the fire and Mick stared along with him. And he saw the village again.

*   *   *   *

June 15, 1966
Village somewhere north of Firebase Bravo

The old lady held her AK-47 at hip level and swung it towards Mick, screaming "Die" in French or English or Vietnamese. Mick could never get it straight in his confused mind, which it was.

"Drop it, drop it, drop it," Mick shouted back. But in his nightmares and waking dreams, she never did. Mick could feel the 7.62 mm slugs whizzing by his head like angry hornets as he screamed for the last time, "I said drop it, damn it you!" and opened up with his M-16, blowing her stomach open and sending her sprawling back into the hut.

Eyes stinging from the smoke or something else, Mick yelled desperately to the old woman's gun-toting, young teenage daughter, "Didn't you hear me you stupid bitch, I said drop it. Now!"

But just as he'd known with a precognition certainty, she wouldn't or couldn't lay down her AK. Instead, with her baby brother still clinging to her hip, she took a wide-legged stance in front of the now burning bamboo hut and locked her finger on the trigger.

Mick saw the slugs leaving the muzzle in slow motion. He could feel them tearing into his body. He was dying and his men were dying all around him. He needed to remember what the colonel had told them to do. No. The colonel had told them that they'd know what to do. What was he supposed to do??

Yes. He was supposed to kill them, kill them all.

He flipped his selector to full automatic and pointed the M-16 towards the VC bitch and her evil little brother and blew them back into the burning hut to take their place next to their dead mother. She was still moving.

Mick entered the hut, his M-16 still hot in his hands. He coughed and wiped a bloody hand across his face, trying to clear his eyes of the smoke that filled the hut. Then he saw the three pitiful bullet ridden figures huddled together bleeding in the corner of the smoldering hut.

Mick gouged a thumb into the corner of one eye and the smoke seemed to clear for an instant, and he saw…the thirteen-year-old girl holding her mother's head in her lap and moaning. Her dead baby brother draped across her mother's shriveled stomach. Mick stood out in the center of the hut, his mouth working but no sound came out.

The mortally wounded teenage girl stretched out her arms to Mick and said in colonial Vietnamese French, "pourquoi? Why, why?"

Mick shook his head from side to side. No, this wasn't real. It was a V C. trick. An ambush. And it was verified three seconds later when private Begley burst through the door of the hut and screamed, "Sarge, watch it," as he opened up on the still weakly pleading young girl and sent her bullet-filled body jerking across the bloody dirt floor of the hut.

"Finished her, Sarge," Begley yelled back over his shoulder as he backed out of the hut.

Mick stumbled to the back of the hut where the figure was still twitching and bent down over her. She was just barely alive and yet she was still whispering over and over, "pourquoi? Why, why?"

Then Walzac and Begley and the rest of the company were standing there beside Mick saying, "Sarge, she's still got the AK and she's getting up to kill again."

"I can't," Mick said blindly shaking his head, until Walzac reached down and pulled his razor sharp, double-edged Fairbairn-Sykes Commando knife out of its sheath and said, "Here, finish it Mick." Numbly, Mick bent down as the golden skinned, slant eyed angel with jet black hair, wept crystal red tears and screamed, "no, no, no," over and over and over again.

＊   ＊   ＊   ＊

"Sergeant?" Came the voice from the figure still back lit from the enormous fire blazing in the hearth of antique mansion perched on the cliffs of Prides Crossing.

Mick snapped back to the present as the rubber band of his own horrible, dark, and paranoid history hit him right between the eyes. He shook his head for a moment and then with an unbearably pain filled animal scream, launched himself at the colonel. He had a split second image of two cold, dark resigned eyes as his hands closed around the rough, sandpaper skin of the colonel's neck, before something crashed into the back of his head and the terror, guilt and pain, winked out.

CHAPTER 22

▼

The Angel came again, but this time she was not alone. There were other things. Things that stood just outside of her golden light. Things that weren't like the Angel. Not at all. They were dark things. Evil things. Things that lurked in the jungle and had come into the village with C Company. They were the things that sat grinning around the huts while the men of Company C had slapped clip after clip into their smoking M-16s and pulled back on their triggers as their automatic weapons had jumped and bucked in their hands like living things.

Mick saw them more clearly now, as the things that lurked in the jungle perimeter of his dreams every night. The things that never came out in the daylight, but laughed and gibbered at him in the half light of each pre-dawn when he woke up suddenly, heart beating wildly and drenched in that same steaming sweat that he remembered from the jungle.

And now they were here, coming out of the shadows. Coming up behind the Angel. Coming for her, as she stood before Mick, a desperate pleading look on her face while the crystal red tears froze and sparkled in hell's firelight.

As the things crept and slithered closer and closer to her, Mick screamed, "Run. Run, I'll hold them off just run. Run!" Where was his weapon? He had to find the M-16. He had to stop them and hold them off so that the Angel could get away. That was the only way. If only he could stop them and save her then maybe all the dreams and the nightmares and waking and sleeping, would stop.

Oh Christ, if he could only make them stop!

His hands flailed blindly, looking for the familiar shape of his M-16, but the things found him and put their dripping red hands on him. Hands that were strong as steel bands. They were all around him now and he struck out, but they pinned him down and he looked up into the eyes of the chief of his tormentors. They were pale and black at the center. Black as coal. Black as death and cold as ice. .

*   *   *   *

Mick drifted through darkness for eternity and out beyond the dark side of the moon. But just before he was about to spin out into the blackness of space forever, a whirling satellite of despair, the Angel took pity on him again and grabbed his hand at the last moment and brought him back.She grabbed his hand so tight it hurt. Dragged him back into the light and forced him to open his eyes as she said fiercely, "Damn you McCarthy, open your bloody eyes and look at me!" And he did. And he looked up into the very concerned, very frightened and very angry face of Bridget Connelly.

"Michael?" She said.

"Yeah? Yeah, oh, Bridge, it's you. How did you get here? With her, and those things. Out beyond the moon."

"Oh, Jesus, Mick," she bit off her concern, "stop it. Now just stop it!"

"Stop what?" Mick asked as he tried to sit up, but the sudden movement brought on a nausea and dizziness that collapsed him back down on…where was he?

He looked around. A couch, a chair, and a beat up old coffee table with cigarette burns left by two lovers who had missed the ashtray one passion-filled night last December. He was home. But how? He closed his eyes as the room swam around him again and the throbbing in the back of his head threatened to turn his queasy stomach inside out.

"What happened, Bridge?" Mick asked, keeping his eyes tightly closed, trying to control the spinning.

There was a long silence, and then he heard Bridget's tightly controlled voice say, "What happened Michael McCarthy, is I've been up all the night worrying and calling every one we know, to see which damn bar you might be off in this time. Or what skirt you might be chasing after, or should I say what skinny, arrogant, little Wellesley snob, you might have decided fitted your mother's world better than the clumsy, tea spilling, servin' girl, who I guess is fit only to wait your family's table!"

Mick forced his eyes open just in time to see the hot angry tears in Bridget's eyes as she turned and ran out of the room. "Oh Christ," he moaned as he pushed himself shakily to his feet and staggered after her. He found her in the small back bedroom, laying on the bed, face down. He could tell by the way her shoulders heaved up and down that she was crying the way he'd never seen her do before.

"Bridge?" He said gently, gingerly sitting down on the side of the bed next to her. "You've gotta' believe me, babe. I didn't know anything about that party. My brother just told me to show up for Mom's birthday. I didn't know Paige was going to be there. I guess Mom just invited her cause our families have been friends and all for so long…" Mick let his voice trail off.

"Bugger all you know about it, McCarthy," she muttered.

"And I absolutely had no idea that they were gonna' hire the catering company you work for. I mean what are the odds?" He finished lamely, as she gave him a look that would have melted lead at five hundred paces.

She said, "You're either the greatest liar from here to County Kildare or the most gullible fool as ever fell down a well. And I don't know as how I might even care which!" And she buried her face in the pillow.

In the end Mick did the only thing he could think of to stop her tears. They made love. Normally, it was an experience far beyond the trite term of 'pleasant' but this time Mick had to concentrate on how much he really did love this feisty, tough, tender, beautiful little girl to keep from passing out, from the splitting pain in the back of head.

"The things we do for love," he thought and would have laughed except:

a) It hurt too much, and b) Bridget would have hit him, and probably right on the back of his head.

When it was over and she finally lay sweet and satisfied in his arms, he thought about the line he'd once read in a Victorian novel in Freshman English at Andover, where a proper British upper class mother had told her daughter on her wedding night to "Just close your eyes dear, and think of England."

"And what are you grinnin' about Mr. 'Cheshire Cat' McCarthy?" Bridget asked, propping herself up on one elbow.

"Just thinking of England, dear," Mick replied, winking at her.

"What??" she said, looking narrowly at him.

"Ah-hhh…" Mick countered, holding up his hands, "it's not nice to hit your lover, especially when he's got a head that feels like someone played kick ball with it."

Her eyes immediately softened again and she said, "Jesus, and shame on me for fergettin', yer like as not to have a concussion. And I should have been takin' ya to the hospital instead of lettin' ya roger me silly, but it was nice all the same," she added with a small smile, as she snuggled back onto his chest and fell quietly to sleep.

*   *   *   *

The sun was high enough up in the sky to pour into the west facing back bedroom window as Bridget woke him by plopping a tray down on his chest, with buttered muffins and hot steaming tea.

"Here, sit up," she said, propping the pillows up behind him, as she fussed him into an upright position. "Drink this," she said, lifting a yellow china mug to his lips.

"Wo-ow!" Mick said blowing into the cup to cool it, "Hot, but good." He added hastily.

She gave a small "Harumph", and then smoothed the sheet and sat down on the bed beside him. As Mick sipped the tea and took a mouthful of muffin, he asked, "you still haven't told me, how did I wind up here last night? The last thing I remember, I was standing in front of the Colonel in that monstrous old pile up on the North Shore, and I guess I sorta' flipped out. And then everything got really freaky and, I…I…don't really know. Or I guess I don't really want to know."

Bridget didn't answer for a minute and then said, "like I told you, I'd worried myself near sick last night till around two in the morning when I heard this thud on the porch and a car driving away, and then a moaning and thrashing sound coming from the front porch. I ran down stairs and there you were. The back of your head all covered in blood and eyes wide open but staring at nothing. I couldn't move you on my own, so I was running up the stairs to call an ambulance, when that nice young lad from India, Gupta I think his name is, you know the medical student, came out of his flat and helped me get you up the stairs. And then he patched yer head and put you on the couch. But you started havin' some kind of nightmare and got up and were screaming, 'run, run' and you fell over the coffee table and I was trying my damnedest to get you back onto the couch, when you finally opened your eyes and came back to me."

CHAPTER 23

▼

April 29, 1968
9:00PM—Just off
Harvard Square, Cambridge

The party was in full swing and even though Chrissie was still pissed about all of the scruffy hippie types who invariably showed up when Bronwyn Prescott (McCarthy) put the word out that it was party time on Palmer Street, it was evident that even 'prissy Chrissie' (as the rest of the girls called Bronwyn's roommate and girlhood best friend) was having a good time. As a matter of fact, maybe too good a time, thought Bronwyn, as she watched her 'best friend'...Or so she thought, rest her hand delicately on Bronwyn's boyfriend Quang's knee. All this while he tried to explain molecular DNA to a group of obviously stoned and semi comatose 'flower children'. "Yeah, right," thought Bronwyn, irreverently, "if the those flower children aren't from the 'Nirvana' of B.U., then I'll eat my hippie beads, one crunchy bite at a time."

However, when a tall, skinny, intense John Lennon look-alike and 'want-to-be', detached himself from the group to ask Bronwyn if she'd ever really analyzed the meaning behind the words to Dylan's 'Desolation Row', she shelved her cynicism, and jealousy (at least for now) and said, "Wow, like right on man," and jumped head first into the 'deep end' of her generation's pool.

Later, after the B U crew aided by a trio of very stoned girls from LaSalle Junior College, had done an impromptu 'love-in dance', to peace and love and worked their way through the collection of 'Vanilla Fudge' and 'Canned Heat' records they'd brought, Bronwyn was finally able to put on some of Eric Clapton's new group, 'Cream' and slide over next to Quang when Chrissie went to the bathroom.

"So have you been having fun tonight?" Bronwyn asked innocently, twirling her long, curly, dark hair around her right forefinger.

"Ah, Bronwyn," Quang said with still the hint of South East Asia lurking under his French, English and Swiss private school education.

Bronwyn looked at him, and thought that even though she knew her father thought that anyone who wasn't Irish was a "God damn sissy" and her mother would have said…" Oh my dear, I know that many of them are terribly nice. But are you really sure that you want to go out with…Well an Oriental gentleman?"

Yes, she almost screamed aloud, she didn't care!

"Well," Bronwyn thought, in defiance of both of her parents, "Oriental or not…He still was very nice and very intelligent and very good-looking…And very much of a gentleman." And just now she admitted to herself, and almost blushed at the thought, between the pot and wine coolers, she almost wished that he wasn't always such a gentleman!

And yet Bronwyn Parker Prescott (the 'McCarthy' quietly put away in the musty attic of 'things past' when her parents got divorced during Bronwyn's final year at the Montessori School) had been raised by her mother to believe that associating with anything but a gentleman should be simply unthinkable.

Once when Bronwyn was 14 and had wanted, 'oh so badly', to go to a dance at St. Bartholomew's in Dorchester, it had precipitated one of their worst fights and had led to one of the few times she'd ever seen her mother 'lose her cool'.

As Bronwyn stared at nothing through the blue haze of marijuana smoke drifting around the tiny party packed living room, she recalled how her mother had gotten wind of the fact that she was meeting a cute boy there from Southie. And the fact that she'd been introduced to him by two of her 'rowdy' McCarthy cousins, made it even worse! She could almost, but not quite, smile about it now as she remembered her mother's voice rising as she forbade her daughter to "go to a dance unchaperoned, where there would undoubtedly be 'hoodlums' hanging about, And didn't she'd understand that her type of 'young lady' didn't go out with 'boys like that'? They went out with young 'gentlemen', and…"

Bronwyn closed her eyes for a moment, briefly regretful at the way she had with self-righteous 14-year-old contempt, turned to her mother and said scornfully, "Oh…You mean just like you, mother?"

"A penny for them."

"Hum…What?" Bronwyn asked momentarily disoriented.

"I mean to say, a penny for your thoughts…that is correct, isn't it?" Quang paused with a slight smile and added, "I never have any doubt where the English grammar is concerned, but I do have to confess that sometimes your euphemisms elude me."

Bronwyn smiled back and said, "Your euphemisms are just fine. And your grammar is much better than mine! I just wish my French were half as good as yours. And the only Vietnamese I know are a few words my brother taught me. And I have a feeling that they're probably not very nice ones knowing my brother," she finished with a giggle.

"Your brother has been to Viet Nam?" Quang asked cautiously.

"Well, yes, for a year. He was in...Well you know."

"Yes, I know," Quang answered quietly, "Many of my new American friends," and he smiled as he gently picked up Bronwyn's tanned but smooth hand and kissed her finger tips while looking over the top of his ever present dark glasses, "have tried to help my poor stricken country."

Bronwyn's pulse did a little rat-tat-tat, before she sucked in a quick breath and said, "Well, yeah, I guess so. I mean, he doesn't really talk about it much. I think he was very affected by all of the suffering he saw there...Just like we all are...Affected I mean...by the suffering...and all," Bronwyn finished awkwardly and blushed.

"It's all right." Quang said quietly and Bronwyn gave him a grateful smile for his understanding. Quang looked back at her, still maintaining his sympathetic, understanding smile, but thinking bitterly to himself, "Look at her. The beautiful, pampered child of a beautiful, pampered nation." He looked closely at her from behind his dark glasses and took in her clear, fair complexion, made all the more interesting by a stardust sprinkling of freckles, long naturally wavy chestnut brown hair and blue-gray eyes that became hazel-green in the sunlight. Despite his cosmopolitan Swiss education, he was still surprised and sometimes titillated by the skintight embroidered bell-bottomed jeans that American girls wore with their low-cut embroidered peasant blouses.

"Now it's my turn," Bronwyn grinned impishly.

"I beg your pardon?" Quang answered politely, momentarily thrown off balance at being caught staring at her.

"I said, it's my turn...You know...A penny for them?" And she giggled at his momentary discomfort.

"Ah..." He suddenly smiled, and then 12 years of French-English private school training and a lifetime of hiding his thoughts kicked in and he smiled urbanely. He picked up her hand, brought it to his lips again and murmured in his most perfect British film star English, "You've caught me again Miss Prescott, lost in the thought of how absolutely, enchantingly lovely you are."

As Bronwym's eyes turned a shade or two brighter and she thought, "I think I'd like to feel those lips somewhere other than on my hand," there was a loud banging at the door. As it crashed open, Bronwyn looked up in horror to see two Cambridge cops followed by a stocky blue-suited figure step into the room where he was momentarily outlined in the blue haze of marijuana smoke. Recognition came an instant later as she looked up into the bull dog face and shocked, angry eyes of her father…Michael Francis McCarthy!

CHAPTER 24

▼

April 29, 1968
9:47 p.m.
Copley Square Boston

"Mr. Ling?" The waiter said.

"Yes?" came the reply.

"I believe your party is here," the elderly waiter assigned to the Copley 'Gold Room' responded.

"Please then, show him to my table," the middle-aged, nondescript-looking Asian man in the drab but expensive Brooks Brothers charcoal gray suit said.

"Ah, Captain Bannon," Mr. Ling smiled as the potbellied, nervous-looking precinct captain was led up to his table and stood uncomfortably shifting from one foot to the other until the ancient waiter had pulled out his chair, seated him, and shambled off.

"So delighted you could join me for a late night snack in this delightful, venerable old restaurant," Mr. Ling beamed, and continued, "This entire area is quite historic, you know. The Back Bay it is called, I believe. And I read in that remarkable Boston Public library that you have available right across the square from this wonderful hotel, that this very area was once underwater. Part of a Boston Harbor's Bay…Hence the name, Back Bay. Remarkable, don't you think?"

Bannon gave a brief uncomfortable smile while darting his eyes side to side apprehensively around the room. "Yes," Mr. Ling continued hooking his thumbs into the twin watch pockets of his Brooks Brothers vest, "Really quite extraordinary when you consider this massive effort was carried out by your Anglo-Saxon ancestors."

"Not mine," Captain Bannon muttered.

Still smiling, Mr. Ling went on as if totally unaware of the interruption.

"Yes, especially when you consider that your Western culture places so much emphasis on the 'value of the individual' rather than the collective good of the whole. Amazing," he said, and still smiling, shook his head from side to side.

"What did you say?" Bannon asked.

"I said...Amazing." Mr. Ling answered.

"What's amazing?" The distracted Bannon answered, still looking nervously around the room.

"That your western race was ever able to accomplish so much, and still seems to be able to," he concluded shaking his head. "You have no collective will...No unity of purpose, unlike our country where the individual exists only to serve the state."

"What the fuck are you talking about?" Bannon snapped at him.

"Please watch your language, Mr. Precinct Captain Bannon," Mr. Ling said in his same measured tones but with his eyes growing hard, "I appreciate the...What is your word...Yes, 'High Class', of this wonderful place, even if you don't."

He was still smiling but something in his expression made Bannon mumble, "ah, ah, yeah...sorry."

Mr. Ling continued his lecture with a slight incline of his head to show Bannon that his apology had been accepted. "However, I still have hopes for your 'cowboy culture'. Yes, very high hopes, because I see your young people...Especially in your province of Cambridge...who seem to be embracing the teachings of our great leader, Chairman Mao."

"What the frigging hell was this God damn Chinaman babbling on about?" Bannon thought to himself, but subconsciously clamped his mouth shut as if to prevent the thought from escaping.

"You see," the beaming Oriental man continued, warming to his subject, "You and men like your former colleague Mr. McCarthy," Ling smiled slightly at Bannon's uncomfortable twitch at the interjection of McCarthy's name, "expend your energy and talent (Ling seemed to sneer at the word) in living your own selfish, individualistic lives. Whereas, this young generation of University students seem to be taking a lesson from our own dedicated young people, in realizing that the wicked old ways of their capitalistic elders need to be ruthlessly stamped out."

"Oh I see," Bannon said, finally turning his head to look at Ling. "You mean, like stamping out Brooks Brothers suits, lobster Thermidor and 12 year-old Scotch."

Ling's eyes narrowed into two flashing points for an instant before he forced his face to relaxed again into his carefully constructed smile.

"Very good Mr. Precinct Captain Bannon, we'll make a philosopher out of you yet. And now to business. Tell me, how are your efforts to direct our friend McCarthy proceeding."

CHAPTER 25

▼

M.I.T.—Boi-Tech Lab—April 30, 1968—1:38 PM

Quang was so engrossed in the images he was observing in the graduate studies Biology labs' electron microscope, that at first he didn't even register the presence of someone standing almost silently and observing him over his left shoulder. But it didn't take long for him to detect the familiar odor from his youth, of fish paste mixed with the gummy sesame seed candies that had been one of his few happy memories from his otherwise bleak and traumatic early childhood.

"Excellent, Doctor Weh, very first rate," came the quiet stilted voice from behind him. "We are all very proud of you. You have more than justified the early faith we have placed in you."

Quang Weh, had the brief hopeful fleeting thought that if he ignored the voice, it would go away. But as soon as the thought took wing, it was shot down in flames by the bland, sing song voice that seemed so innocent and yet as Quang knew only too well, was laced with menace. Finally without taking his eyes away from the electron microscope, he sighed and asked, "What is it that you want now?"

For what seemed like an eternity, there was no response except for the shallow breathing behind him. And then finally…" Now?…Now, Mr. Engineer/Doctor Quang? Now we would like you to remember the great, un-repayable debt that you owe to our glorious People's Republic," and the voice paused for emphasis…" that has sacrificed so long and hard to bring you to the position of power and prestige that you occupy today…Or did you forget all of that, "the formerly soft and lyrical voice added in the same polite tones which had now become a hard as ice crystals.

An eternity passed before Quang finally let his voice out and said resignedly, "No, I didn't forget," and added, "and if I ever did, I'm certain you would remind me." Silence. After a few moments, Quang looked up from the sub atomic universe displayed in the electron microscope and looked around. The lab behind him was empty. He let the pent-up breath he'd been subconsciously holding escape through his nostrils and turned back to the comprehensible order he observed every night through the 10,000 to one eyepiece of the incredible electron microscope.

"It is incredible," he thought as he settled in to play his nightly 20 questions game with himself. It always went something like this:

Quang # 1: (questioner)—"Are you sure you've found the answer to ending world hunger?"

Quang # 2—"Almost"

Quang # 1—"And what will you do with this?…Who will you share it with?"

Quang # 2—"I'm still not sure."

Quang # 1—" And what about the terrible parts…Are you going to share those?"

Quang # 2—"I shouldn't…But I must. It's too much for…"

Quang # 1—"So again, who will you tell?. Who?!! You must answer me or…"

Suddenly Quang's world went black as a pair of hands clamped down over his eyes. He drew in a choking gasp and flailed with both hands in a vain attempt to pull away, while screaming, "leave me alone, leave me…What?…"

He whirled around and looked up into Bronwyn Prescott's green, gold and hazel eyes.

The seconds of silence stretched away until Bronwyn finally said in a small contrite voice, "I was going to say 'peek-a-boo'…But maybe I'd better just leave it at…Oops!"

CHAPTER 26

▼

Harvard Square Cambridge
October 28, 1966—in front of the Harvard Co-op

It was almost too warm to even think about Halloween and then Thanksgiving less than a month later. So Mick decided not to think about it at all. He was becoming a very good at that. He was almost pleased with the way he'd managed to wipe everything out of his mind that had happened before he woken up in his Fort Benning hospital bed sometime just after the fourth of July. The 4th of July in Georgia. Way too hot…He didn't want to be hot or think about memories laid down in the stifling, choking heat. Not now…Not ever again.

He shook his head to rattle the miscreant memories away and thought, "but an unseasonably warm October afternoon in New England…Well, that was OK."

He wiped the sleeve of his old olive drab Army shirt across the blue and gold paint of his brand new BSA motorcycle's gas tank.

"So I guess there are some good things you can do with a mysterious 'mustering out' bonus check," he mused to himself.

"Sure," the wayward voice in his head answered, "good for you…And how come you've yet to run across anyone else who got a five figure check for 'mustering out'?"

"Oh screw you," he said irritably to the now annoying voice that wouldn't shut the hell up. It kept up a steady stream of unpleasant questions during his sleeping, and now somewhat alarming waking hours.

"Shut the hell up Mick," he said to the voice, "and enjoy the day." But he knew, as always when this happened, he needed to talk to someone, anyone, if he was going to get the god damned voice to shut the hell up. He glanced at his watch. Four p.m. and it was already getting dark. He knew he wasn't going to be able to stick with his self-imposed rule about no drinking before 5:00 p.m. He needed to anesthetize the voice…and quick. He stretched his arms over his head and drew his knees up to his chin as his boots slipped off the chrome handlebars of the 750 BSA.

He thought about pulling on his denim jacket as he primed the BSA's carbs in preparation for starting, but decided against it thinking to himself, "Christ, it's only a block and a half and its warm as summer or warm as the jungle in…No! Damn it, I'm not thinking about that place! "And he savagely kicked his foot down on the recoil foot crank. Nothing." Great play Shakespeare, "he muttered to himself…" You flooded the damn thing." And putting both feet down onto the pavement, pulled the BSA backwards to rest on its kickstand until the gas fumes could clear the carburetor so he could try a restart.

In the meantime…well there was that cute little blond playing with two talentless hippie burnouts in front of the Harvard Co-op. Mick swung one booted foot over the right side of handlebars and slowly ambled across the square, just daring any car to challenge his slow, "Hey I own this road, man," shuffle. Mick crossed the square and propped his butt up on the back of one of the bus stop's faded peeling benches, as the wispy, pale little bond finished up a credible if somewhat uninspired version of Judy Collins' 'Daddy you've been on my mind'.

"Well, 'Big Mama' Thornton certainly did it better," Mick thought to himself, "but on the other hand, she looks a hell of a lot better than 'Big Mama'!" One or two people passing by, stopped long enough to give a few sporadic claps which Mick took upon himself to improve upon with almost a full minute of sustained, measured applause. The pale girl with the long white blond hair in the flowing flowered dress blushed and smiled gratefully back at Mick before launching into a thin, sweet high version of Dylan's 'Masters of war', and…Yes! That was where he seen her…almost three weeks ago at the Club 47! Yeah, that was the night, he'd got in a 'bug up his ass' and broken Danny's nose 'cause he'd been running his mouth while Mick wanted to listen to this pale little doll. What was her name? He racked his brains. And then it started to come back. He'd never gotten it. Because, just as he was about to ditch his two cousins and go up to the stage where the dozen performers of the evening were taking their intermission, a dirty cardboard coffee cup had been plopped down on the table by a slim, white, silver ringed hand and he'd forgotten all about the shy little folk singer.

"And crap," he thought ruefully, "I've been looking for the owner of those soft white hands and green eyes for over three weeks now, and still nothing…So what is it about the' bird in the hand'?" he thought as he slipped off the benches back, while reaching into his pocket to find it $5 bill to put in her empty guitar case.

But before he could cover the 10 steps that separated them, he heard a pair of nasal whining voices say, "Hey—you...Hippie bitch, play some Beach Boys!"

And as Mick watched, eyes narrowing, and mouth clamping into a thin hard line, two half-in-the-bag, frat boy types, swaggered up to the folk trio.

"Play, 'Help Me Rhonda', the beefy guy at in the SAE sweatshirt yelled and his grinning frat buddy said, "Yeah, and then...And then play that song about, 'fun, fun, fun, fun...' he slurred the words, "until her Daddy...Does something with the T-Bird?..." He trailed off looking up at his equally drunken friend for completion.

"Takes it away."

"What?"

"I said, takes it away, asshole!"

"Takes what away?"

"The T-bird, numb nuts!"

"Oh, hhh, Yeah...The T-bird. Yeah, play that!"

Throughout this drunken exchange, the blond girl's two long-haired accompanists had been quietly packing up their guitars. Now as the tipsy pair finished up their tortured dialogue, the musicians slowly began to back away while whispering to the stricken looking blonde, "See you later, Holly...yeah, we'll practice tomorrow...Ok?"

"Hey, faggots!" yelled the shorter of the two, "come on back here!"

"Aw, let 'em go, "the football type in the red SAE sweat shirt said, "We've got our own little songbird right here." He stepped with one sockless, Bass Weagin-clad foot into her open guitar case and putting a meaty arm around her thin shoulders, pulled her panicked face close to his.

"Please...I...I really have to go now," she gasped.

"No, you don't," said the smaller of the pair, "You're gonna' play us some Beach Boys...Right, little hippie girl?"

"Actually...No," came a hard voice from behind him. He whirled around and saw a medium height, medium build, gray-eyed guy in a faded army T-shirt and jeans, leaning against a bus stop bench, one cowboy-booted foot hooked over the lower rungs of the bench.

"Hey, screw off, pal," the big guy in the sweat shirt said, "this ain't none of your business."

"Then I guess I'm making it mine," Mick smiled remembering how a Kentucky coal miner's son had, 'made it his business' in that South Boston army base locker room, what seemed like a thousand years ago.

"Yeah," Mick said to himself, as he pushed his booted foot off of the bus stop bench, "I guess I owe the 'wheel of karma' a little payback."

In retrospect, Mick reflected, it really hadn't been much of a fight. Certainly not enough to earn him the trembling, dewy-eyed gratitude of the still shaking little blonde who sniffled softly into his now damp T-shirt. As a matter of fact, after the first, adrenaline rush of 'combat' wore off, he felt almost guilty about how easy it had actually been. They had, incredibly, been even drunker than they'd looked. And a quick 'take down' move from right out of basic training had done for the smaller of the two, while one sharp jab to the gut had doubled over the big SAE jock, and sent the contents an afternoon's beer binge at the Oxford Alehouse splattering all over the brick walls of the Harvard Co-op.

Now Mick was gently shushing the still frightened girl as he helped her do up the clasp on her guitar case. "Come on," he said picking up the case in his right hand as she still clutched onto his left, "I'll give you a ride home.

"Thank you, she smiled, wiping the corner of her eye with her long, flowing sleeve. And then added, "my name is Holly."

CHAPTER 27

▼

**Harvard Square
Cambridge—October 28, 1966—
Third story window overlooking the Harvard Co-op**

Michael 'Big Mike' McCarthy looked away from the window overlooking the Square and sat back down at the big, scarred, old roll top desk and smiled to himself. "Well, Mickey," he thought, "It's damned certain you don't need the help of a beat-up old beat cop!" He grinned and said out loud to himself, "I gotta' say that a year in the army has turned Mrs. Prescott's prep school boy into a 'kick ass' McCarthy." He reached into the top drawer of the old rolltop desk and pulled out a half-empty bottle of Bushmill's Irish whiskey. Mike blew the dust and dried coffee grounds out of an old cardboard coffee cup that had seen better days and poured out two fingers of Bushmill's. He turned back to the window, lifted up the paper coffee cup saying, "Here's to ya', Mickey lad," and tossed back the shot. He continued standing and watching at the window overlooking the square, and his grin widened as he saw his youngest son put his arm around the pretty, thin blond and lead her to his motorcycle.

He smiled sadly and said to the small figure below, "Be good boy-o…and if you can't be good, for Christ sake, be careful!" A sharp rap on the pebbled glass door that read, "McCarthy and Associates: Private Investigations," interrupted his musing.

"Come in, it's not locked," Mike said, still staring out the window.

The door creaked open and a soft voice said, "Mr. McCarthy?"

"You got him," Mike said not turning around.

"Yes…then, thank you," came the strange cadence, causing Mike to finally turn around, where he saw a blank Chinese face smiling back at him."

"So happy to have found you, my name is…Mr. Ling."

*   *   *   *

The chair from the old oak desk squeaked in protest as Mike swiveled it back towards the window and stared out at the now dark October street.

He wondered for the hundredth time since the smiling oriental man had left his office, if he'd done the right thing by accepting the job. On the other hand, he shrugged, what real choice did he have? After all, it wasn't as though he had hordes of well-heeled clients breaking down his door with hundred dollar bills in their hands. And this guy actually did, he reflected…have hundred dollar bills in his hands!

"Mr. Former 'Police Detective McCarthy'," he'd said in that curious sing-song voice of his, "I've heard many very fine and worthy things about you"

"Yeah, from who?" Mick had snorted. "My mother died ten years ago and my brother moved back to Ireland after he became a priest."

"Ah," Mr. Ling smiled uncomprehendingly, "It is obviously my misfortune not to have made the acquaintance of either of them, but I was referring to your former colleagues, Mr. Precinct Captain Bannon and Detective/Sergeant Morrison."

"Bannon!" Mike snorted again. "And what 'fine and worthy' things does that little 'cousin to a weasel' have to say about me?

"He speaks very highly of your diligence," the little man smiled his unreadable smile and added, "He says that once you have accepted an assignment, you never slacken your diligence until it is completed." Mr. Ling sat back in the hard wicker chair across from the desk and clasped his hands over his small round belly and stared, still smiling, back at Mike.

"I guess you could say that," Mike shrugged noncommittally.

"That is excellent, Mr. Detective McCarthy," Ling beamed and pulled out a large roll of hundred dollar bills, "because I have a small but very 'special' and very important commission that I wish you to accept."

CHAPTER 28

▼

The Blue Parrot
Harvard Square—Cambridge
October 28,1966
9:00 p.m.

The candlelight flickered and cast strange but attractive shadows across Holly's thin, aesthetic face, Mick thought. He watched her through the smoky air that swirled and drifted around the tiny tables crammed between the rough stone whitewashed walls of the 'Blue Parrot'.

"Why do they call it the 'Blue Parrot' Mick?" Holly asked with her shy, sweet smile. After a moment's pause she added, "everything here on the East Coast is so different than the Midwest. It's so exciting and different, and so free. I guess that's why I love it so."

"Yeah," Mick answered in a tired, cynical voice, "it sure is that all right," and then smiled back at her, "Maybe that's why sometimes I think that some day I just might fire up the BSA and head for one of them Midwestern corn fields. And when I finally get to where no one has ever heard of Harvard Square, codfish or chowder then I'll turn off the bike and marry me the first pretty little blonde haired, blue-eyed, corn-fed Midwestern farm girl I see."

"Oh stop it Mick," Holly blushed as she quickly made the connection of the romantic innuendo, "Why would you ever want to leave a place where there's culture and music and art and freedom to express yourself and..."

"And drunken frat boys," Mick interrupted with a wry cynical smile.

"Mick," Holly drew in a breath with a stricken look and then steeled her trembling lower lip with a smile and finished with..." But you just proved my point.

For every drunken frat boy here, there's a noble knight in shining armor." She beamed back at him through the 'Blue Parrot's' smoky haze.

Mick smiled back at her with the same self doubting but 'wishing-it-were-true' smile curling up the left corner of his mouth and answered, "I'm afraid the armor's a bit tarnished...And by the way there were two."

"Two?" Holly crinkled her nose in puzzlement.

"Two...Two drunken frat boys." Mick answered.

"Oh, Yes...Oh yes," Holly smiled face beaming with gratitude. "There were two, and you just came to my rescue all the same." And reaching across the tiny table, took his hand and pressed it to her lips, said with a sigh..." My brave, brave knight."

"Holly..." Mick said, suddenly uncomfortable "it really wasn't all that much...I mean they were just full of piss and beer muscles. Hell, if they were stone cold sober, I probably would have gotten my ass kicked."

"Hush," she said and put one thin soft finger up to his lips. "It was the bravest thing I've ever seen...and I won't hear a word against my own brave, true knight!"

"Okay, kid," Mick thought, "Hey, if you're looking for a hero to warm your bed tonight, then I guess you've found him."

He had a brief guilty twinge as he looked into her sweet, admiring and trusting face. He thought, "You bastard, are you really take advantage of the 'accidental hero' bit to get her into the sack?"But he answered himself a moment later with, "yeah...And you know why. Those beautiful blue Midwestern corn-fed eyes, will keep those jungle demons back in the shadows. And I'd do anything for that," he added grimly to himself.

"Mick?" Holly looked at him across the barrel tabletop, "Is there anything wrong? "Mick snapped back and looked into her guileless eyes. He shook his head and said, "Sorry, babe, I was just drifting out there in the ozone for a minute." She smiled back at him with concern.

Mick drew in a breath and shook his head to clear the cobwebs and said, "Hey, what were you asking me...before?"

"Before what?" Holly answered.

"Before you started dressing me up in all that shiny, clanking armor," "Mick grinned back.

"Oh stop," Holly blushed, "I meant it...every word," and she turned even redder and as she looked down at the candle wax-scarred table top.

"Wait," interrupted Mick, changing the subject. "I remember...you wanted to know why they call this place the 'Blue Parrot'.

"Oh yes," Holly answered, "It's such an exotic name. There must be a story behind it."

"Well," Mick began, "If you noticed, when we came, there's a restaurant upstairs, called Casablanca. Ring a bell?"

"Why, yes," Holly smiled with recognition, "That was that wonderful old black-and-white movie that starred Humphrey Bogart and Ingrid Bergman. Oh," she sighed, "that was so-o-o romantic!"

"OK," Mick said, "then you must remember the name of the bar that Humphrey Bogart owned."

"Was it Casablanca?" Holly asked hopefully.

"Nope," Mick shook his head, "That was where it was located. Do you remember what Bogey's name was in the film?"

"No," said Holly shaking her head.

"It was Rick," Mick answered, "And the club was called 'Rick's'."

"But," he continued, "Sidney Greenstreet also had a club and that was named…?"

"Sidney's…?" She answered still hopeful.

"Uh, uh," Mick shook his head again, hoping he wasn't coming off like a big know-it-all'. but he couldn't resist a grin when he finished with… "It was called," and he paused dramatically…"The Blue Parrot!"

"Oh!" exclaimed Holly clapping her hands as recognition dawned, "That's so perfect." She sighed. "That's why I love it so much here in Boston and everything is so exotic and interesting and…Romantic. I mean, we don't have anything like that back in Iowa!" she smiled again and squeezed his hand, "It's all just so, so…perfect."

And in spite of a now rapidly receding, vague sense of guilt, Mick smiled and squeezed her fingers back.

"All right then, are you wantin' anything…Or maybe you'd just like me to move you to a quieter tabled in a nice dark corner, so you can finish yer conversation without any interruptions from an annoying…and I'm afraid…very busy waitress."

Mick barely noticed a petite dark haired form standing just slightly behind his right shoulder. He looked at Holly and said, "have you ever had the Sangria here?"

Holly shook her head and answered wide eyed, "I've never even had Sangria…Anywhere!"

"Harumph, welcome to the big city, darlin'," came a derisive snort from behind Mick's right shoulder.

Ignoring the sarcasm, Mick said without turning around, "Bring us a pitcher, okay?"

"You got it, Romeo," the strangely accented voice answered. And Mick turned to look just as the small lithe form slipped back between the tightly packed tables in the direction of the crowded bar.

"So you're from Iowa," Mick said raising his voice to be heard above the din as the cellar club filled up with more and more college bodies as another Harvard Square Friday night got fully underway.

"Yes," Holly answered, "just me, Mommy and Daddy, and my two brothers...and 500 acres of corn...But it was awfully good corn," she added with a tentative twinkle in her eye.

"Hey," Mick bantered, "if it was half as good as you look, the then sign me up for a bushel!"

"Oh, stop!" Holly blushed and changing the subject said." Oh look, they've got entertainment. Oh, that's great. Maybe I can pick up some new songs." And then added with a suddenly serious expression, "You don't think I do too many Dylan songs, do you?"

"Na'," Mick answered, "Not at all." And as the skinny guy in faded jeans and work shirt stepped up to the microphone on the club's small stage and launched into 'Baby, Let Me Follow You Down', Mick laughed and pointing at the stage with his thumb said, "See, everyone does Dylan."

"Thanks," Holly smiled gratefully, adding, "You always seem to know just the right thing to say Mick," and added looking into his eyes with adoration, "and do...My brave, brave knight."

"Well, if 'Sir Casanova' here can move his fist off the table top so I can set down this bleeding pitcher and manage to cough up $3.50 for the Sangria, then I can leave you and your 'brave knight' here, in peace."

Holly blushed furiously and looked back down at the tabletop while Mick looked up, half pissed and half intrigued, at the owner of the mildly mocking but pleasantly accented voice.

And saw...It was her!

"Holy shit!" he thought, stunned, "my fucking cup runneth over!"

There standing in front of the tiny barrel top table, a frosted picture of dark red Sangria in a one silver-ringed hand, was the black-haired, pixie-faced owner of the emerald eyes that he'd been searching for ever since that night three weeks ago in the Club 47. The same night he'd first seen Holly, who was now looking at him with a tentative expression of uncertainty.

"That's $3.50, Luv, "the green-eyed, gorgeous little elf said, planting one dainty white hand on her slightly cocked hip.

"Oh, man," Mick moaned to himself as he reached for his wallet and thought ruefully, "when it rains…It really frigging pours!"

CHAPTER 29

▼

Boston—China Town
November 2, 1966

"Mr. former Police Detective McCarthy," Mr. Ling smiled, "Please come in."

Mike stood in the doorway of the red and gold decorated room in the back of the Dragon Palace Restaurant on Harrison Avenue. Out of long habit, he paused before stepping through the imitation jade beads strung across the door way.

Mr. Ling watched and still smiling his bland guarded smile said, "Ah yes, I see, as always, the complete professional…cautious and thorough. We have indeed chosen well, have we not, Mr. Feng?"

The elderly Chinese man in a black silk robe embroidered with red dragons just smiled and inclined his head towards Mr. Ling. But the younger Chinese man slouched against the far wall cleaning his long nails with a jeweled letter opener in the shape of a miniature sword, narrowed his eyes and scowled.

Ling's gaze took this all in with a barely perceptible flicker of his eyes and without changing expression, motioned again for McCarthy to come in.

Mike stepped through the beads, unbuttoning his jacket as he entered, allowing the movement of his coat to lightly press his back with the reassuring weight of his newly 'obtained', if not quite legal, .380 seven shot automatic.

"Please, sit." The elderly Chinese gentleman that Ling had referred to as Mr. Feng, said as he pulled a black lacquered chair out from the lone table that stood in the center of the room.

"Thanks anyway," Mike said with a nod to Feng who was still standing expectantly behind the offered chair, "if it's all the same, I'm a lot more comfortable standing. And as a matter of fact, right here is fine," he finished taking up a position with his left shoulder lightly resting against the wall facing the now scowling even more, young Chinese man.

Mr. Ling pretended not to notice the increased tension and beamed, "yes of course, as you wish Mr. former Police Detective McCarthy, what ever you wish."

"Great," Mike smiled back without warmth, "and since you seem to be so hung up on titles, let's drop the "Former Police Detective"…It's Mike, or McCarthy, or P.I."

"P.I.?" Ling asked with a puzzled frown.

"Private Investigator. Licensed by the state of Massachusetts and the Boston and Cambridge police." Mike snapped back. The red silk-clad Feng padded over to Mr. Ling and whispered something in his ear with concern in his eyes. Not taking his eyes off of Mike, Ling shook his head and snapped out a rapid stream of Chinese of which Mike could only make out one word…Bannon. Mr. Feng bowed twice and backed away, apparently satisfied, but the young Oriental man slouching against the wall pushed himself upright with a derisive snort and muttered, "a frigging old has-been retread."

Mr. Ling crossed the room with three quick, silent steps and without even seeming to move, backhanded the young man across the mouth with one short, sharp movement. It happened so fast that the young man had no time to react before several drops of blood from his rapidly swelling lips stained his shiny sharkskin suit. Never changing his bland, pleasant expression, Ling glided back to his spot at the head of the table. Without turning his head he said, "Mr. Feng, it seems that your son Ritchie happily continues to adopt the ways of your new home, but sadly seems to have forgotten the most important lesson of his heritage…and the last three word snapped out like a whip. "Obedience and respect!"

Feng moved rapidly forward and bowing low in front of Mr. Ling, put his long nailed hands over his eyes. Still not looking at the shame faced Feng, Mr. Ling smiled expectantly at Mike and said, "Mr. Feng wishes to express his sorrow and humble apologies for the rude behavior of his son. Two cultures war for his young soul, but still…no excuse."

"Hey, no skin off my teeth, I've been called a hell of a lot worse," Mike shrugged still leaning against the wall.

"You are most gracious," Ling smiled with a small bow and snapped a few unintelligible words back to Feng, who backed away still bobbing his head up and down. He rounded on his son with a string of hissed commands in Chinese and the younger Feng slouched out of the room, still holding a now red silk handkerchief to his bleeding lips and casting a murderous glanced back over his shoulder at Mike.

Mike shook his head and said, "Okay, if we're through with the family feud, here, can you get on with this and tell me just why the hell you asked me to come here?"

"Yes, certainly," Ling replied, with a slight incline of his head, "this is the 'small commission' that I mentioned when I visited your office last week."

"What is?" Asked Mike looking around the room suspiciously. "Ling snapped out another command and Feng clapped his hands sharply twice aa a panel in the dark ebony inlaid wall swung outwards and a beautiful young Oriental teenage girl gently led a frightened young man into the room.

Mike looked the newcomer over as his dark eyes darted apprehensively back and forth around the room. He looked, Mike thought, about 19 or 20 years old, just about Mick's age…Except he had that scared rabbit looked of people who have had their world turned upside down once too often. He was certainly Oriental, but somehow didn't look quite the same as the Chinese around him.

"Mr. Private Investigator McCarthy, may I introduce you to the very brilliant and promising young student and ward of my government, Mr. Quang Weh."

*   *   *   *

Driving back over the BU Bridge to Cambridge, Mike reflected that these damn Chinamen must have thought that he'd just fallen off the turnip truck, if they seriously felt that he was gonna' buy that BS story about the frigging Chinese government sponsoring a 'deserving' Vietnamese war refugee out of their common benign universal bond with the suffering of Asian people everywhere.

"Bullshit!" Mike muttered to himself, "they could put an end to the suffering in Vietnam a hell of a lot quicker if they just stop sending them frigging AK-47's!"

"The crux of our commission with you," Ling had stated with his perpetual blank and unreadable expression, "is that we would like you to use your connections with your former police associates as well as your 'blood' connection with the prestigious law firm of Hayward, Elliott and Delbert, to secure young Quang entrance into the country and his acceptance as a graduate student at the world renowned University of MIT."

"Why the hell don't you just go through the INS and trot the boy genius there across the river to MIT to fill out an application like anyone else?"

"Because as you must be aware, the wait for refugees from Southeast Asia can be years and the work of this… 'young genius' as you say, a is too important to wait that long."

"What's he working on," Mike snorted, "a cure for cancer?"

"Oh, more, Mr. McCarthy," Ling answered, momentarily losing his concentration, "much, much more. A salvation and a shield," and added dreamily, "yes, a salvation, shield and perhaps...A sword."

"What kind of sword?" Mike had asked narrowing his eyes at Ling.

"Ah, just another bit of inscrutable Chinese metaphor Mr. McCarthy. You know, like those silly little sayings in the fortune cookies that always began, 'Confucius say' he finished with a smile. But somehow Mike didn't think so. However after another full minute had passed, he'd looked back at Ling and said, "and what's the bit about my blood connection', with Hayward, Elliott..."

"And Delbert? Mr. Ling finished for him. "I refer of course to your eldest son of whom you must be justifiably proud."

"You mean Frankie?"

"Of course."

"Well, he just started working there six months ago for Christ sakes, what the hell do you think he can do?"

"Our sources tell us that, not only is your esteemed son a well thought of new member of the firm, but he has also recently been seen escorting one Clarissa Elliott, the pampered and favored daughter of the firm's president."

"Your frigging sources had better be careful how far they stick their 'informed noses' into my family's business if they know what's good for them," Mike growled.

Ling continued on as though he had not heard Mike, "and the three important and worthy gentleman who head that firm, also have the honor of sitting on the Board of Admissions of both Harvard and MIT!" he finished triumphantly.

"Okay," Mike conceded, "I guess I can speak to Frankie, about getting your little South East Asian brother into the country. Lord knows, I've no love for the damn INS, they keep enough good Irish lads waiting for years to get in, but they're sure not about to do me any favors."

"Perhaps," Ling smiled, "but they are prepared to 'look the other way' thanks to another good comrade of yours, Mr. Police Captain Bannon."

"Bannon!" Mike spat the word. "What the hell does that prick have to do with this? And what do you mean 'my good, Comrade'?"

"Are you not so? Perhaps I was mistaken, but he speaks very highly of you. Yes, very highly indeed."

"I'll just frigging bet he does," Mike muttered, and added, "You know, Ling, this whole thing is starting to smell like last Friday's mackerel. Maybe I'll just give you back your thousand bucks and we'll call it quits."

"A thousand...dollars?" Ling's brows knitted in feigned perplexity and then rapidly cleared as he said, "Ah, my most sincere apologies, my dear Private Investigator McCarthy. How inexcusably remiss of me. I obviously failed to mention that the paltry $1,000 was merely a poor down payment. A simple gift to compensate you for your valuable time."

"No, Mr. Private Investigator McCarthy, the fee which we are pleased to re-numerate to you for this small service for a most worthy endeavor is...$10,000!"

CHAPTER 30

▼

Harvard Square
Cambridge
May 3, 1968
8:02PM

"Oh, no, you don't, McCarthy!" Bridget exclaimed, backing away from the dirty gray chipped stone steps that lead down to the cellar cafe. "You promised me dinner at the Casablanca, not a pitcher of beer and a shared bowl of Yugoslavian stew at the Blue Parrot!"

"It was Sangria," Mick smiled

"What was Sangria?" Bridget asked.

"The pitcher you brought to our table…The first night I met you here," Mick answered still smiling at her.

"What,…you call a leering grin and a $2 tip a 'memorable' meeting?"

"Well, it was for me at least," Mick responded and then, a bit miffed added, "and a $2 tip on a $3 bill, is a pretty good tip. In case your math is a bit rusty since your Parrot waitress days, that comes out to a 66 percent gratuity," and he drew himself up in a mock pompous pose and added, "Miss Connelly."

"Oh, and it's beggin' your pardon I am, fine sir," Bridget shot back in her best 'over exaggerated' Irish brogue, and finished up with a deep curtsy to which Mick responded with his best sixth grade dancing school bow.

"Uh, excuse me, man. Hey, can we get by?"

Mick looked up and realized that a small audience had collected in front of the steps leading down to the cafe.

"Oh, yeah…Sorry," Mick said sheepishly moving out of the stairwell.

The student in the tweed sports coat and jeans just shrugged his shoulders and said, "no problem." His date in a sweater and tie-dyed jeans added, "hey, don't stop on our account...You're probably better than the entertainment inside!"

Bridget's normally pale white skin turned a bright crimson as she muttered from between clenched teeth, "nice going McCarthy, you've got us playin' the village idiots to half the population of Cambridge."

Mick immediately crossed his eyes, put on a vacant expression and answered, "...Uh-h what?"

A split second later, they both burst out laughing, and the more people who filed past them into the Blue Parrot looked at them strangely, the harder and more hysterically they laughed. They laughed until their sides began to ache and Bridget turned away groaning, "Stop, stop! Oh, my face is starting to hurt," and put her two tiny hands on the sides of her cheeks to ease the strain. It almost worked until Mick looked over at her, burst into uncontrollable laughter, tears streaming down his cheeks, and her hysterical giggles started all over again.

When Mick had finally wiped his streaming eyes and Bridget's giggles had subsided to hiccups, they both slumped down onto the sidewalk and leaned weakly against the wrought iron fence.

"Well, Miss Connelly," Mick said still dabbing his eyes with the heel of his palm, "do I take that as a 'no' to sharing a pitcher of Sangria and a bowl of Yugoslavian stew at the Blue Parrot?"

"I'd be delighted to share a pitcher and a bowl of anything with you McCarthy," Bridget smiled back at him, adding, "under two conditions."

"Which are?" Mick queried, raising his eyebrows.

"One," Bridget said holding up her index finger, "that it's not some place I've waitressed at."

"Well, that leaves out the Parrot," Mick said.

"And your mother's house," Bridget added in a low voice.

"Ouch!...Boy, you play rough babe," Mick responded, but after a few seconds she answered his smile with her own.

"Okay, then," Mick asked cautiously, instinctively knowing that he was going to regret it, "I'll bite...What's number two?"

"That it's not some place you've taken one of your old girlfriends!"

"Bridge!" Mick gasped in mock horror, "do you realize that this means we're gonna' have to start taking all of our meals with the Brothers out at B.C.?"

"Just kidding, just kidding," he said holding up his hands to catch the soft but well aimed punches she was peppering his shoulders with.

"Well, Mr. 'Don Juan' McCarthy…You better think fast, or as me' ol' Da' used to say, 'I'll beat you like a redheaded stepchild.'"

Bridget advanced on Mick, striking a classic turn of the century boxer pose as Mick backed into and almost tripped over, a row of padlocked bicycles.

"Okay, okay, he cried still holding up both hands and looking across the square added in a very bad German accent, "Okay, mine little strudel…Do you like knockwurst?"

✳   ✳   ✳   ✳

"You know," Bridget said, spearing another plump bratwurst from the steaming platters of knockwurst, bratwurst, sauerkraut and hot German potato salad, "I do like these."

She spread a generous helping of spicy brown mustard, and began delicately working her way through her second piece, adding "they're sure a damn site better than those dried out 'banger's and mash' we had every Saturday night at home."

"Bangers and mash?" Mick asked skeptically crinkling up his nose.

"That's sausage and mashed potatoes to you lad," she laughed.

"See," Mick said grinning, "I told you you'd like it here. And you're the first girl I've ever brought here…Scouts honor!"

"Yeah, sure McCarthy, I don't think you ever were a Scout."

"You're right, but it's true. I never found a girl who liked sauerkraut before!"

Later, after an ancient dour waiter had cleared away the remains of the sauerkraut and bratwurst, Bridget paused in mid sip of her second Heineken, and looking across the table at Mick said, "Something is bothering you. What is it?"

"You mean besides your beautiful green eyes and sinfully delectable body!?" he grinned.

"Yes," she smiled back and then added seriously, "I've felt it ever since you got dumped on the front porch a week ago, more dead than alive."

"Well, then chalk it up to a case of badly scrambled brains," Mick shrugged.

"Uh—uh McCarthy," She shook her head, "you're not brushing me off that easy. I want to know what happened in that house up at Prides Crossing. Just what went on between you and this famous 'Colonel' that I've been listening to you mumble about in your sleep every night for the best part of two years?"

For a long time Mick didn't say anything. He just stared at her the tabletop, quietly peeling off the label of his St. Pauli Girl Beer. Finally he looked up at Bridget and he started to talk.

*   *   *   *

When he finally finished, Bridget wiped her eyes and blew her nose with the now damp Kleenex and said softly, "Mick, why didn't you ever tell me...?"

"I did...sort of," he shrugged.

"Bits and pieces," she said, leaning across the table and taking his hand, "but never the whole thing...what happened at that village."

"Bridge...I still don't know what happened at that village! That's why I went to find the first Louie, and he sent me to the Colonel. Which is where I always knew it would lead. But now...now I think I know that it doesn't end with the Colonel. As a matter of fact, I think now that it goes way beyond that sad sorry murdererous old bastard hiding out in Prides Crossing. I know that a lot has happened to make me...both of us for that matter...paranoid. But I think that if I find out what I feel I have to know...I may wind up wishing I didn't."

CHAPTER 31

▼

Boston
China Town
May 3, 1968
9:07PM

The young Chinese man sensed, rather than felt, the butterfly soft touch on his suit coat's right shoulder. Without turning around, he said, "yes Jade, what is it?"

"There are three men here to see you," she said in a voice that was so soft it was almost a whisper.

"What token do they bring?"

"The paper dragon," honored son of my uncle, "she whispered close to his ear.

"You're sure?" He asked getting up and turning off the projector that had been showing the latest Kung Fu movie from Hong Kong in mid frame.

"Yes, honored cousin."

"Where are they?"

"In the bar where Jasmine Lilly serves the two large ones Scotch whisky, but the small man with the dead face and dead eyes, drinks only black tea."

"Can you see anything…Behind his eyes?"

"No, cousin," she paused…" I don't think there is anything there to see."

Moving his head a fraction of an inch he looked at her out of the corner of his eye and said, "Tell your mother I wish for her to join me in the bar while I speak with these men."

Again he sensed, rather than felt, her gliding out of the room as he crossed the floor and slightly parted the beaded curtain that separated the bar from the private office. As he peered through the curtain at the table beyond, he heard the soft click of a panel opening in the carved ebony wood. But before it could close, he snapped out, "Jade!" Several seconds passed and he felt her warm breath on the back of his neck.

"Yes, cousin."

"When you tell your mother to join me, also tell her that I do not want to see your sister, Jasmine Lilly, dressed again like a cheap slut in my home and place of business!"

He heard a sharp intake of breath, and then an accusatory, "But honored son of my uncle, she does no more than dress like the other girls of her age do in this city...As perhaps I too would like to. This is not Shanghai." For a moment there was no response as his eyes remained fixed on the table in the red lantern lit bar where a beautiful golden skinned Chinese teenage girl dressed in bellbottoms, a tight half opened silk blouse and high-heeled boots, sat laughing and flirting with the two goons who slammed down the shot after shot of Chivas Regal.

Suddenly he reached back over his shoulder with his left hand and grabbed a handful of silky perfumed hair. He heard one sharp gasp of pain as he pulled her head forward until her face rested against the right shoulder of his expensive Hong Kong tailored suit. "You will tell your mother is exactly what I said. And never forget this, Jade, I can have you sent back to Shanghai, anytime I choose, where once the Red Guards had finished raping you and your sister, you would most likely spend the rest of your short miserable lives, whoring in some back alley."

"If your father—our honored uncle, were..." came the brief rebellious hiss, before it was cut off with...

"But he's not...I am."

"Yes, cousin," came the now meek reply, "I will tell my mother. "And once again he heard the swish of silk, the click of the panel, and she was gone.

He parted the curtains and walked into the bar.

"Hey Ritchie, how are you doing, man," the fat thug in too tight bellbottoms yelled as the slim young Chinese man sat down at the table. He looked at the sweating, fat pig who threw back another shot of Chivas, letting the amber drops dribble down his almost double chin and over the half dozen massive gold chains embedded in the fleshy folds of fat in his neck. Masking his contempt, he just smiled and said, "Not bad Tony...Not bad at all."

"Yeah," Tony laughed, "I bet you do just fine...Doesn't he, baby?" As he slipped a meaty arm around Jasmine's tiny shoulders.

She laughed and swirled the ice cubes of her Coke and then licked the dripping straw with the tip of her tongue in a slow sensuous movement, as she said in almost perfectly unaccented English, "oh yeah Tony, you can take that to the frigging bank. Ol' cousin Ritchie here does real fine, for himself…Don'tcha' Ritchie."

Ritchie smiled as his hands clenched under the table, but before he could say a word, there were two sharp claps behind him and a staccato string of Chinese rang out ending in Jasmine's name.

Jasmine stared over Ritchie's shoulder with smoldering resentment and snapped back, "Jeez Ma, why don't you speak English. You sound like one of those goddamn coolies back in the kitchen!"

"Jasmine," came the now icy voice, "leave us."

Sullenly, she pushed her chair away from the table and said, "I'm going over to see Chang and Amy. I'll see you…Whenever." She pushed one black lock of hair back up under her beaded headband, adjusted the skintight bellbottoms and with a wink at the grinning Tony and a wiggle of her butt, was gone.

With knuckles still whitely clinching the side of the table, Ritchie smiled and said, "Gentleman, this is my aunt, Mrs. Wu. Her family is still in mainland China and therefore is the most important part of our operation."

"So like how are you doing Mrs. Wu," Tony said.

"And," Ritchie continued, his eyes moving around the table to a badly acne-scarred, sallow faced man with long greasy hair and tight butter colored leather jacket, "This is…Bingie."

Mrs. Wu's expression flickered slightly as her eyes moved to the third and final face staring expressionlessly back at her across the black lacquered table, as Ritchie finished with, "and this of course is…Mr. Sloan."

The seconds stretched away into minutes as Tony played with his empty shot glass, Bingie picked at old acne scars and Mr. Sloan…just stared.

Finally Sloan said in a voice so low that Ritchie almost had to hold his breath to hear him. "We have the paper dragon…and he's come to drink."

Ritchie smiled a hard smile at his Aunt and replied, "From our golden bowl."

CHAPTER 32

———————▼———————

Washington DC
May 2, 1968
11:21PM

"Mr. Sloan."

"Sir."

"I've read your report and while I find the majority of it very encouraging, there are some parts of it that are quite...Well, disturbing."

The entity that was known only as Sloan, said nothing. He just sat in the hard backed armless chair with his hands folded gently in his lap. A deceptive picture of calm and attentiveness.

"What about this McCarthy?" The deep voice with a cultured Northern Virginia accent asked.

"Which one sir?"

"Excuse me?"

"Does your inquiry refer to the father or the son?"

"Ah, yes...I see. No, I was referring to our veteran, the young Sergeant. How is he...adjusting? Is he...well...stable?"

"In some ways it's hard to tell, sir. Our research has determined that he had some very rebellious, unstable traits, long before we ever came in...contact with him."

"So then what is your recommendation? Should we cut him loose?"

"No sir, I don't think so. I feel that he remains very important to the project." Sloan looked at the portly figure sitting behind the large mahogany desk, monogrammed with the seal of the Central Intelligence Agency and added,

"They both have parts that have yet to be played out sir. Both the father and son," he finished with a flat note of finality.

CHAPTER 33

▼

Cambridge
Inman Square
May 4th 1968
3:03AM

"Jesus, McCarthy, if this is how your gonna' be after just five or six…"

"Seven or eight," Mick belched.

"All right then…whatever, ya' drunken pig," Bridget said as she pushed her shoulders under Mick's arm so she could help him up the three flights of stairs of the Inman Square apartment.

"God damn!" Mick muttered drunkenly, "what kind of a little girl, pussy do you think I am? Drunk on five or six measly little St. Pauli girl beers? Ha!"

"I guess the same kind of 'pussy' who tries to drink a girl born and raised in County Cork under the table! Mind ya' darlin', I was drinkin' Guinness with dinner when you were drinking Ovalteen or Coca-Cola or…"

"Nestle's Quick," Mick said smiling. "What?" Bridget asked as she guided him past the second floor landing.

"It was Nestle's Quick, you know, the chocolate milk, that I used to have with dinner every night," Mick smiled as he let Bridget direct him up the last flight of stairs.

"It's a wonder you've got any teeth left at all then," she hissed as she supported his wobbly weight and turned the key in the apartment lock.

"You're beautiful you know," Mick whispered nuzzling her neck.

"Yeah right, McCarthy," Bridget said steering him to the couch where he collapsed, "and seven or eight beers . ."

"Nine or ten!" Mick exclaimed proudly.

"Whatever," Bridget responded with a wry smile, "make me all the more beautiful. And I suppose another six-pack would turn me into the 'Queen of the bleedin' 'May'."

"The Queen of County Cork...and my heart," Mick said as he caught her slim white wrist and pulled her towards him.

"Don't start something ya' can't finish, Boy-o," she smiled as Mick began nosily lapping her left ear lobe.

"Ha!" He answered with drunken bravado as he jumped up from the couch. "I can, and will...Love you my girl, till the frigging cows come home...from wherever the frigging cows go...when they're not home?" He finished staring at Bridget with a totally befuddled expression.

"Oh come here, you great sot," she laughed at and held out her arms to him.

Mick grinned back foolishly and fell down on his knees beside her. He let his head drop next to hers on the yellow and green print pillow propped up on the arm rest of the couch, and opened his eyes wide for a moment, "I mean it," he said, suddenly serious.

"What do you mean Mick?" Bridget asked, eyes bright and shining.

"You know," he smiled.

"Tell me," she breathed wrapping her arms around his neck," tell me true...Now and forever, "she recited recalling the verse of an old song her father had sung to her mother.

"I love you Bridget Connelly. Now," Mick said holding her tiny white face between his hands, "and forever."

"Oh God, Mickey," Bridget said, the words catching in her throat, "please...make love to me now."

"Why?" Mick asked, his eyes focused dreamily on hers.

"Because...I don't think I've ever loved you as much as I do this moment."

Mick lowered his mouth to hers as he gently pulled her towards him and they sank down onto the threadbare rugs of the hard Inman Square floor, and felt nothing but each other.

The silly little plastic clock, shaped like a pewter tea kettle had buzzed and sputtered its way through 3:00 a.m. and they were still kissing, locked in an unbreakable embrace on the floor next to the couch, cushions and clothes scattered like dry leaves, in untidy heaps.

Mick lay on his back and was only dimly aware of the worn scratchy carpet beneath his shoulder blades, as his entire attention was focused on the center of his universe. Bridget gazed down on him with lips slightly parted and eyes glazed by love and lust.

"Sweet Christ, Mickey," she half sobbed, "oh God…I do love you so."

She rocked forward and flicked her tongue over his lips before burying it deep in his mouth. Mick ran his hands down the soft white skin of her back as she shuddered on top of him and their world exploded into stars.

Bridget fell exhausted on top of him and said with a small sigh, "that was grand McCarthy…Can we do it again?"

Mick laughed deep in his throat and asked, "do you think you're up to it my 'Queen of County Cork'?"

"Me, up to it?" Bridget laughed. "Oh no Mickey lad…It's you darlin' as has got to be 'up to it'!"

They both laughed as Mick said playfully, "and you're just the girl who can make sure that I am!"

"And I will McCarthy," Bridget breathed, taking his face back between her hands and licking his lips like her favorite taffy candy.

"Love me darlin'…Please love me. Love me again…now." She reached up again and pulled her soft delicious body onto his and…The co-mingling of their breathless sighs were shattered as the old black telephone rang.

They both froze.

"God damn!" Mick cursed, "who the hell is calling at 'three frigging thirty' in the God damn morning!"

"Shush Mickey," Bridget said rolling off him. "Maybe it's something important. It could be your Da' has had a relapse…Or, oh sweet Jesus…It could be me own Da' or Collin as something has happened to."

"Mickey," she said in a small voice, "answer it. I'm afraid to."

Mick pulled on his jeans and stepping over the coffee table, plucked the phone out of its cradle and said, "McCarthy here and this had better be fuckin' good!"

With a strange precognition of fear she watched Mick stiffen and lower the phone back into the cradle without saying a word.

Mick carefully picked his way through their clothes that had been strewn between the couch and the coffee table and said, "so where were we?"

"Who was that Mick?"

"No one…Wrong number," Mick answered, his eyes going cold.

"But it must have been…"

"I said it was no one," Mick repeated his eyes growing even colder.

"Maybe we should just go to bed Mick," Bridget said gathering up her clothes and stepping around the coffee table towards the back bedroom.

"No!" Mick said with a grin that bared his teeth, "you made me a challenge I believe, Miss Connelly, so let's find out, as you put it, if I'm 'up to it'".

"Mick, I don't think..." But she never finished her statement as Mick knocked her clothes out of her hands and pulled her roughly down to the floor.

"Still think I'm not 'up to it' Darlin'," he leered sarcastically as he climbed on top of her.

"Mick...No!" Bridget said trying ineffectually to push his weight off of her.

"Hush, my little 'Queen of County Cork'," Mick hissed, seeming to mock the tender words of just an hour before.

"Mickey...Please...Don't...," Bridget gasped, tears of fear and confusion smarting in the corner of her eyes.

Mick just laughed, enjoying her fear as he mockingly repeated her words. "Please don't..."

"What's the matter, my sweet colleen, I thought you were worried about me being able to...'keep it up'!" And he squeezed her face between the iron hard fingers of his right hand.

"No!" Bridget shouted crying in earnest now, "not like this—never like this! Mick, there's something wrong with you....you're..."

"I'm what darlin'?" Mick hissed. "I'll tell you what the fuck I am. I'm the bad ass Sergeant of Company C, and I'm going to fuck your dirty little VC brains out and then..." he drew in a breath as his eyes glazed over and spittle ran down his chin as he finished with, "I'm gonna' kill you!"

Bridget froze with fear as somehow she knew that this was no longer—" her Mick."

Whoever he was, he was going to rape and kill her.

Mick grabbed the back of her hair and savagely pulled her mouth into his, cutting her lips with his barred teeth, relishing the taste of her blood.

He smiled a death grin as he pushed into her and as he did, he began scrabbling for something on his bare leg. Something that wasn't there, and hadn't been there for two years. And she suddenly knew what it was in one heart chilling instant as she remembered back to his confession of the horror in the jungle. He was looking for his double-edged Fairbairn-Sykes combat knife! Whoever he was, or thought she was, he intended to cut her throat!

"This isn't Mick anymore!!" She yelled to herself, "fight...save yourself god-damn it, and save whatever may be left of him...If there is anything!"

And as Mick dug his fingers into her shoulders, Bridget brought her right hand up to his face and raked her fingernails from his forehead to his left eye.

At first, he didn't even seem to register the pain. He just kept grinning his 'death's head' grin, but Bridget hadn't grown up in at a small cold cottage in County Cork with five brothers, without learning how to take care of herself.

As he tried once again to crush his face into hers, she dug her thumb into the corner of his left eye. At first, as with everything else, he seemed oblivious to the pain, but out of desperation she increased the pressure all the while gasping, "no, no—Mick—stop—goddamn it—listen to me!"

The face above her grew flushed with rage and he back-handed her.

Her head rang but still she held him off. And then, he put both steel hard hands on her throat and began to squeeze.

"Oh Christ," Bridget thought, "this can't be the way…The way I die. Raped and murdered by the man I called my lover…and my best friend."

"No!"

She gave a final push and gouged both thumbs into his eyes as the oxygen was slowly but surely being cut off to her brain, and black and gold dust motes swam in front of her eyes.

And then suddenly…It seemed—yes! The pressure was easing. Bridget looked up to where her thumbs were still locked at the outside of his eyeballs and saw…Confusion—disorientation—bewilderment, pain and a light of horrified recognition slowly coming back. And she knew…It was Mick.

Whoever he had been, and wherever the Mick she knew and loved had gone, she could tell…he was coming back. To her.

Cambridge
Inman Square
May 4th 1968
4:00 AM.

"Oh Christ Bridge," Mick asked in bewilderment, "what the hell happened?"

Bridget leaned back against the worn couch still massaging the bruises around her throat, as Mick held on to her knees, oblivious to the tears running down his face.

"Where were you Mick?" She managed to croak out. "Who were you?"

"I…I was back in the village—at the village. With the VC…Or whoever they were. Or…" and his face went chalky white," whoever I thought they were."

"But why did you put me there Mick?" Bridget grasped his shoulders. "I was never there, and you aren't any more...are you?" she asked with a growing sense of horror dawning on her.

"Oh sweet Jesus, you are still there aren't you?!"

"Yeah,"came a Mick's wooden reply. "I should have known. I'll never be able to leave that village—ever!"

"Mick!" Bridget asked, "that phone call...who was it? What did they want?"

For a minute Mick said nothing as he stared off into the empty space where the angel and the things of darkness still waited for him.

Finally he said with the tears still dripping unnoticed down his cheeks, "it was the Colonel...And he said...' that I'd know what to do'."

CHAPTER 34

▼

Prides Crossing
May 4, 1968
3:39 AM

The hollow eyed, sallow faced former senior officer replaced the phone in the antique brass ornate cradle and looked down at the floor.

"Thank you Colonel," the slight figure dressed in black said from the shadows,

"I must tell you that there were some in Washington who had lost faith in your ability to maintain a command and leadership role in this project. I am pleased to tell you, that I was never one of those."

"What about you Captain?" the voice in the shadows called out to the feminine uniformed form that stood staring out through the open French doors, outlined in the moonlight.

"What?" The soft, but hard voice answered.

"I said, don't you agree Captain, that the Colonel still retains the ability to perform a useful and important role in this project?"

There was a long silence, broken only by the logs popping and hissing in the giant fireplace grate.

Finally the emotionless, hard female voice answered, "Oh yes, without a doubt, the Colonel still has a very important role left to play."

*   *   *   *

Commonwealth Avenue—Allston
May 4th 1968 1:00 PM.

The worn, frayed old shade snapped up with a crack like a cannon shot, allowing a blast of sunlight to shine into Boomers face like a flashbulb going off.

"Aw-w shit," he groaned while trying to scramble away from the bright sunlight like some sort of hippie vampire.

"Hey, 'lieutenant space cowboy', up and at 'em," Starr's voice rang out as she punctuated her statement with a sharp slap to Boomers skinny butt which was still clad in his ratty old army boxer shorts.

"Starr, knock it off, damn you," Boomer moaned, his voice becoming muffled as he pulled the pillow over his head. "I'm trying to sleep here."

"Yeah? Well that's tough titty darlin' cuz you got company,"

"I don't want to see anyone!"

Then he peeked owlishly from under the pillow and said..." Who?"

Star folded her arms and leaned against the wall, momentarily creasing the psychedelic poster of Jimi Hendrix.

She smiled down at Boomer with her sardonic smile while lighting a joint from his stash on the purple painted Salvation Army bureau, and said, "it's your old army buddy...General 'Curly' himself.

She flicked her eyes back towards the bedroom door as Mick walked in and with an uncharacteristically serious expression said, "hey, lieutenant...Man, we've got to talk."

*   *   *   *

The mid afternoon sun poured in through the tiny kitchen window of the fourth floor Commonwealth Avenue apartment.

"Here Curly," Starr said pulling a multicolored-chair out from the cheap Formica kitchen table that was covered with sociology textbooks and small squares of aluminum foil half filled with pot.

"So what's your pleasure Sarge," Starr asked crossing to the counter littered with last night's beer bottles and half burnt roaches. She pointed to a once white and now steadily gasping old refrigerator, and said, "you've got a choice of Colt 45 malt liquor or even 'choicer' Acapulco Gold."

"Thanks anyway," Mick answered recalling all too vividly his stomachs' protest earlier this morning against the six-pack he'd put away the night before.

"I think I'll just have some of that herbal tea you gave me the last time I was here."

"Sure thing Curly," Starr smiled, putting a beat up old yellow whistling tea kettle on the left hand front burner. She picked up a small wooden a spice rack filled with tiny tea cans and crossed from the stove to the table. Starr pulled out a purple Day-Glo painted chair left over from the previous tenants and turning it around, pulled herself up towards the table while proceeding to roll herself another joint. One by one she opened each tiny metal can and sniffed its contents.

"Hey, Boomer...This is good shit, where did you get it?"

"A friend," he answered evasively, adding, "hey baby...don't smoke up all the profits."

Boomer paused as Mick shrugged across the table saying, "hey don't mind me, just do your own thing man." He then added, "I just need to know man, what do you remember about that night?"

"You mean besides, the fact that it was hell on earth?"

"Yeah, that too."

"I remember the jungle, the Hueys, the smell of burning flesh and...You."

"Me?"

"Yeah," said Boomer with a small shudder. "I remember the way your eyes looked...All flat and dead."

"But," Mick asked, "you were there when...when, the colonel gave his orders..." he trailed off.

"No!" Boomer shook his head as Starr watched him with a strange intensity.

"No, I came back in on the re-con chopper. I didn't know what happened. I didn't know anything, until...until...You came up to the chopper Mick. And then, I went back with Smitty, and I...I saw..." Boomer put his face into his hands. "I...I can't get it out of my mind. Every night. Every frigging night, I see it again. Over and over and over again, and it doesn't matter," he moaned, "what the hell I smoke, or drink or snort...it just won't ever, ever go away!"

"Okay baby...easy," Starr cooed rubbing the back of his head with her left hand while rolling a joint with her right.

Then she turned back to Mick with a cold penetrating stare and said, "hey Sarge, I think it's time for you to hit the bricks again. You know," she smiled her cold smile, "you seem to have this nasty habit of getting my little Boomer here all worked up and bummed out and," she added turning back to Boomer, running her chipped, purple painted nails through his long tangled hair and smiling at him like a nurse in a cancer ward, "we can't have that, right baby?"

"So, adios Curly," she said swiveling her gaze back on Mick, "and make sure you come back and see us real soon…Like, let's say right after the moon falls out of its orbit and lands in Boston harbor."

Mick stared back a minute and then shrugged his shoulders and pulled back his chair. He had his hand on the doorknob when he heard Boomers voice behind him saying quietly…" No."

✳   ✳   ✳   ✳

Allston/Cambridge line
May 7, 1969
6:03 PM

Three days later, Mick slowly guided the BSA through the rain slick streets of Allston. And as he headed towards the BU Bridge to cross back over into Cambridge, he thought about what Boomer had finally told him and how Starr had looked first at him, and then back at Boomer, while he talked to Mick in a low tortured monotone.

Mick wasn't sure of what the expression was on Starr's face, but one thing he was pretty damn sure of…It wasn't love.

The other thing he was sure of was that if looks could kill…" Well Mick my boy, you'd be deader than last Friday's mackerel."

He shook his head to clear the water drops off the visor of his helmet and said to himself as he crossed over the Charles River, "next stop, MIT."

CHAPTER 35

▼

MIT
Cambridge Mass
May 7, 1968
6:22 PM

Mick pushed his wet boots down on the BSA's foot brake as he slowed in front of the now mostly dark and unpleasantly foreboding, MIT biology lab.

He sat there in the thick, fitfully sputtering rain, his booted feet on either side of the 750 cc motorcycle as he searched the dark windows for any sign of life.

There was nothing. Not a light, or sign of activity, except...

Mick looked around the left side of the building where he thought he saw the barest glimmer of light peeking out from a second story window.

He slowly let the clutch out and still keeping both feet out for balance, gently eased the bike around back until he was directly underneath the lit window.

Mick turned the key off and slipped it into the watch pocket of his now soaking wet jeans. He pulled the bike back onto its kickstand and walked towards the rear entrance of the building. It was locked. He really hadn't expected that it wouldn't have been.

"Fortunately," Mick thought, "one good thing about Ivy League schools is that they actually do tend to be covered with ivy."

He pushed the pointed toe of his right cowboy boot into a crack in the red-brick front and grabbed at the tough ivy with both hands and began to slowly pull himself up...one course of bricks at a time.

As he climbed, he thought back to what Boomer had told him and he saw the former 'First Louie's' face as he quietly told Mick what he knew...Or rather could still remember, about, "The Project."

Boomer had stared down at the table top as he told Mick about his first meeting with the colonel from Special Opps and the strange un-introduced black suited figure who stood back in the shadows of the the DaNang Quonset hut, hands folded in front of him, just listening. "Yeah," Mick said to him self, "some of the little puzzle pieces from around the edges are starting to fall into place. But there are so many, I'm still missing. And maybe if Boomer is right, I'm gonna find a great big fat one right here," he finished as he pulled himself up and into the second story window ledge.

Boomer had told him to check out the MIT biology lab on the second floor of the grad studies building...And that was really the last coherent thing he'd said.

"He had,"Mick reflected, "been doing great." Then Starr had pushed a long pipe stuffed with hash over to him but he pushed it away, saying "no, I'm gonna tell this straight, not all fucked up."

He turned to Mick and said, "Mick, do you remember the first time you saw me?"

"Sure Boomer."

"Call me lieutenant," he said quietly.

Mick had sat up straighter.

"Yeah sure, lieutenant, it was at firebase Bravo, right after I got my sergeant's stripes and you came in to congratulate me and give me command of the first and second squad of C Company."

"What did I look like then Mick," he asked almost pleading.

Mick thought for a moment and then said, "you were tall, blue eyed, blonde haired—crew cut," Mick smiled "and very, very Army, all the way."

"The epitome of the corn fed midwestern farm boy gone off to serve his country, right Mick?" He said almost plaintively.

"Yeah, God damn, yeah," Mick said back, "sure as shit, right lieutenant," he finished with a smile.

"And I didn't cry, and I didn't shake and I didn't have to get fucked up just to get through the day...did I Mick!"

"No sir, lieutenant!" Mick barked out without thinking and then they both smiled realizing how they had slipped back into a, "what used to be."

For the first time Mick noticed that Boomer was looking hard at Star and behind her cynical smile, Mick could almost make out an expression he'd never seen on her face.

It looked like fear.

Boomer continued staring at her until she dropped her eyes and went back to measuring out teaspoons of pungent marijuana and rolling them into aluminum foil twists.

Boomer turned his gaze back to Mick. "You remember the night before the raid when I called all the sergeants to the mess hall tent for the briefing."

"Yeah," Mick answered simply.

"And you remember I said we were gonna' be under the command of the Special Ops colonel."

"Sure," Mick answered, "I remember."

"Well," Boomer continued, "what I didn't tell you was that the colonel was under the command of someone else."

"A guy in a black suit, with bone white skin and dead black eyes?"

"Yeah," Boomer slowly breathed out the word "so you knew?"

"No," Mick shook his head, "not really...Not until just this moment...But now it's starting to make some sense. Where was this guy from?"

Boomer shrugged, "CIA, SPCA or some other God damn alphabet soup government agency. Who knows. All I do know was that there were two objectives in that village."

"Right," Mick replied, "find the 'big mugoo', and the other...?"

"The other?" Boomer said, shaking his head, "the other I think...Was you."

"What the hell do you mean man?' Mick leaned forward grabbing Boomers hand. But the sudden movement seemed to spook him and he looked up at Starr with panicked eyes.

"Easy babe," she said and opening a big old steel Zippo lighter, dragged the flame across the open mouth of the hashish packed bong pipe. She drew in a single deep breath of the pungent smoke and then reached down and pulled Boomers lips to hers and exhaled a lung full of the sickeningly sweet smoke into his mouth. For an instant his eyes opened wide and it looked to Mick like he was going to turn away. Then he drew in a breath and Mick could see the resolve and the former first lieutenant Benson, drift away on the sweet, drug smoke. Boomers eyes started to glazed over again.

Star pushed her chair back from the table and came over to Mick. Her hard eyes locked on to his. "I'm not gonna' tell you again 'Curly'...Hit the bricks. And you know what? This time, even if the moon does drop smack into Boston harbor...Just keep right on going!"

Mick looked over her shoulder at the lieutenant, "hey, lieutenant...Steve...Is that what you want?" The sallow faced, skinny ex-officer didn't look up. He just mumbled, "Yeah...Sure."

But as Mick turned to go, Boomer looked desperately up at him and mustering up the last drops of who he once been, half whispered, "go to M.I.T. The biology building. The second floor lab."

Mick's eyes widened in surprise as Boomer grabbed his arm one final time and said, "and for Christ sake man, be careful!"

Then Boomer, seeming to have exhausted what was left of himself, slumped back into the rickety peeling chair and with shaking hands, greedily grabbed onto the pipe that Starr held out in front of him.

Mick slowly walked down the hall from the kitchen and out through the apartment door. All the way down the hall he could feel Starr's eyes burning into his back.

*   *   *   *

Mick reached the second story window ledge and gently eased the unlocked window open. For a moment he leaned his head back and let the gently falling rain wash the cobwebs out of his brain. Then he swung his booted feet over the windowsill and entered the lab.

CHAPTER 36

▼

Central Square
Cambridge
May 7, 1968
6:33PM

The dozens of layers of peeling paint, scraped Bronwyn's knuckles and gave the old muddy-brown door a muted, hollow sound when she pounded on it for the third time in half as many minutes.

"Damn," she muttered to herself, "where is he!"

After she'd spooked Quang at the MIT lab, and he'd almost freaked out, he'd called her the next morning and profusely apologized, citing stress, overwork, and just the sheer surprise at, "looking up from 10,000 power microscope and into the eyes of someone so lovely."

"Yeah right," Bronwyn thought cynically," boy, he wasn't even from this country but it sure hadn't taken him long to learn how to 'B.S.' with the best of them."

"On the other hand," she thought to herself, "it was certainly nice to know that he thought enough of her to care to feed her a flattering line…even if it was nine tenths B.S."

She stepped back from the still silent doorway to apartment 4C and looked around the dingy fourth floor landing of the rundown five story walkup located in an equally rundown section, of almost always run down…Central Square, Cambridge.

She felt a momentary small chill shiver down the middle of her back as she realized how quiet and dark it really was in the silent, musty hallway.

"Wow," she half whispered to herself, "this is just the kind of place you'd expect to find the Boston Strangler lurking in the shadows, just standing there, all dressed in black, with that creepy black knit cap he always wore. Standing there with that nylon stocking that he always used to strangle those poor girls, and...stop it!" she said to herself, "get a grip girl or next you'll be seeing..."

And something from the other end of the hallway, moved.

Her intake of breath caught in her throat and she froze stark still.

She didn't know how long she stood there, petrified in that same position, straining her eyes to pierce the gloom on the other side of the fly and dust darkened forty-watt bulb.

After what seemed like hours, but could have only really been twenty or thirty seconds, she realized that there was nothing there and was actually glad that no one else had been around to see how stupid she was acting. She let her pent up breath out with a whoosh, raised her hand to knock on the door again and...

The shadow darkness at the other end of the hall moved again.

This time there could be no question, because the movement was accompanied by a soft but unmistakable shuffling sound and Bronwyn could see rising dust motes floating in the forty-watt gloom.

She stood paralyzed. Rooted to the spot with terror. Frozen. Hypnotized like a bird in front of a snake. She tried to scream and was actually surprised when the only sound that came out was a little mewing sound, like a kitten about to be drowned

The slowly approaching shadow was now starting to coalesce into man form and her wildly darting eyes moved back and forth, looking for the nylon stocking she was sure he held in his hand. And as the form stepped into the periphery of the dim hallway light, Bronwyn's most horrible nightmare...came true!

The form was dressed in black, right down to the black ski hat and ski mask and...the nylon stocking looped around one hand.

"Oh my God in heaven," Bronwyn mumbled hysterically to herself, "please don't let it end like this! Oh please, God help me!"

Suddenly her mother's voice came back to her, snapping through her paralyzed terror.

She had a flash of remembrance, when she had wanted 'oh so badly' to make the freshman cheerleading squad and had beseeched divine intervention. "Oh please God," she had prayed fervently with fourteen-year-old intensity in her pink and gold bedroom, while clutching her favorite girlhood stuffed Pooh Bear for moral support, "let me make the JV team."

God hadn't answered, but her mother had. Felicity Parker Prescott (formerly McCarthy) had answered sharply with all of the self assured certainty of three hundred years of Puritan heritage, "Bronwyn, don't ever call upon the Lord for something trivial and silly. He is quite used to answering the important prayers of Parker's and Prescott's. But let me also remind you my dear, of the first rule of your heritage, before you call for the divine intervention that your lineage entitles you to. In fact it was engraved on your christening cup…and those of your brothers too. Here, come with me dear," her mother had said leading her down the grandly sweeping staircase to the high ceiling living room below, where she paused in front of the floor to ceiling fireplace.

Bronwyn hesitated and her mother had pointed to the tarnished old silver cup and said, "take it down my dear and read it."

Bronwyn had reached up to the cracked and warped mantle of the Brattle Street house's parlor and plucked the small silver cup with her name engraved on the front. She had slowly turned it over and read the spidery, ornate script… "The Lord helps those who help themselves."

All the memories and childhood reminisces passed through her brain in a split second and seemed to bounce off the inside of her skull as her shaking tongue mouthed the words…" Oh God, please help me."

Then all her childhood memories answered back for the Lord and reminded her in the imaginary voice of her mother, that the lord was most favorably disposed towards those who, "helped themselves."

The memory broke the scream loose from her throat, and as the black clad form reached for her, she found her voice and screamed…" No!"

The shadow hesitated for a moment, seemingly stunned by the force of the scream…but when only the silence of the dust motes around the forty-watt bulb answered, it came on again.

A hand reached out across the weak hall light, clutched Bronwyn's arm, and the spell of immobility was broken.

Suddenly she remembered a night from last year's Thanksgiving, after the food and dishes had been cleared away, when amid the laughter and teasing wrestling of childhood, her brother Mick had showed her some army judo moves that he said were "guaranteed to make any horny, rat-bastard, SOB, forget all about 'bothering my baby sister'."

Older brother Francis had shaken his head as he walked away, but Brom had listened while she laughed, and now…She remembered.

As a black gloved hand came out of the glare induced shadows to fasten around her throat, instead of screaming and running away, as every instinct told her to do, she took a step forward, pulled the black gloved hand towards her and fell backwards, letting her own momentum drag her over and away from the apparition.

The respite was only momentary as the terror form twisted and slithered like some kind of cat\snake and almost instantly, righted itself again. But Brom had used that instant of pause to good advantage and vaulted the fourth floor landing railing. She hit the stairs in between the third and fourth floor and broke into a desperate, dead run. She ran down the creaking, wooden treads two and three at a time, too terrified to look back at what she sensed was behind her.

She reached the second floor landing and now could hear the pounding of feet just inches behind her. A hand grabbed her shoulder causing her to lose her stride for an instant before she twisted out of her Lowden coat and with a desperate push, rolled herself over the second floor landing railing falling heavily on to the cracked linoleum tiles of the apartment foyer.

She lay there for a moment…stunned, and out of breath. Then as she desperately pushed herself up on to her knees, she saw to her horror that the black clad shadow was between her and the buildings entrance door.

Bronwyn looked at the now impossible and impassible front door for an instant and in one final desperate gamble, launched herself into a dead run down the first floor corridor towards the apartment buildings back door. She heard the feet pounding after her and prayed she would make it…

But she didn't.

A black-gloved hand caught her by her long, dark, curly hair and dragged her down with a short, sharp, sudden tug.

Brom stumbled and crashed down onto the filthy linoleum, knocking the breath from her. When she looked up again, she was staring into to cold, black, lifeless eyes, and she felt something slip around her throat, constricting her windpipe and slowly but inexorably, start to squeeze.

She tried to scream but couldn't. She managed to slip two fingers between her throat and the strangling tool. It brought her a moment's respite of air and a tiny, desperate breath, but in the long run she knew, it would only mean that her fingers would be crushed, right along side of her windpipe. Her vision was blurring as she stared up into the two shiny black, lifeless, dolls eyes.

"Dear God...This was it? This was the end?" All the things that she wanted to do...and had never...or told anyone about, and now never would. And now...

The blood flow was cut off from her fingers and throat. She couldn't fight anymore. She was going out...like a candle in the wind.

There was a loud thud of footsteps in the hallway. Then a sudden shift of the weight off her chest and shoulders. A light, shuffling sound, a click and slam of the back door to the apartment building. And then...strong arms lifting her up. The smell of peppermints and Lucky Strike cigarettes. A smell from her childhood.

Bronwyn slowly opened her eyes and saw her own gray/blue green eyes reflected back from those of a timeworn, broken nosed, but still loving face.

Her father.

CHAPTER 37

▼

"What the hell are you doing here?" Michael McCarthy growled, though never loosening the solid but tender grip he still maintained on his only daughter's quivering shoulders.

"I...I, just wanted to see him. I...I had a present for him." She took a small brightly wrapped square package from the pocket of her Lowden coat and held it out to her father. The ex-Boston cop (now private detective) Michael McCarthy took the small package from his daughter's loose grip and turned it over and then sniffed it. "Christ Bonnie," he rumbled under his breath, using her childhood nickname, "tell me this isn't pot!"

Bronwyn's eyes flashed and she snatched the small parcel back. "It's just incense, damn you!" she snapped, "can't you ever stop being a cop for 10 minutes and just be a..."

"A what?" Mike answered, eyes narrowing. Brom paused for a moment and answered in a small voice, "just...a father."

Silence filled the dusty hallway. Even the dust motes seemed to pause in their endless dance around the forty watt bulb.

Finally 'Big Mike', McCarthy sighed and said in an uncharacteristically quiet voice, "okay Bonnie...I'll try."

He reached down and gently lifted her up off the dirty floor. He kept his arm around her small shoulders as they walked back up the stairs to apartment 4 C and paused in front of the door.

"Would you like to do the honors or shall I?" Mike tried to ask in what he hoped was his most reasonable voice.

"I will," Brom said and raised her knuckles and then stopped suddenly and turning to her father asked, "just what are you doing here anyway?"

Mike didn't answer. He just raised his left arm and with one meaty fist, gave three sharp raps on the old wooden door. The sound echoed hollowly up and down the dingy stairwell and ended in…Silence.

Bronwyn shifted her weight from one foot to the other and chewed the inside of her lower lip.

Her father gave her a quick look and then dropped his eyes back down to the door as he took out a small leather case from his raincoat pocket.

Without looking at her, he unzipped the case and with years of practiced ease, selected a small slim steel probe and inserted it into the antique lock.

He gave a few twists of his wrist and then a grunt of satisfaction as the old spring mechanism gave a protesting squeak and clicked open.

Mike started to ease the door open when something made him pause.

His eyes narrowed, hardening into the too-many decades of beat cop experience, as he reached around to the back of his belt and eased out his newly replaced snub nose .38 revolver.

He put his shoulder against the door as he slowly pushed it open and then stopped and looked back at his daughter.

"Bonnie, stay here", he said in a low, grim, clipped tone and stepped into the apartment, half closing the door behind him.

Bronwyn stood there on the threshold to the apartment, frightened and worried. She wanted to go in, but something she'd seen in her father's eyes, stopped her. She just stood there. She knew she shouldn't go in, but…She slowly pushed the door open all the way and took a half step inside. She couldn't see her father. Everything was so quiet and strange. She had been here before…many times, but this time something was different. Something was wrong. Very wrong. . It was…O my God!

The smell!!

It hit her all at once, almost like a physical force. Her hand went to her mouth as she bolted through the apartment door and falling to her knees, vomited all over the faded black and white hallway tiles.

She rose shaking from her knees and felt her father's hands go around her shoulders.

"Oh Jesus, Dad…What is that…O my God, what's happened in there? Where's Quang? What…?!!?"

She tried to push past him into the apartment but Mike held on to her with an iron-vise grip.

"Don't go in there Bonnie. Go downstairs and wait for, me out in front of the building."

"No!" Bronwyn cried as she gave a sudden twist and slipping out of his grip, stumbled across the threshold.

Without knowing why, she ran through the long living room and back into the single bedroom. The smell was so bad that she almost couldn't breathe, but it was what she saw on the unmade, blood stained, double bed that froze her stark still and started her shaking her head back and forth as she moaned, "no, no...No!" over and over again.

Two strangely small and seemingly shrunken forms lay wrapped in each other's bloody arms.

It was Quang...And her best friend...Chrissie Elliott.

*   *   *   *

Bronwyn couldn't even remember her father, gently but firmly, pulling her out of the bedroom and pushing the door closed with his foot.

"Oh my God, Dad," she hiccupped with dry racking sobs, "what...Who...Who could have...?"

"That's exactly what we'd like to know Missy," came a hard nasal voice from behind them.

Bronwyn spun around. Mike turned more slowly. Almost as if he knew who he was going to find standing at the entrance to the apartment, wearing a big nasty grin on his face.

His old pal...former Sergeant, now Precinct Captain, Dennis Bannon.

CHAPTER 38

▼

Cambridge Mass.
MIT
May 7,1968
6:31 PM

Mick closed the window behind him and moved into the MIT lab.

He wasn't exactly sure what he was looking for but he had a strong hunch that he'd know it when he saw it.

He moved through the silent lab, his nostrils tickled by the sharp, acrid, piercing scent of chemicals and unwashed test tubes.

He paused and looked through the pebbled glass half-window of the lab door, reading the backwards 207 number as he listened for any hint of life or movement in the outside corridor.

"Silent as the frigging tomb," he muttered to himself in what he hoped was not a flash of prophecy.

He eased the door open and quietly stepped into the hallway. He looked warily from one end to the other.

Nothing.

"Do I have a damn clue what I'm doing?" he asked himself, shaking his head.

He stood there for a moment, trying to remember, and read between the meandering lines of Boomers last few cryptic, mumbling sentences...

"Go to MIT," the ex-lieutenant had said. "Look in...look for..."

Look for what?!

Mick closed his eyes, trying to read Boomers lips in his mind's eye, as Starr had stepped between them and shut off whatever Boomer had been trying to tell him.

"Look for…"

And then Mick saw through his closed eyes, the words form on Boomers (a.k.a. First Lieutenant Steve Benson) lips, "look in the biotech lab…And look for…The paper dragon and…The golden bowl."

CHAPTER 39

▼

Central Square
Cambridge
Precinct 5 Station House
7:18 PM

So missy…"

"It's Bronwyn, you black-Irish, bog-trottin' piece of trash," Mike growled from the other side of the scarred table in interrogation room # 3, that took up most of the space in the small basement below Cambridge's Precinct Five.

"My pardon, 'Miss Bronwyn', and I forget…Is it Prescott or McCarthy?" Bannon added with a smirk.

Bronwyn just pulled her knees up to her forehead and pressed them to her still leaking eyelids, making herself into a tiny ball of sadness and misery as she huddled silently in the cheap steel and vinyl chair.

Bannon nudged his chin to the right and a big beefy detective stepped out of the shadows at the back of the interrogation room and into the glare of the harsh unshielded two hundred-watt bulb that hung over the table.

Mike rose half out of his chair and rasped…" Morrison."

"McCarthy," was all the bulky form acknowledged with a cold smile.

"So," Mike said to Bannon, his eyes narrowing, "you've been dredging up the bottom of the barrel with the feeble minded and baby-rapers.

The hulk that Mike had identified as Morrison, gave a lurch towards him, his gravel voice rumbling, "I'll rip your balls off you son-of-a-bitch!"

"Come right ahead, hot shot," Mike invited, standing up and pushing the chair back and over.

They both stood on either side of the table, breathing hard, with the fight or flight adrenaline flowing for seconds that stretched into minutes and seemed to everyone in the room, like hours.

Finally Bannon said to his chief-interrogator detective, "take a deep breath Johnnie…and sit down. Michael isn't going to do anything…Especially when he's got sweet little Bonnie to look after. Isn't that right Michael?"

Mike breathed hard through his nose for a few seconds and finally answered, "Yeah…But just remember this you slimy son-of-a-bitch, if you or 'Paddy's pig' there, so much as lays a finger on her, I'll…"

"Michael…darlin'," Bannon mocked in a parody of an Irish brogue, "there's no need for threats between friends."

Bannon planted his knuckles on top of the scarred table and leaned close to Mike's flushed face, "and that's why you and me need to have a friendly little chat…Alone."

Bannon lifted his left hand in a lazy gesture and pointed his thumb towards the door.

Two uniformed patrolman moved in and each put a hand on one of Bronwyn's shoulders. Mike started out of his chair. Bannon made a chopping motion to the two patrolmen and they stepped back into the shadows.

Mike paused in a half crouch.

"Bonnie dear," Bannon said, "would you be a good girl please and go with these nice officers so that me and your dad can have a pleasant little chat."

Bronwyn looked across the table at her father.

His jaw clamped tighter for a few moments and then he drew in a deep shuddering breath and slowly nodded his head.

Bronwyn gave a last look at her father, then turned and walked to the door.

"Just remember what I said," Mike growled to their retreating backs in a voice cold as ice.

There was a slight pause, the click of the interrogation room door.

And then…Silence.

Bannon smiled at Mike and the big detective identified as Morrison, stood with arms folded, staring across the table at Mike.

"So boy'o," Bannon said, "now we can have our nice little chat…Just between old friends. And speaking of friends, we seem to have one in common."

"If we even had one of anything in common, it would be a frigging miracle," Mike growled back.

Morrison reached over the table and backhanded Mike, splitting his lip.

Mike pulled back, shook his head, spat blood onto the dirty linoleum floor, and said, "Everyone gets one sucker punch, but I guarantee, that will be your first …and your last."

Morrison just sneered and folded his hands as he stepped back into the shadows.

"Now," Captain Bannon smiled, "let's begin again. You've taken a rather large retainer from a very good friend of mine. A Chinaman."

Mike looked up, and wiping his mouth with a dirty linen handkerchief, spat blood again.

Bannon continued without acknowledging Mike, "and as I understand it, the only requirement for this rather large fee, was to keep a certain young man well and alive…Which quite evidently, "he shook his head in mock sadness," you have most miserably failed to do. And as a matter of fact, I hate to tell you old friend, that it appears to all of us here in Precinct 5, that you may have even had a hand in it."

Mike's face hardened and then Bannon added the 'coup de gras', "and I'm even sorrier to say, it appears that you may have even dragged your sweet, lovely and innocent…" the hulking Morrison sniggered in the background, "Bronwyn into this sorry affair too."

Even though Dennis Bannon had known Mike McCarthy for almost fifty years, he still wasn't prepared for what happened next. Almost before the words had left his mouth, Mike had somehow thrown himself across the table and fastened his hands around Bannon's throat. For one of the few times in his life, Captain Dennis Bannon found himself sincerely terrified as he realized that he was looking into the eyes of someone who was truly ready to kill.

"Listen to me you miserable son of a bitch," Mike hissed from between clenched teeth. "If you or anyone who works for you, so much as lays a finger on Bronwyn…I'll hunt you down. From beyond the grave, or Hell or wherever I am, and I'll kill you in ways which will make you pray to the sweet Virgin Mary, that you had never been born…Do you understand me?"

And Dennis Bannon did. He knew the family and their history. 'The McCarthy madness' was legend in Southie. He nodded his head.

"Send the goon out of here," Mike growled.

"Go," Bannon croaked.

Only when the door clicked shut did Mike finally release his Gila-monster-like grip on the precinct captains throat.

Bannon slumped back in his chair and rubbed his bruised larynx with his left hand.

Mike drew in a deep breath, held it and then let it out slowly, saying, "okay, you cousin to a weasel, what's this about the Chinaman and just how the hell do you fit into all of this."

CHAPTER 40

▼

**Cambridge, Mass
MIT
May 7, 1968
7:57 PM**

Mick paused before the last door on the second floor group of labs. He'd been through each one and couldn't find anything except a bunch of ordinary science-geek places where they played with test tubes in white lab coats.

If there was nothing in this one, he was gonna' climb back on the BSA and go back to Inman Square and Bridget…and bed.

"Maybe Boomer had sucked up one too many tokes, on one too many of Starr's hash pipes," he thought morosely, as he gently turned the doorknob under the lettering on the last door that read, "Genetic Biology Lab # 2".

Mick slipped into the lab and closed the door behind him.

Right away he noticed that something was different. He couldn't put his finger on it, but somehow he felt that something in this lab just wasn't quite right. He didn't know what it was but there was something about this lab. A smell. A vibration. A feeling. Something evil.

He stopped in front of a small narrow door at the back of the lab. It looked like a broom closet or someplace for supplies, he thought. But he'd already been through every room on the second floor lab complex, so if there was nothing here, well then it was back to bed and Bridget…in just about that order he grinned to himself as he twisted the doorknob.

Damn…locked!

Well what else was new on this rainy, bizarre, futile-quest night.

"Might as well go all the way." he muttered to himself.

"What I need is a hairpin or a piece of wire, or a…paper clip!" he smiled to himself as his eyes fastened onto a lab report on the stained granite topped work-table behind him.

Mick quickly pulled off the paperclip holding the report together and smoothed it out between his fingers.

He grinned to himself again and thought," Pop, you'd be proud of me. And to think, all those times that I sat around Station B as a kid while you and your buddies discussed the finer points of B&E with Boston's best lock pickers. Hah!…and you thought I wasn't listening, just because I always had my nose buried in a Bugs Bunny comic book, but…"

Click

Mick pulled the paperclip pick out of the lock and turned the doorknob.

It swung open.

It was pitch black inside. No windows.

Mick's left hand fumbled around for a light switch. His fingers found the switch-plate and…the room was flooded with fluorescent light. He looked around. It was much bigger than it had seemed from the outside. Maybe twenty feet long and at least a dozen feet wide.

Mick slowly walked towards the far end of the room and stopped in front of an immaculate lab table with rows and rows of neatly labeled Petrie dishes. At the far end, on the right of the table, an immense camera-like gadget that Mick remembered from a quick pass through the Harvard science labs, was an electron microscope.

He walked up to the left hand end of the table up and lifted up the first Petrie dish. There was a light, yellow colored mold growing in the dish. He read the label, "X P-AR-DR-GN Phase one".

He picked up each successive dish. They all had the same prefix letters, only the numbers were different…

Phase two, Phase three…And so on.

Until he came to the end of the table and the last dish.

This one was different. This was a large metallic dish. Almost like a giant cooking-bowl. It was filled with a huge, thick mass of the bright, yellow fungus…Or mold, or whatever it was. There was a faintly ghostly glowing fluorescent light over the bowl, that gave it a…Golden glow.

Mick stopped as if someone had thrown a brick against his head.

His memory flashed back to Boomer and what he'd been trying to tell Mick when he left the Commonwealth Avenue apartment.

He read Boomers lips again in his mind.

"Go to MIT…The second floor Bio Tech labs. Look for…The 'Paper Dragon' and…And the Golden Bowl."

"The Golden, frigging Bowl!" Mick breathed as he reached out his hand to touch it and then for some instinctive reason, pulled it back.

"But if that's the 'Golden Bowl'," he thought, then where's the God damn 'Paper. ..."

The thought floated away as he walked back to the head of the table and picked up the first Petrie dish and read, "X P-AR-DR-GN"

Suddenly it clicked and he spun around and picked up the report that he'd taken the paper clip from and looked at the heading at the top. It read, "Confidential Introduction to Series X P-AR-DR-GN" across the top of the first page.

He stared at the words on the snowy white, expensive, 60 lb. rag-bond paper, written in broken Army stenciled script, "…X P-AR-D R-G N".

The Paper Dragon.

CHAPTER 41

▼

Harvard Sq.
Cambridge, Mass
May 7, 1968
8:56PM

Bridget sat on the barstool in the Oxford Alehouse house just off Harvard Square and smiled distractedly as the bartender asked her for the third time, what she wanted to drink. She finally answered more from embarrassment than thirst, "Whatever you've got on tap."

"Schlitz okay, then?" The bartender asked and Bridget thought, "I wouldn't know a Schlitz from a cocker spaniel if it walked up and bit me on the bum," but answered with a weak smile, "sure fine."

"Sweet bleedin' Jesus," she thought, "what was she doing here?"

The phone had rung about an hour ago and a tentative, soft, almost bland, American voice had asked, "is this Bridget Connelly?"

"Yes," Bridget had answered suspiciously, "and who is this?"

"A friend, I think," and after a short pause, "I hope."

There was a moment of silence and the voice said, "we need to talk."

"About what?" Bridget asked, a small knot of dread forming in the pit of her stomach.

"About someone that we both care for, very deeply," the thin, sweet voice responded.

"Do you know where the Oxford Ale House is...Just off Harvard Square?"

"Yes," was the only word that Bridget could squeeze out.

"Meet me there in one hour."

"How will I know you?" Bridget asked, not quite believing that this strange conversation was real."

I'll be wearing a yellow headband, "the voice responded..." But don't worry, I'll find you."

And the line went dead.

CHAPTER 42

▼

Boston's financial district—Hayward, Elliott & Delbert—41st floor

"Francis, please get Charlton a glass of water…Or would a Scotch be better Charlton?" Preston asked his partner with well modulated and well practiced solicitude.

Charlton Elliott didn't answer. He sat at the end of the polished oak boardroom table, head buried in his hands.

"Mr. Elliott?" Francis (Frankie McCarthy) Prescott said tentatively, holding out a heavy lead crystal glass in one hand and a water carafe in the other.

Charlton Elliott never even looked at him. He just sat there and stared at the head of the table. "Preston," he said in a barely audible, broken voice, "she's dead Preston. My baby. My Chrissie is dead."

"I know Charlton," Preston Hayward said, "and no one could be more devastated then I."

"Don't say that to me you bastard," Charlton Elliott snapped, "you're the one who got us into that devil's bargain with that, that…" His voice shook as he pointed his finger at the dumpy, innocuous figure seated in the shadows. Silently watching from the corner next to the floor to ceiling picture window facing Boston Harbor.

"Charlton, please…You're upset and I can't blame you, but it was a horrible, unfortunate accident and…"

"Don't you understand?" He screamed…" my little girl is dead and this Commie piece of scum is responsible…I'd like to…" and Charlton Elliott lost total control for the first time in his privileged life. Picking up the ornate letter opener, from the side table, he launched himself at the unmoving figure seated in the chair next to the window.

But before he'd covered even half of the distance, another figure had detached itself from the shadows next to the window and Charlton Elliott found the letter opener ripped from his grasp and pressed against his throat.

Tears of rage and frustration, traced down his cheeks as he found himself held helplessly in a deceptively soft but unyielding grip.

"Ling!" Preston Hayward snapped, and the dumpy little figure slowly rose out of the chair next to the window.

He paused for a moment and then slowly said, "Ritchie, please release Mr. Elliott."

With a snort of contempt, Ritchie lowered the ornate letter opener from Charlton Eliot's neck and with a seemingly lazy flick of his wrist, tossed it in one smooth motion into the boardrooms oak tabletop.

The room's occupants froze.

The short man in the light colored silk suit, just smiled slightly.

Charlton Elliott found his voice again and hissed, "I don't care how many knife throwing thugs you have, my little girl is dead and I'm going to see that all of you go to prison or hell or wherever…"

"Charlton!!" Preston Hayward cut him off and then tried to lower his voice, "you don't know what you're saying, we're all…"

"Please, Mr. Hayward," the short man said in his quiet, slightly accented voice, "we know that Mr. Elliott's grief is understandable from the consequences of this tragic accident, that was beyond even our powers to control. There are greater forces at work here then you can comprehend…Nor do you want to," and the seemingly mild eyes sharpened and turned cold.

"Yes," he repeated, "unimaginable forces at work."

Preston Hayward look cowed.

Francis (Frankie) looked bewildered, but Charlton Elliott looked defiant, so the small man added, "but in case, you forget Mr. Elliott, remember that you still have one other lovely, blonde haired daughter.

I believe her name is…Paige".

CHAPTER 43

▼

Oxford Alehouse
Harvard Square
Cambridge
May 7,1968
9:37 p.m.

"Bridget? Bridget Connelly?"

Bridget spun around on her barstool and looked into the pale frightened eyes of a wispy, thin blonde with long straight hair held place by a yellow headband. They just looked at one another for a moment that seemed to stretch on and on.

"I've seen her before," Bridget thought, "I know I have. And she knows Mick, and…"

And then it hit her.

"Yes! It was right here…in Harvard square!"

She racked her brains for another moment and then snapped her fingers and said out loud to the serious, frightened looking girl in front of her, "the Blue Parrot! Two years ago!! You were there with Mick!!!"

"Yes," she smiled shyly, "and you were our waitress," and added…

"My name is Holly."

*   *   *   *

MIT
Cambridge, Mass
May 7, 1968
10:10 p.m.

Mick looked down at the lab report that he'd spread out on the granite workta-ble. He could only comprehend one word in ten but it seemed to refer to an experimental project that the world renowned science lab was conducting for...Who?

Mick shuffled through the papers looking for something. Anything. A clue...Something...anything...And there it was.

On the last page of the report. Under the cryptic..." X P-A R-D R-GN," Phase 1—Observations from Station 613, Vietnam. Map coordinates, M 22—S37.

15, June 1966.

Mick's breath froze in his lungs. His hands started to shake and despite the cold, clammy damp of the lab, a sick, fever-like sweat, moistened his forehead and ran into his eyes.

He rubbed his hand over his damp face distractedly as he stared at the date...The 15th of June 1966.

Mother of God. Could he ever forget that date. It was burned into his soul. That night...In the village.

This was friggin' it!

This was the key, the answer to what had happened.

All the nightmares, waking and sleeping.

He frantically riffled through the papers again. But it was all just a bunch of a meaningless chemical formulas.

There had to be more!

He looked at the last page again.

And there, just below the code letters and that bone chilling date...

"Conclusion. See;.. LX.—BX. 733 MIT-Reference-Deposit-Building...4-B, Mem. Drive .

"Okay," Mick said to himself, trying to calm his breathing, "I can do this...just think. 'L X-B X', obviously lock box 773. At the campus reference library, building # 4 B...On Memorial Drive!"

Mick folded up the lab reports and paused. He looked back at the long granite lab table and then walked back to the large bowl, which was still glowing under the fluorescent light at the end of the table. He pulled open the drawer under the counter top and rummaged around for a moment before pulling out a pair of rubber gloves.

Mick pulled them on, and then taking a small stoppered test tube from the rack on the table, carefully opened the bowl's cover and scooped up a tiny bit of the golden, yellow mold. He gently deposited it in the waiting test tube and pushed the stopper back in tightly. Then he carefully slid the test tube into the inside pocket of his denim jacket and a snapped it closed.

He started for the door again, but vowed to himself that he was going to take it very easy on the short ride over to Memorial Drive. Because somehow, he instinctively knew, that whatever was in that test tube, he didn't want it to break.

*   *   *   *

Commonwealth Avenue
Allston
May 7,1968
10:36 p.m.

The last strains of Procol Harum's 'Whiter shade of Pale', died away and with it the fine fuzzy edge that Boomer had gotten from his last hit off of Starr's hash pipe.

"Starr…Hey…" he called, but there was no answer .

"Where the hell has the party disappeared to?" He idly wondered.

The last he remembered, the Commonwealth Ave apartment had been filled with the usual eclectic mix of students and street people. All grooving to the sounds of Jefferson Airplane, Procal Harum and Cream .

But now? All gone…poof!

He laughed quietly to himself and getting shakily to his feet called out again,

"Starr…hey, where the hell are you? I need you Babe ." he half whispered to himself. He tried to get up. To walk to the kitchen. He needed water. Or something. But his legs weren't working very well.

"Man," he muttered, "that must have been some heavy shit that Starr put in the pipe."

He shook his head again, trying to clear away some of the mist. And then…He seemed to remember. A dream? He'd been sitting at that same table, staring at the Jimi Hendrix poster. It had seemed alive under the party's black light and then Terry, the guy from downstairs, had come over to him and shouted over the music, "hey man, you've got a phone call."

Boomer had just shaken his head, still mesmerized by the poster and Jimmy dancing for him under the black light.

Terry had shaken him.

"Hey Boomer, man. Some chick on the phone for you. In the kitchen…"

He'd paused and then winked, "she says, she's your sister."

Somehow, Boomer had stumbled into the kitchen and managed to pick up the dangling phone.

And it was…his sister.

*   *   *   *

Memorial Drive—Cambridge Mass.
May 7, 1968
10:39 PM

The cold drizzle had tapered off to a fine mist, but it still didn't make it any easier for Mick to see.

He'd finally broken down and gotten one of the new "Visor" gadgets, after Bridget had complained about him "comin' home with dirt on his face and bugs in his teeth."

Well it kept the bugs off his teeth, but until someone invented a windshield wiper for the damn thing, the beading water droplets from the mist, made it worse than useless.

He deliberately slowed at the next stoplight so that he could unsnap the pointless contraption, and get it out of his way. "I may get a face full of rain," he muttered, "but at least I can see."

The light changed and he clicked the foot shift into first and then quickly into second gear, as he kept shooting glances to left, trying to determine which of the imposing, cold, grey granite faced buildings was # 4B. Suddenly, he saw a semi-circle of four stone buildings on his left, facing the river and a stark, utilitarian sign that read, "University Complex B—Reference Center".

"That's it," Mick said aloud and gave a quick check to his left as he prepared to change lanes and hang a U-turn at the next curb cut.

That split second glance was probably the only thing that saved him from getting broadsided by a monstrous two-tone Lincoln Continental that swerved from the left lane, directly at Mick.

He only got out the first, Sh—, of "shit!!", before the big piece of Detroit steel was right on top of him and Mick locked up the back brake, leaning desperately right in a futile effort to avoid being squashed like a bug. The BSA fishtailed wildly to the right as Mick pushed his left leg back and flat over the bikes rear seat a millisecond before it would have been ground between the BSA's frame and the big Lincoln's right front fender. He looked through the Continental's rain streaked windshield and had a split second image of two grinning faces before the bike hit the curb next to the river, flipped over twice, and careened into the cold, gray waters of the Charles River.

▼

CHAPTER 44

Oxford Ale House
Harvard Square
Cambridge, Mass
May 7, 1968
10:43 p.m.

"I said," the guy in the faded college T-shirt and beat-up old cowboy boots, repeated, "would you like to dance?"

Bridget looked up from the table that she and Holly had moved to…over an hour ago?

"Sweet Jesus," she thought to herself, "I can't believe we've been talking that long."

She looked up from the table and past the slightly drunk, but still optimistic, probable college boy, and over to the corridor leading to the restrooms where she could just make out Holly through the smoky barroom haze.

Holly was still on the phone call that she'd left the table ten minutes ago to make. She was talking to someone who was obviously upsetting her from the way she was clutching the phone and shaking her head.

Although Bridget couldn't hear a word she was saying over the noise of the bar and the band, she could tell, even through the smoke, that whoever Holly was talking to and whatever she was hearing on the other end of the line…it wasn't good.

"Ah, um…if you don't want to dance, can I buy you a beer?"

Bridget shifted her eyes away from Holly and looked back at the college cowboy who had just pushed his battered, dirty white straw cowboy hat back on his head while wiping the sweat off his forehead with the back of his hand. She tried to hide an amused smile as she saw him take a deep breath for what she instinctively knew, would be the next in his repertoires of bar pick-up lines.

"Well little lady," he began with an accent that couldn't quite seem to decide if it belonged in Texas or Boston, "you're just too pretty to be sitting here all by yourself."

"Oh, but I'm not," Bridget smiled.

The accent and self-confidence leaked out of the blue-eyed, curly haired, 'Cambridge Cowboy' like a punctured balloon.

"Your not?" He said.

He looked so disappointed, that if it wasn't for Holly and her disturbing story…and Mick off God knows where, she almost might have let the poor puppy dog buy her a beer.

Instead she mustered up her best noncommittal smile and said, "no, I'm not and as a matter of fact, here's my friend right now."

As she spoke the words, Holly came back to the table and sat down.

Suddenly the college cowboy brightened again with renewed hope. The accent and confidence were reignited as he said, "well lovely ladies, that's just fine. In fact," he grinned readjusting the brim of the old white cowboy hat, that Bridget decided, he probably thought made him look like one of the Byrds, "that's twice as good!"

He grinned and made a 'come on' motion towards a table full of guys sitting with a half dozen empty beer pitchers scattered about them.

A dark eyed guy with a mustache, long sideburns and shoulder length hair got up and came over to their table.

"Well you see, that's just perfect, "the blue eyed boy with the cowboy hat repeated," cuz' this here is my buddy Steve."

The guy with the mustache and sideburns grinned and reaching over to the next table, started to pull a chair over, in obvious preparation to sit down.

"And," the college T-shirted cowboy continued, "my name is Rick, and yours is…?"

"I'm Bridget, Luv," she answered with a half smile, "but…"

"And who is this foxy chick?" The longhaired guy with the sideburns asked? Holly looked up from where she'd been drawing designs with her forefinger in the beer-wet tabletop.

She looked at Bridget, and then back at the two young men and finally said in a very small voice, "my…my name…is…Holly."

And she burst into hysterical tears.

*   *   *   *

Commonwealth
Avenue Allston
May 7,1968
10:52 p.m.

Boomer was running through the jungle. Someone...something was after him. And it was gaining.

He ran on blindly, tripping over roots and vines. Branches were whipping into his eyes, half blinding him so that he had to keep wiping the sweat and dirt away with the sleeve of his torn Army fatigue shirt.

But every time he paused to do that he could hear what ever it was, gaining on him.

Getting closer.

He had to get away. Get to...Where?

He stumbled and almost fell. And then steadied himself on a half rotted tree.

He leaned against the tree for a moment and looked around frantically.

He could hear it quite clearly now. It was right behind him. It would. .

Suddenly his wildly swiveling eyes caught sight of a clearing through the green wall of jungle. There was a loud noise behind him. It was almost on top of him.

He ran.

He ran through the jungle. The vines and branches tearing at his clothes and skin. He was almost to the clearing when he felt sharp talons tearing into his flesh.

He looked back at his shoulder and saw five purple claws had buried themselves in his shoulder blade and were contracting, to rip out muscle, skin and bone.

He screamed. Over and over.

His eyes flew open and he saw the snakelike fingers of Jimi Hendrix reaching out from the poster for him.

He screamed again.

"Hey Boomer," Terry had laughed, "having a bad trip man? Here take a slug of this Ripple wine, that'll clear your pipes."

Boomer grabbed for the bottle and sucked down a long swig of the sweet, rank wine and then leaned his head back on the old torn couch.

Then the phone had rung and it was his sister.

The sound of her voice had brought back so many long forgotten happy memories of home, and cornfields and a bright blue sky that seemed a million miles from dark, evil jungles.

He'd told his sister everything. As he spoke to her, more and more had started to come back to him. But far more disturbing…for better or worse…and it was probably worse, all of the pieces were starting to fall into place.

He told her all the things he remembered and all the things he supposed. And the truth washed over him like a clammy jungle rain.

Then he told her about the dream. But this time, he thought he knew what the dream really meant. So he told her about that too.

She was frightened for him and wanted to come to him but he knew instinctively that was something she shouldn't do.

"Where are you?" he'd asked. And she told him.

"Stay there," he said. "I'll come to you. I just need to get my shit together and then, I'll take the Green Line and…I'll get there somehow."

"Okay?" he'd asked.

"Ok," she said.

And then just as she was hanging up, he'd added, "Sis…I love you."

Boomer rolled the still cool bottle of Ripple wine over his forehead and muttered to himself, "man, I gotta' get my shit together and get out of here." He started to push himself off the old couch when it a pair of cool hands slipped down over his shoulders from behind and gently pulled him back down on the couch. He turned to look and those same cool fingers lightly pushed something past his lips and onto his tongue. It tasted bitter. He started to spit it out but a voice said, "hush baby. Close your eyes. Go to sleep and dream."

And he did.

He was back in the jungle, at the edge of the clearing.

He looked to the center of the clearing where a ring of burnt and blackened huts still smoldered and he saw…The colonel.

And Mick was there and Smitty and Walzac and Begley…And a man in black, who stood in the shadows.

The man in black with bone white skin and dead black eyes, prodded a small blackened lump with the toe of his shoe. It began to move. It started to crawl. Then it unsteadily got on two feet, and slowly began to walk…towards Boomer. Towards first lieutenant Steve Benson.

He wanted to scream but nothing would come. He turned back to the colonel and was a surprised to see that the colonel was grinning. The colonel had his arm around someone. A smiling young Oriental man.

"You bastard!" Boomer shouted at the colonel, "you murdered them all…the entire village. And you fucked up Mick and Walzac and Begley and all the men…and me, so that none of us will ever be right again!"

The colonel just kept smiling and said, "casualties are a part of war lieutenant, but please don't worry. You see our young friend here," and he squeezed young man's shoulder so tightly that he winced, "has something which is going to make it all worthwhile. Yes, something that will make everyone happy and put everything right."

The Colonel gave the young Oriental man a gentle push and said, "show him." The young man smiled shyly and took a step forward. He held something out to Boomer. It was a large bronze bowl. And it was glowing. A pale yellow, golden glow.

First lieutenant Steve "Boomer" Benson took a step backwards. "Keep that thing away from me!" he shouted. "I know what it is. And I know all about you and 'Paper Dragon' and by Christ, you're gonna' pay you son-of-a-bitch!"

"I'm sorry you feel that way lieutenant," the colonel replied shaking his head.
"I truly am."

And then the colonel turned in towards the swirling smoke of the smoldering village and was gone.

In fact they all were gone.

Mick, Smitty, Walzac…all except for the man in black and the twitching blackened lumps that were starting to rise again.

Boomer backed away, deciding he'd rather risk the jungle than stay there.

As he started to turn away…the man in black, for the first time, spoke.

"Goodbye lieutenant," was all he said and he nodded his head to something behind Boomer. Boomer swung his head around and screamed as he saw the purple talons burry themselves in his shoulder again. He screamed and tried to run but the five purple talons held him fast. A soft husky voice whispered,

"I'm sorry," and then grew colder and repeated the words of the man in black.
"Goodbye lieutenant."

First lieutenant Steve, "Boomer" Benson's eyes shot open one last time as he stared at the form silhouetted against the black lit poster of Jimi Hendrix.

"I should have known..." he managed to get out before something sharp jabbed into his arm, and all the bad dreams winked out.

Forever.

CHAPTER 45

▼

Oxford Alehouse
Cambridge Mass
May 7, 1968
11 06 p.m.

Holly's hysterical sobs had finally subsided to a, dry hiccupping sound, which was a damn good thing, Bridget thought. It wasn't that she didn't feel concern for Holly or want to comfort her…even if she was one of Mick's old girlfriends. It was just that she was starting to get damned worried herself.

She knew that it wasn't the proper Christian feeling, like the nuns had tried to drill into her, about self sacrifice and concern for others, but the more Holly sobbed out her fear for her brother, the more uneasy she started to feel about her own, trouble-prone, 'bad-boy'. And just where the hell was Mick!

"Do you think it would be too much to ask, Bridget?"

Bridget snapped her spaced-out gaze back to Holly, momentarily embarrassed because she hadn't heard a word that Holly had been saying.

"I'm sorry Luv," Bridget said, "I was…"

Holly smiled a quick understanding half smile and said, "don't be sorry Bridget, you've already been so sweet. To meet me here and listen…and care."

Holly continued, "you don't know how long it took me to get up my courage to call you tonight. I mean," and she looked down at the table, "I know that you know, that Mick and I went out for a month before he met you…Or saw you again, that night two years ago, at the Blue Parrot. I mean, I knew when he saw you that night that something clicked," she said softly, "and that even though I wanted to hold on to him, I never could."

Bridget didn't say anything. She just looked at Holly. Very carefully.

Holly looked up at Bridget and gave her a shy said smile. "Yes," she said, "I guess I still am a little in love with him. You see I never had a boyfriend back in Iowa. Just two brothers. So Mick was really the first boy, I ever fell for. And he was so sweet and funny, and a brave and nice and..." She broke off when she saw the way Bridget was looking at her, and quickly added, while grabbing Bridget's hands across the table, "but please, you've got to believe me, that's not why I called you tonight. I told you about my brother and how I didn't even find out till long after Mick and I stopped dating, that he knew Steve in Vietnam."

Bridget slowly nodded and Holly went on. "And then I told you how worried I was about my brother and the people he was involved with, and the drugs and his nightmares and..." The tears began to drip down Holly's cheeks again and Bridget felt her feelings of jealousy dissolve as Holly twisted her drinks' paper coaster into small nervous shreds.

"But what I didn't tell you," Holly said, "looking back down at the table," was the nightmare that Mick had..." She blushed furiously, "the first night I stayed with him."

Bridget stiffened and pulled her hands away from Holly's.

"Bridget...Please!" Holly begged," he didn't even know you then. "Bridget's face remained stony.

"I'm not telling you this to hurt you," Holly said, "or trying to break you up. It's only because my brother has been having the exact same nightmares, ever since he got back from Viet Nam. He says that he has the same nightmares almost every night. And they're getting worse. And...now Mick is in them."

She stopped and looked up at Bridget who was still watching her warily, and continued, "but that's not even the worst part. It's what Steve, my brother, just told me on the phone.

Holly's hands as well as her voice, were shaking now. "Steve told me that lately, whatever was after him in the dream each night, seemed to be getting closer and closer. And he said that in the one he'd had tonight, just before I called him, it had almost gotten him. He said he knew, that if it ever did, in the dream...He'd never wake up."

Holly gave a small shudder and looked into Bridget's sea-green eyes, trying to get past the slow, peat-fire of anger that she could see, still smoldered there.

"You've got to believe me," she implored. "Do you remember what I told you about Steve's commanding officer in Vietnam. Colonel Chalmers, I think his name was..."

Yes, Bridget thought, she did remember that name…From Mick's mumbled shouts during his own sweat drenched nightmares.

"Well," Holly went on, "tonight when I called Steve and he'd just woken up from that nightmare, he said he'd remembered something from the dream…About the colonel and the people who were close to the colonel. And Bridget," Holly grabbed her hand back and held on to it, "whatever he remembered, terrified him. He kept saying over and over again that it was all starting to fit, and he should have known. That they could destroy this whole country…And the world! Then he seemed to make up his mind about something and said that he had to leave Boston, and he wanted me to go with him. He said we could go back to mommy and daddy's farm. The last thing he said was that I should stay here. That he'd come to me. Then just before he hung up, he said something he'd never said to me before…Not right out loud.

He said he…loved me."

Bridget smiled slightly, but Holly continued, white faced and serious.

"Bridget…The way he said it? It was like…it was like he never expected to see me again."

CHAPTER 46

▼

Inman Square
Cambridge, Mass
May 7,1968
11:17 PM

Bronwyn had just raised her knuckles to knock on the faded, non-descript brown door of the top floor apartment in the old triple-decker, when she saw the note..."Gone to Oxford Alehouse—meet me there," it read. It was signed, "Luv Ya! Bridget."

Obviously not meant for me, Bronwyn smiled wryly to herself.

She wondered for a moment if she should wait here for Mick, but then realized that he could have already been there, seen the note and gone to the Oxford Alehouse.

She sighed as she thought of another long bus ride back to Harvard Sq. and started back down the stairs.

She had just passed the second floor landing, when she thought she heard footsteps behind her.

She froze.

"Oh my God...No!" she thought, "Not again. This can't be happening again. Not twice in the same night...it couldn't be! Oh dear God, don't let it be..."

A hand brushed her shoulder and she screamed.

The hand was snatched back as Bronwyn spun around and saw...a very frightened looking Indian student who held up both hands and said, "Please, I was only going to tell you that if you were looking for Miss Bridget, upstairs, she is not here. She left several hours ago, and Mick is not here either."

"Oh yes," Bronwyn gasped, finally able to take a breath again. "I saw Bridget's note and was going to find her. Do you know what time the next bus comes?"

"Ah," he smiled, "you are going to Harvard Sq.? Then maybe I can make amends for frightening you so. I am going there and would be honored to take you."

"Oh, That's great!" Bronwyn exclaimed. "You just saved me a long bus ride."

"It is most certainly my pleasure, Miss…?"

"Bronwyn," she smiled. "I'm Mick's sister. And you are…?"

"Gupta," he inclined his head slightly, "and if it's not too rude of me to ask, what made you scream like that when I touched your shoulder? Surely," he smiled, "I cannot be so terribly frightening?"

"Oh, no," Bronwyn smiled back as they continued down the stairs and out the front door, "It wasn't you, it's just been a very weird and kinda' scary night up till now."

The front door closed with a click and everything inside the tired old frame building was silent for a moment.

Then slowly a figure stepped out of the shadows on the third floor landing.

The black clad form stood silently in front of the third floor apartment's door for a moment as if reading the note on the door…and then stepped back into the shadows

*   *   *   *

Inman Square
Cambridge, Mass
May 7, 1968
11:56 p.m.

Mick trudged slowly up the last two steps to the triple-decker's top floor and shuffled towards his apartment door, his boots making a soggy little squishing sound with each step.

He stepped in front of the door and read the note. He stood silent for a moment, head down, looking at the floor.

Suddenly he banged his fist squarely into the middle of the note pinned to the door and barked out, "shit!" with an equal combination of pain and frustration.

"God damn it Bridget," he muttered, "of all the nights to pick to go drinking. I'm fucking cold and wet and bruised and…" he let his voice trailed off. "And you don't even know, do you Bridge, 'cuz I never even had the decency to put a dime in a damn phone to let you know that I just spent the last two hours fishing me and the BSA out of the Charles," he finished quietly.

He dug his keys out of the right front pocket of his sopping wet jeans, turned the latch and stepped inside.

He stood still for a moment, dripping on the braided floor mat, and then peeling off his soaked denim jacket and wading it into a wet cloth ball, threw it into the old wicker basket that Bridget used as a clothes hamper when they made their weekly trip to the laundromat. Next came the boots, T-shirt, jeans and underwear. Finally stark naked, he crossed over to the old second hand hutch that Bridget had bought for $12 at a yard sale in Somerville. He picked up a half empty bottle of Bushmill's Irish whiskey and pulled out the cork stopper. As he raised it to his lips, he gave a slight smile and a nod of his head and as he murmured to himself, "guess the apple doesn't fall far from the tree, does it Pop," and took a long shuddering pull.

Wiping his lips with the back of his hand, he put the bottle down, crossed over to the bathroom and stepped into the cracked old porcelain tub. He turned the tap marked 'H' on full and was rewarded with a pathetic trickle of lukewarm water. But he stood under it gratefully all the same, letting the tepid warmth leach some of the chill out of his bones.

"Damn," he thought, "I guess I'm lucky to even be able to stand up in this crappy old tub and feel anything at all. If it wasn't for that split second glance to the left, I'd have been squashed like a bug under that Continental or at the bottom of the Charles.

He stepped out of the tub and pulled an almost clean towel off the rack. He wiped his face and then wrapped the towel around his waist and padded into the tiny alcove he and Bridge laughingly called the kitchen.

He opened the old fashioned Frigidaire refrigerator and pulled out the last can of almost-cold Papst Blue Ribbon beer. Mick opened it and let half the contents slide down his throat in one thirsty swallow. This was of course followed by a huge belch to which he added, "Oops, sorry Bridge," before he realized that she wasn't there.

"Better get changed and get over to the 'Alehouse'," he thought as he ambled into their single bedroom and pulled his other pair of jeans from his favorite clothes storage space…the closet floor.

He found some clean, dry underwear on the chair next to the bed, along with an almost-clean T-shirt, but try as he might, he couldn't find his sneakers.

"Crap!" He thought. That meant he had a choice of sandals or boots. He heaved a sigh and went back into the living room to pull on his soggy boots.

And as he pulled and struggled to work his feet into the wet leather, he thought back again to that moment two hours ago that had almost been his last. One thing that was for damn sure...It was no friggin' accident!

He knew whose faces those had been, grinning sadistically at him through the rain streaked windshield of the big Lincoln. The 'gruesome twosome', in the flesh and twice as ugly. And the fact that they'd caught him there out on Memorial Drive, with nothing between him and the river but a five inch curb and seven feet of grass, meant that they must have been following him.

For how long? And from where?

He needed to get down to the Alehouse and find Bridge. He reached into the closet and pulled out a worn, brown leather 'Bomber' jacket, a 'legacy' from his Uncle Tommy in Southie who brought it back from his B-17 days spent in the skies over Germany.

He ran his fingers over the cracked leather and smiled, remembering all of his uncle's war stories of ME-109's brought down, wearing the same jacket.

Mick smiled as he slipped it on and thought, "I'll try to bring down a few bad guys for you tonight, Unc'."

He stuffed his wallet into his pocket and admitted to himself that it was a damn miracle that he was able to walk away from flipping the bike with nothing more than bruises and...He looked in the small, cloudy mirror on the wall that Bridget had picked up in a dusty old antique shop just off the square because, she "felt so sorry for the poor old 'Gran'," that ran the place. He stared at the wavering image, bisected by an angry, red, oozing scrape that ran from his right cheek to just below his jaw line.

He smiled at his hazy, banged up reflection and thought, "hey between my face and the World War II bomber jacket, I look a little like a fighter pilot who's been through a battle...Yep and lost," he added with a shake of his head.

He grabbed his keys off the table, snapped the catch of the apartment door latch and clattered down the stairs. He still couldn't believe that the BSA was even able to run after they'd both gone for a swim in the Charles River.

Well actually, he'd gone for more of a swim than the bike. When he hit the curb and flipped the bike, he'd gone headfirst into the river which was probably all that kept him from breaking his neck.

The bike on the other hand, had skidded across the wet grass, gotten caught on an old half sunken wooden packing crate and come to rest with the front wheel in the water and the engine and the back wheel on the muddy grass at the river's edge.

After Mick had pulled himself out of what the popular Boston song referred to as that 'Dirty Water', and had finally managed to pull the bike out of the mud and upright, he'd spent an hour with his tool kit pulling the plugs out and trying to dry them on his sopping wet T-shirt. The plugs were still too wet to fire and Mick knew he never get the big 750 cc machine up the embankment under his own power. But finally fate had smiled on him in the form of a pair of scruffy old timers in a beat-up Chevy. They'd stopped when they had seen him trying to manhandle his bike up the slope and had helped him push it back up onto Memorial Drive. When Mick explained it wouldn't start, one of the old guys winked and said, "I used to ride around on a big old Indian cycle back in the '40's. Let me show you a little trick we used to use when it wouldn't start."

They'd gotten back in the car and told Mick to put the BSA in neutral and hang on to the right rear door. Right away Mick had figured out their plan and nodded. The car slowly started to move with Mick on the bike hanging onto the doorframe of the open rear window with one hand. As their speed approached about 15 mi. an hour. Mick suddenly let go and pulling the clutch lever in, stamped the foot lever into first gear. He opened his hand and let the clutch handle spring open. The gears engaged, rapidly forcing the pistons to turn and…The engine fired…And caught.

Mick quickly shifted up into second gear and gave the old guy's a wave, three toots of his horn, and turning the bike around, rapidly headed back towards Inman Square.

Mick stepped off the porch and climbed on the bike. As he turned the key, he thought, "shit, I never did get to the "Reference Center" to try to find, "Paper Dragon", but at least I got a sample of…" He froze with his foot poised over the recoil starter.

The sample!

It was still in his…his jacket! His jacket that went into the Charles with him and was now a soggy, rolled-up ball, lying in the bottom of a Bridget's whicker clothesbasket.

He jumped off the bike and ran up the stairs, two at a time.

He got to the apartment door, fumbled for his keys, grabbed the door handle and…The door slid open.

Mick paused for a moment. "Damn, I could have sworn I locked this."

He looked around the room, then crossed quickly to the basket and pulled out the wet clothes. He reached into the jacket pocket, felt a large, soggy lump, and groaned, "oh shit I broke the damn thing."

Then he almost laughed with relief, as he drew out the lump and realized it was a mass of wet Kleenex and in the center as he gently pulled the soggy tissue away…The test tube.

Intact!

He started to put it into his inside jacket pocket and then crossed to the old hutch and grabbed a handful of dry Kleenex from the box that Bridget always kept there.

He carefully rolled up the test tube in the tissue and gently eased it into the inside pocket of his jacket.

He crossed back to the open door and looking at it, snapped the latch back and forth twice before he was satisfied. He then closed the door with a solid click behind him, twisting the doorknob to make sure it was locked.

As Mick leaned left out of his street and headed the big BSA towards Harvard Square, something still kept nagging at him.

There was something…

Something in the apartment wasn't quite right.

He tried to force his mind back there, momentarily looking around the room again. He looked left and right in his mind's eye and tried to remember.

He'd gotten the test tube, crossed over to the hutch. Gotten some Kleenex and….

The hutch!

That was it. He'd left the bottle of Bushmill's Irish whiskey on the right side of the hutch, next to the glasses placed on the little lace doily that Bridget had brought with her from Ireland.

But now of the bottle was on the left hand side. Next to the Kleenex!

Someone had moved it.

Someone had come into the apartment. That was why the door was open. Someone had been there, and he had a sinking feeling that he knew who that someone was.

He twisted the throttle open and leaned forward as the bike roared down the rain damp street.

Whoever had been there, had been looking for what he had in his jacket pocket. But they had also read the note on the door.

He had to get to the Oxford Alehouse…And fast!

CHAPTER 47

▼

**Oxford Alehouse
Harvard Square
Cambridge, Mass
May 8th 1968
12:37A M**

Mick would have known he was in the 'Ale House', the moment he opened the door and pushed his way inside, even if he'd been wearing a blindfold. The smell of spilled beer and cigarettes (with just a little pot mixed in) was that strong.

He stood in front of the entrance for a moment as he tried to acclimate his tired eyes to the tear-smarting cigarette smoke.

He unzipped the faded leather bomber jacket and turned down the now-too-hot, fur collar, as he took two steps into the noisy, smoky college bar. Mick looked slowly left and right, taking another two steps into the beer soaked haze. And then…Yes, the table over on the far left, next to a yellow and green psychedelically painted window…There was Bridget and…and…Holly?!!

"Oh my frigging word," he murmured to himself, "am I dead meat or what!"

Numbly he crossed the floor, towards their table.

How the hell had this happened?

What were the odds? It was like the bad old joke about the wife and girlfriend. Except, hey, Bridget wasn't his wife…Yet. "And besides," he rationalized, "me and Holly were, before there was a 'me and Bridget'. And I mean, she doesn't own me. Well, maybe she does now, but that was then and anyway, it's not like we're married or anything. And we technically still could see other people, and…"

He stopped short.

He was approaching the table just slightly to the left and outside of Bridget's range of vision. But he could see just fine. And what he saw stopped him dead in his tracks.

All of the arguments he'd been preparing about being broad minded and understanding about, "affections for other people," evaporated like the spilled beer into the sawdust on the floor. Because as Bridget sat there, deep in conversation with Holly, a sandy-haired, blue-eyed guy in a ridiculous looking white straw cowboy hat, came up to the table, put his hand on a Bridget's shoulder and whispered something in her ear.

Bridget smiled, tipped her head back until her cheek almost touched his and whispered something back.

Mick felt like he'd been punched in the stomach. Bridge!

And then the red 'McCarthy rage' washed over him and he covered the ten feet to the table in three angry strides.

He grabbed, 'kid cowboy hat' roughly by the shoulder, spun him around and growled, "I don't know who you are, but I do know, that if I count to ten and you're still here, your name is gonna' be shit!"

The college cowboy Lothario looked confused, like a deer in the headlights. Bridget looked angry and amused, all at the same time.

"7, 6, 5, 4, 3, 2," Mick put each finger down and balled them into a fist as he counted down to his ultimatum. When he reached 'one', his right hand cocked back (it had bent a long frustrating night and he was more than ready to get really pissed) but before the fuse could burn any shorter, Bridget stood up between Mick and the bewildered cowboy and said, "stop it, you damn fool, before you make a bigger idiot out of yourself then you already are."

Mick breathed hard through his nose, still ready to, "go" when Bridget reached up and put her hand around the back of his neck and pulled his lips down to hers in a quick kiss, made all the more arresting when her humming-bird-quick little tongue, darted between his lips.

Then she turned back to the still bewildered, but now starting to get angry, college-boy and took his hand saying, "I'm sorry Luv. You're actually very sweet, but this really is, the 'very special friend' I've been waiting for."

The college kid looked confused, angry and embarrassed, all at the same time. But now the other five guys from his table had appeared behind him saying things like, "hey Rick, we got trouble here...huh?"

Mick took a half step forward, saying, "yeah, there's all you want right here."

A big guy with shoulder length hair in a faded 'Greatfull Dead' T-shirt and denim jacket said, "okay tough guy, you want to start with me?"

Mick grinned back and started to slip out of his leather bomber jacket, but before he could even formulate the next wisecrack that he'd throw along with his first punch, a familiar voice from behind him said, "no fatso, I want you to start with me!"

Mick whirled around and, yup…It was Kevin and Danny, his Southie cousins.

The two groups, now three vs. six, and in reality pretty evenly matched, glared at one another, until Bridget clapped her hands sharply, like a third grade teacher and said, "all right, that's enough. Mick…sit down. Kevin, Danny? Put your hands back in your pockets or wrap them around a beer glass and join us." Kevin winked at Danny and answered, "Sure thing…'Luv'."

Bridget just rolled her eyes. Then turning back to the still confused, but just starting to get wiser, college boy, she said, "I'm afraid that you just happened to walk into the middle of something that has nothing to do with you 'Luv'." She gave a challenging glance at Kevin and Danny, who tried unsuccessfully to look innocent. "You're a very sweet boy and under other circumstances…Well maybe in another life."

"Uh, sure. . I guess," he shook his head and drifted back to his table with his friends, feeling that he'd probably learned some great cosmic lesson, but was damned if he could figure out what it was.

Mick sat down next to Bridget as Kevin and Danny pulled up chairs on either side of Holly and started simultaneously telling her their life story.

Mick picked up the remains of Bridget's beer and finished it in one swallow.

"Okay, my lady love," he said wiping his mouth with the back of his hand, "let me finish out my act of being a complete jealous, jerk and ask you, what the hell were you doing with him?"

"Oh you mean whispering in his ear?" She answered.

"Yeah," Mick said draining the last drops from her beer and motioning the occasional waitress for a refill.

"Well" Bridget demurred, opening her sea-green eyes wide with an innocent expression, "I thought that seeing as how we just made love under the table, the least I could do, was thank him."

Mick went chalky white and stood up so fast, that his chair went flying backwards.

"I, I…You…" He stammered.

And now Bridget stood up too, and putting her tiny hands on her hips, glared up into his face and snapped, "and so that's what you think of me Mr. Michael Prescott McCarthy? Well let me tell you, I am most definitely not you. And I do not sleep with every member of the opposite sex who crosses my path!"

Holly turned a bright crimson and stared down at the tabletop.

Mick just stood there, his mouth soundlessly opening and closing until he found his voice. "But I saw you…You were…Whispering in his ear and…"

"Watching you." Bridget said folding her arms over her small, firm breasts.

"What…how?" Mick asked.

"There," Bridget said pointing to the multicolored painted window, and as Mick bent down to look, he realized that he could see his reflection in the half painted window pane that faced the door, catching every movement between the entrance and the table.

"So," Mick said slowly, "you were watching me…"

"From the moment you came in, you great bloody fool," Bridget finished .

"I'm sorry baby," Mick said quietly.

"So then, now you know how it feels when you think that someone you love is…" she drew a deep breath, "except in my case, it wasn't true, but in your case…"

Now it was Mick's turn to just look at the tabletop.

Holly suddenly pushed back her chair and grabbing her macramé pocketbook, said in a stricken voice, "I . . I have to go. Thank you for listening Bridget. And remember, everything between Mick and I, was before 'you and Mick'."

There were tears in her pale blue eyes as she squeezed out between Danny's chair and the wall. But Bridget stopped her before she could get any further. This time it was Bridget who took Holly's hand and said, "Holly, I am sorry. I didn't mean for it to come out like that. Of course, you did nothing wrong. Or even this big idiot here." She glanced back at the still sheepish Mick. "I was just being a jealous little bitch and I apologize for it."

Holly looked uncertain until Bridget smiled and hugged her.

"It's okay," Bridget smiled at Holly, "tell Mick about what's been happening to your brother, and then tell us," and she emphasize the word, "how we can help."

CHAPTER 48

▼

Oxford Alehouse
Harvard Square
Cambridge, Mass
May 8,1968
12:52 A.M.

When Holly finally finished her story, the table was silent. After a minute, interrupted only by the background noises of clinking glasses and semi-drunken laughter, Mick slammed his beer mug down on the stained table top with a clipped but loud exclamation of, "shit!"

The people at the tables around them looked up, and at the one next to them, a chunky girl with frizzy red hair held in place by a bandanna that read, 'Make love not War', poked her even chunkier boyfriend and whispered something to him with an outraged expression.

"Yep," sighed Mick to himself up, as the beefy guy hoisted up the belt buckle of his corduroy bellbottoms until the large bronze piece of metal, cast in the shape of a peace symbol, stuck into the top of his jelly-roll, fat gut. He waddled over, but Mick didn't even bother to get up. Maybe if he ignored this one, he'd just go away...Quietly.

But it was not to be. It usually wasn't.

The big guy stopped just short of Mick's chair and stood there, breathing bad breath and stale beer.

Bridget was still trying to comfort Holly and Mick had a whole lot of things that he had to do...like right now. And he had no time for college boys with beer muscles and bad breath. So he just gripped the cheap glass handle of his beer mug and tried to concentrate on the "angels of his better nature," as Bridget would have said, while 'big-gut/bad-breath', sprayed, "hey buddy, first of all, watch your mouth, you're bothering my girlfriend. Second, why don't you take your bitches," he looked at Bridget and Holly…"Big mistake," thought Mick…"And your baby killer T-shirt…And he poked Mick right in the center of his G.I. olive drab Army issue T-shirt, "and get the hell out of here."

Mick started to push his chair back from the table, as Bridget covered his white-knuckled hand with her own. But before he could even decide whether or not to complete the movement, Kevin had pushed his chair back, grabbed the big guy by his tie dyed T-shirt with his left hand, while shooting his right hand onto his bulging corduroy covered balls and squeezing.

'Mr. corduroy bellbottoms' started to say, "hey what the f…" before his voice went up three octaves, ending in a high shrill "yow…!"

Kevin pushed him back until his beefy butt hit his own table where he fell back heavily, overturning beer, glasses and popcorn.

"Listen up, you fat piece of crap," Kevin snarled in his flat, nasal, South Boston accent, "that's my cousin and my friends you just insulted, you butt fucking lump of shit, and you've got exactly three seconds to apologize or I'm gonna' break your freakin' nose."

Kevin pressed the now gasping, ex-tough guy, down onto the beer soaked table and counted down, "one, two…"

Smack…Crunch!

"Owwww-w!!' You broke my frigging nose man. And you never even said three!"

"Three," Kevin said quietly and hit him again. Right in the same place.

The big guy was reduced to a bloody faced, blubbering mass of big, beefy tears. His frizzy red-haired, girlfriend, opened her mouth to scream until she looked at Kevin's face and then shut it with an audible snap.

They quickly picked up their things to go but Kevin still held on to the now bloody tie-dyed T-shirt. "I didn't hear that apology," he said quietly but with a voice laced with menace.

"Shit…Jesus Christ…I'm fuckin' sorry…Okay? God damn, you're frigging crazy!"

"Aren't I though?" Kevin grinned at him with a lazy left-handed salute.

He pulled over the now vacant table and two more chairs, saying, "stretch out boys and girls…I think some more space just became available."

Bridget tried to give him a disapproving frown but it broke into a head-shaking grin instead. "Sweet lovin' Jesus,"she smiled reluctantly, "I've just got to bring you into Callahan's back home in County Cork, on a Friday night."

"Hey, comin' from you Bridge," Kevin laughed and tipped his beer mug in her direction, "I take that as a compliment."

"Okay," said Mick banging on the table with his beer mug. If the 'Oxford Ale-house Marching, Chowder and Fighting Society', would please come to order, we've got something serious to take care of."

The smiles fell off everyone's faces as they turned back and looked at Holly who had remained staring down at the table, tearing her napkin into small thin strips, during the previous exchange.

"Holly," Mick said turning towards her, "what time did you call Boomer…Steve…tonight?"

"I don't know," Holly said quietly, about 10:30 I guess."

Mick looked down at the cracked, scratched crystal face of his old army issue watch and frowned.

"Christ it's almost 1:00 AM…even with the worst connections of the Green and Orange lines, he should have been here at least a half hour ago."

"That's if he's coming at all," Danny muttered half to himself.

Holly's white cheeks turned, yet another, what 'Procal Harum' would have called, "a whiter shade of pale."

Mick jerked his head at Danny and hissed, "shut up!"

But not talking about it wouldn't change anything, Mick thought. He and just about everyone else at the table, knew that something had happened to former first lieutenant Steve 'Boomer' Benson.

And what ever it was, it wasn't good.

CHAPTER 49

▼

Harvard Square
Cambridge, Mass
May 8th 1968
In front of the Harvard Coop
1:07 a.m.

The night was turning cool for May. Mick glanced up at the clock and thermometer next to the big Harvard Square newspaper kiosk.

The drizzle had let up, but the temperature had kept dropping to a damp, bone chilling 47 degrees.

"Damn," Mick thought blowing on his hands, "it's gonna' be one cold figging ride over to Allston."

As if reading his mind, Kevin and nudged him in the ribs and said, "hey Mick, it's freakin' freezing out here, what you say we take the Mustang…Ok?"

Mick bit his lower lip trying to plan three moves ahead as in his mind he saw his platoon in 'Nam looking back at him and waiting for the decision that might mean the difference between life and death…His and theirs!

Suddenly Mick looked across the square at a single glowing third story window.

"Come on Kevin," he said pulling on his cousin's jacket as he started crossed the square.

"So that's the whole story Pop," Mick finished, leaning back against the tiny office's single window, "or at least all that I've been able to piece together so far."

Michael senior hadn't said a word for the past twenty minutes as Mick had laid out the whole convoluted web of seeming coincidence that now seemed over-laid with menace and conspiracy.

Finally, 'Big Mike', took a deep breath and heaved himself out of the old wooden swivel chair in front of the roll-top desk.

"Mickey,' he asked in his rumbling whisky voice, "do you think that those people know, that you know, what you do?"

"Yeah," Mick said shaking his head, "for what I actually do know,"and then added, "and for whatever that's actually worth."

"It may be worth a whole lot more than you even know yet, laddie-buck," Mike said softly.

There was silence for a moment. Then Mike walked over to the old-fashioned wooden coat rack, pulled on his weather-stained raincoat and opened the office door.

"Okay boyo-s," he smiled grimly, "are you up for some excitement?"

"Always Uncle Mike!" Kevin answered with a wide grin.

"Okay then hot shot," Mike responded, "bring, that 'muskrat' thing you drive around in, up to the front door."

"You got it!" Kevin answered," and by the way Uncle Mike, it's a 'Mustang', and it's the fastest little pony in Southie!"

"All right Kevy," Mike smiled using Kevin's boyhood family nickname," I'm sure it is, so now just be a good boy and go bring it around front. And Kevy…?"

Halfway out the door Kevin turned back towards his uncle expectantly,

"Make sure you take out all those beer cans and whatever else you've got in the trunk, so your lovin' uncle doesn't have to remember that he used to be a cop."

"Sure thing Uncle Mike," Kevin answered and then added with a 'McCarthy' grin, "whatever the hell it is your talking about!"

"Go with him Mick," Michael Sr. said motioning to the open door, "I'll be down in a minute."

"Sure Pop," Mick said raising one of eyebrows quizzically.

Mick walked through the office door and started down the stairs but paused as his eyes drew level with the third floor landings' floor and looked back into the office at his father's broad back. Mick saw him reach into one of the roll-top desk's small inside drawers and pull out a compact, blue-steeled .380 automatic. He watched as his father popped the spring on the gun's butt, and the clip dropped it into his hand. He put his thumb down on the bullets, checking for a full load by the firmness of the feel. Satisfied, Mike snapped the clip back into place, took the .380 in one meaty hand and dropped it into his inside suit jacket pocket.

Mick whistled softly under his breath. "Whew, carrying an unlicensed piece Pop. You are taking this seriously aren't you?"

He slipped quietly down the stairs before his father could spot him.

"Okay Mickey…Kevin?" Mike asked as he settled his bulk into the Mustang's bucket, front seat, "just where does this, 'Captain Bloomer' live?"

"It's Boomer Dad," Mick answered. "And lieutenant. To be precise, first lieutenant, Steve."

"Good boy Mickey," Mike grinned, "accuracy is always the sign of a good cop."

"Hey…No way Pop…I…" Then Mick just smiled from the back seat and shut his mouth.

Kevin gave a snorting laugh from the driver's seat as he shifted into third and headed over the BU Bridge.

Turning his attention back to the question, Mick leaned forwards to the two front bucket seats and said, "he lives on Commonwealth Ave just before Harvard St."

"And," Mike countered, "what if he is ok, and shows up at the Oxford Alehouse after all?"

"That's why we left Bridget and Holly there," Mick answered.

Mike snapped his head around and gave his younger son a hard stare.

"You've left two girls, to wait for him…Alone?"

"Jesus no Pop!" Mick came back defensively.

"Yeah," interrupted Kevin, "that's right Uncle Mike, don't worry…We left Danny with the girls." "Oh sweet suffering Jesus," muttered Michael Sr., "the other half of the 'idiot twins'."

"Uncle Mike!" Kevin exploded in a wounded voice.

'Big Mike', paused for a moment before he finally smiled and said, "my apologies nephew, yer' both a pair of ragin' geniuses…Now shut the hell up, and drive!"

CHAPTER 50

▼

Commonwealth Ave.
Allston, Mass
May 8,1968
1:28AM

Mick never did get a chance to show his father how well he'd learned those lock-picking lessons all those childhood years ago spent hanging around Station B, because when they got to Boomers apartment and knocked on the door...it swung open.

Mike started through the door but Mick put a hand on his father's arm and said, "wait a minute Pop, something isn't right. Every time I've been to this place, Boomer had it locked up like Fort Knox."

Michael senior looked up at the peephole set into the steel covered door and paused for a moment. Then he grinned back at his son. "I told you Mickey, we'll make a cop out of you yet."

Mike reached his right hand into the left inside pocket of his suit jacket and pulled out the .380 automatic. He pulled the slide back, chambered a round and stepped carefully into the apartment.

The first sound they heard was a steady, rhythmic, "click. click, click."

Mick and Michael Senior froze but Kevin just smiled and shook his head.

"Hey, no sweat guys, I know what this is," he said as he walked into the dimly lit room living room.

Kevin stopped in front of the beat-up stereo in the corner and called back over his shoulder, "this is what I woke up to at every party where I passed out."

He lifted the stuck record needle off of the last track of the .33 1/3 long-playing album, Jefferson Airplane's "Surrealistic Pillow", and the clicking noise abruptly stopped.

Everything was quiet except for…a faint drip, drip noise coming from a small alcove between the living room and kitchen.

Mike motioned Kevin and Mick back as he elevated his right hand, and clutching the .380, steadied it by wrapping his left hand around his right wrist, and carefully edged into the alcove.

Mick and Kevin followed close behind, which is why they both bumped into the former cops broad back when Mike stopped short.

Mick blinked twice, trying to adjust his eyes to the gloom that was relieved only by a ghostly glow coming from where the eerily illuminated Jimi Hendrix poster, pulsed and shimmered in the black strobe light.

Mick's vision finally focused and traveled to the other side of the alcove where he saw that someone else was watching Jimmy pulsate and dance, with a seemingly single-minded intensity.

Mick suddenly realized with a sad, certainty, that the glassy-eyed, skinny figure, would be watching Jimi dance and play 'Purple Rain', throughout eternity.

The form seated silently on the couch in the corner, an almost empty bottle of ripple wine clutched in his hand, which slowly drip, drip, driped onto the floor, was Boomer.

And he was dead.

*   *   *   *

Harvard Square
Cambridge Mass
Oxford Alehouse
May 8th 1968
1:31 a.m.

Gupta Singh took off his thin wire rim glasses and wiped them with his pocket handkerchief in the vain hope that the action would somehow help his vision penetrate the Alehouse's swirling eddies of smoky haze.

It didn't work.

Gupta sighed as he readjusted the glasses and myopically peered through the man-made smog in an increasingly futile attempt to find his friends, Rami and Ali.

He swiveled his head back and forth in his fruitless search, but he'd either come too late or they'd moved on without him.

"Ah well," he mused to himself, "the time would probably be better spent in studying, than drinking beer with fellow student refugees from the Indian subcontinent." He turned back towards the door when out of the corner of his eye he noticed…

"Ah, Miss Bridget!"

A familiar, pleasant accent made Bridget pause and look up from the increasingly worried conversation that she'd been having with Holly and Danny.

"Gupta! What are you doing here?" Bridget said in a voice that she realized as soon as the words left her mouth, was too tense and strident.

Gupta smiled uncertainly as he tentatively approached the table. "Well," he replied, diffidently, "I was hoping to meet my friends Rami and Ali here, but it looks like they have left. Do you mind if I sit down for a moment?" He finished shyly.

"Oh for certain. Sorry, and please excuse my bad manners," Bridget added hurriedly. "It's just that I'm that worried about Mick and…"

"Please, please." He said holding up both hands. "It is I who am presuming on your hospitality."

He pulled one of the empty chairs over to the table and sat down, adding, "and so Mickey's lovely sister Bronwyn found you all right…Yes?"

CHAPTER 51

▼

Commonwealth Avenue
Allston Mass
May 8ᵗʰ, 1968
1:33 a.m.

Mick sat quietly in one of the cheap steel and vinyl kitchen chairs he'd probably sat in the first time he'd come to the Commonwealth Avenue apartment, and just kept staring at the unmoving, glassy-eyed, waxen-faced dummy that used to be his C.O. and friend.

He kept remembering their last meeting and everything had led up to it.

The nightmare in the jungle. The dreams…waking and sleeping. Boomer's paranoid but sometimes, right-on tips that had sent him to Prides Crossing and the…The God damn mother…Yeah, the colonel.

Mick ground the knuckles of his right hand into the scarred palm of his left and thought, "Yep, and I'm gonna' bet, that this is just one more thing in that big long cosmic list, that the son-of-a bitch has to answer for."

He paused for a moment and stared at his former friend. His eyes smarted as he remembered the poor strung-out skinny bastard when he'd been First Lieutenant Steve Benson. And he remembered the big, honest open face and pale blue eyes holding on to Mick's own crazy, half mad eyes on that horrible June night in the jungle.

"If it hadn't been for you Steve," Mick whispered softly to himself, "I would have blown my fucking brains out that night."

He had taken Mick's demons and turned them into his own, and they'd cut deeper and tormented him more than they had ever done to Mick. They'd driven the former lieutenant into the, "wonderful world of drugs," and into the arms of 'the Junkie Priestess', ...Starr.

"Where the hell do you suppose she is?" Mick wondered idly. "And how much will she really care when she finds out that her surrogate 'dependent child', had finally gone to meet his, 'connection in the sky'.

Mick shook his head cynically and then froze as he realized with a sick feeling in the pit of his stomach, just who would be devastated by the news that Mick knew he was going to have to deliver...Holly.

"Mickey, come 'ere," 'Big Mike' called.

Mick slowly got up from the kitchen chair and crossed the six feet back into the alcove.

"Yeah, Dad." He answered quietly as he stood in front of the dead white staring corpse and folded his hands. He looked back into the unseeing eyes as if hoping they could give him the answers to another belated casualty of war.

Mike looked up at Mick from where he knelt next to what used to be 'Boomer', and asked almost gently, "are you OK son?"

"I don't know Dad," Mick answered slowly shaking his head. "I really don't know."

Mike didn't say anything. He just let out a long breath through his nostrils, and his voice turned back to the 'professional cop' mode.

"Okay, Mickey," I'm gonna' need your help for a few minutes...Ok?"

There was no answer.

"Okay. .?"

This time the question was sharper, just like Boomer had said that night in the jungle when he'd barked, "Sergeant report!" in an effort to draw Mick back to sanity...At the eventual cost of his own.

Mick shook his head and angrily wiped at his left eye. "Yeah, Pop. I'm here. What do you need me to do"

Mike looked back at him and gave a slow nod. "Okay, grab a-hold of his arm and try to pull it out straight. It won't be easy, or pleasant. 'Rigger' has started to set in. But there's something I think I see...that I need to get at."

Mick shifted around and slowly pulled the stiff arm of his former friend, into an open position. "Doesn't hurt a bit, does it lieutenant," he murmured.

"Mick," his father said sharply, "hold it steady."

Mick put one hand on the cold, waxy wrist and the other supporting the elbow as Mike took out a pair of tweezers from his jacket pocket and twisted the corpse's bicep around until it was fully exposed. With a small grunt, he clamped the tweezers around a tiny metal sliver and pulled.

Michael senior gave a snort of satisfaction and as he held the tweezers up to the light and said, "what do you make of this Mickey?"

Mick peered down at the thin piece of steel about an inch long and said, "it looks like a broken needle."

"Yep," Mike said, nodding his head. "That's exactly what it is. And unless I miss my guess, when I take it to my old buddy, Charlie Hayes, who used to be our medical examiner, it's going to' test real positive for heroin...or maybe even something stronger."

Mick didn't say anything for a minute and then snapped out in a quiet angry voice, "hell of a way for a nice All-American farm boy to end up, isn't it Pop?"

Mike stood up and dusted off his pants. "He might have died that way Mickey, but I don't think it was from any habit he had."

"What do you mean Pop?" Mick asked turning his head.

"I mean," Mike answered slowly, "that I pulled this broken needle out of the far right side of his bicep...Here." Mike pointed and turned back to Mick. "Now pretend you've got a needle and tried to inject yourself in there."

Mick moved his left hand holding the imaginary needle and tried to pop it into the right side of the bicep, almost underneath the arm.

"I can't reach it Dad," he said, as the truth dawned on him.

"Exactly," Mike said. "You couldn't and wouldn't shoot yourself up like that. The only way that could happen would be if someone standing slightly behind you and to the right, did it. And then...why would you want them to?"

"So that's why the needle was broken off in his arm!" Mick hissed.

"Yeah," Mike said. "He was murdered."

Mike took the broken sliver of needle and wrapped it carefully in his handkerchief and started for the door when Mick suddenly said, "hey Pop...Come here for a minute."

Mike crossed back to where his youngest son stood, staring at Boomer, whose glassy eyed gaze stared back from eternity.

"What?" Mike asked.

"There." Mick pointed to a small bright yellow-gold dot on Boomers lolling tongue. The dot glowed almost luminescent, but the tongue around it had turned black.

Mike looked at it for a moment and then took out his pen, and gently scraped the glowing dot into a clean portion of the handkerchief and carefully rolled it back up and into his pocket again.

"Come on," Mike said, "let's get out of here."

The phone rang.

Neither one of them moved but the phone kept ringing.

Kevin came out of the back bedroom where he'd been 'exploring' and looked quizzically from Mike to his cousin.

Finally Mike said, "Answer it Kevin."

Kevin slowly picked up the phone and said, "yeah?"

Then he held the phone out to Michael Sr. and said, "Uncle Mike...Its for you."

Mike took the receiver and listened, grunted a few times and finally said, "yeah, I got it, thanks Billy."

"Come on," he called over his shoulder, and as he walked towards the door, yelled back, "we've got to move...Fast."

"What's up Uncle Mike?" Kevin asked as he gave the apartment one last, 'look-see', for any interesting objects that might be 'looking for a new owner'.

"That was an old pal of mine from Station B, who owed me a few favors and was giving me a heads-up that Bannon was on his way over here...And is planning to try to pin this...On us!"

He pulled the apartment door handle and was just stepping into the dingy hallway when the phone rang again.

"Get it Mickey," Mike said, "it'll be Billy again. Tell him 'thanks', and we're just leaving."

Mick quickly crossed back into the living room and picked up the phone.

But it wasn't Mike's old pal Billy on the phone.

It was an almost quiet, sing-song voice, but laced with incredible, potential menace.

"Mr. Former Detective McCarthy?" The voice on the other end of the line said before Mick had a chance to answer. "You have a son, who has something which belongs to us. We want it back. We likewise have something that belongs to you. That we are sure you will likewise want back...before it's too late. Be at this address in one hour," the voice said and gave a street and number in downtown Boston. "And do not be late, or you may find that your merchandise has been...damaged"

And the line went dead.

CHAPTER 52

▼

Harvard Square
Cambridge Mass
Outside The Oxford Alehouse
1:38 a.m.

It had been the final but all too familiar cry of, "last call," from the Alehouse's sole remaining bartender that had prompted Bridget to turn to Danny and Holly with a resigned sigh and say, "come on guys, we've got go."

"But where Bridget?" Holly asked. "Mick told us to stay here…In case Steve comes."

Bridget knew that Holly didn't really believe it anymore than she did.

And of course Danny had to squash even that tiny, fantasy into the pavement by adding, "hey babe, if he ain't here by now, he ain't never comin', you know what I mean?"

That blunt statement was almost instantaneously punctuated with a, "yow" as Bridget took the third knuckle of her right hand and jabbed it into the upper bicep of Danny's right arm. "It does do a marvelous job of getting their attention," she mused with satisfaction as she watched it Danny rub his upper arm.

"Jesus Bridge, cut it out, will you," Danny complained, "what the hell did I do for Christ sakes. I…"

Bridget gestured with her chin towards Holly, and hissed, "shut your bloody mouth about her brother you damn fool!"

"It's all right Bridget," came the sad, quiet voice from behind her. "I guess I know he won't be coming."

Bridget looked back at the dejected little pale blond ghost and said, "okay Holly, if your brother isn't gonna' come to us, then let's go to him."

"How" Holly said miserably, "we don't have a car and the T' has stopped running."

Bridget smiled a cynical smile and looked at Danny.

"Well, 'Cousin Danny' what do you think you can do about getting us some 'transportation'?"

Danny grinned and answered, "well 'almost cousin' Bridget, why don't you two, wicked-fine chicks just wait right here and let me show you what kind of wheels 'Old Cousin Danny' can come up with."

Sure enough within five minutes a cherry-red Camaro pulled up to the curb with a squeal of tires and the smell of burning rubber.

"Not bad for a second generation Irish lad," Bridget smiled as she opened the passenger door so that Holly could climb into the back seat.

"Hey," Danny said with a mixture of pride and defense, "short notice Bridge, otherwise I could've come back with a 'Caddy'."

"You know Danny lad," Bridget returned with almost sister-like affection, "I do believe you could have."

She got in, pulled the heavy door shut and added, "I'll just bet that Colin and me 'Da could make good use of your talents back in Ballykill on a Saturday night 'action'."

"Anytime Bridge," Danny laughed as he put the Camaro into first gear, popped the clutch and pulled away from the curb in a cloud of blue smoke and a screech of tires..." Any time!"

Almost a full minute passed as the smoke dissipated and sound of tires and roar of the Camaro's four barrel carburetors began to fade into the distance.

Inside of a darkened, two-tone Lincoln Continental, a large lumpy figure poked a smaller lump who dozed over the steering wheel and grunted, "go."

The smaller lump shook his head while wiping the sleep out of his eyes. Then he put the big Lincoln into Drive and headed out in the same direction as the Camaro...Across the BU Bridge, into Allston.

∗   ∗   ∗   ∗

Michael Jr. and Sr. sat quietly in Kevin's car under the shadowy protection of a tired old elm tree that poked it's spindly trunk up through the Comm. Ave. sidewalk.

"Look," Mike said quietly.

Mick and Kevin followed Mike's pointing finger to the recently vacated build-ing across the street where they saw a black Ford Fairlane pull up and disgorge three obvious plain-clothes cops.

"And there's the friggin' the back-stabbing prick himself," Mike breathed from between clenched teeth as Cambridge's newest precinct captain, climbed out of the unmarked Ford

"Okay Kevy," Mike said in a low voice, "let's get moving."

"Mick," he said, "do you have that address downtown? The one that…the man gave you?"

"Yeah Pop," Mick answered, "it's right here," and he reached into the pocket of his leather jacket to retrieve the slip of paper that he'd written the address on. As he passed it back up to his father in the front bucket seat, something that had been stuck inside the paper, fell out and landed on the floor of the back seat. He'd noticed the strange object back at the apartment, sticking out of a slight tear in the back of Boomers T-shirt, and he plucked it out and wrapped it in the piece of paper.

Mick groped around on the dark floor of the back seat until his fingers closed around something long and sharp.

He held it up in front of him as the Mustang paused at a stoplight in Kenmore Square, and in the glow of the streetlights that penetrated into the back seat, saw that it was sharp…And purple. It looked like…A fingernail.

*   *   *   *

**Boston
Clarendon St.
Back Bay
May 8, 1968
1:43 a.m.**

Paige Elliott was having a bad dream.

In fact, as far as her REM sleep brain was concerned, it could be officially clas-sified as a nightmare.

There were men. Horrible, scary, frightening men. And they were putting their hands all over her.

And not in a nice, sensual way. The way that she sometimes enjoyed, but in a nasty, cold, rough and unfeeling way.

She tried to knock their hands away, but they were too strong. They grabbed her and dragged her from her warm bed and down comforter and smooth, cream colored satin sheets.

They hissed back and forth at one another in some rude, harsh language…And they smelled.

They smelled of fried food and fish and sour spices. Like some cheap restaurant she'd been in once…and didn't like very much.

"Stop it!" She screamed. "I want this dream to end…Now!"

And the dream part did end. Because suddenly she was wide awake, and she realized with a scream suffocating, throat constricting horror…That this was no dream.

$$*\qquad*\qquad*\qquad*$$

Boston Mass
The Financial District
Hayward, Elliott and Delbert
41st floor 1:46 a.m.

The silence and tension in the boardroom seemed like a thick, stifling, blanket, France's (McCarthy) Prescott thought. He looked across the semi-darkened room, at Charlton Elliott who sat unmoving in his chair, seated at the long mahogany boardroom table, head buried in his hands.

The tomb-like hush was finally broken when the voice belonging to the figure who had remained quietly seated, said in a voice barely above a whisper, "it is time we left here. We have an appointment on Harrison Avenue."

"I'm not going anywhere with you…You damn Communist son of a bitch!" Charlton Elliott snapped out.

The figure in the corner got up out of the chair and meticulously adjusted his expensive Hong Kong tailored suit and silk tie.

"Perhaps you should have thought of that Mr. 'legal counselor' Elliott before you and your colleagues accepted so much of our 'damn Communist' 'money to represent our interests."

"I don't care what sort of devil's bargain my partner…And former friend," Charlton Elliott added bitterly, glaring at his life-long, now ex-friend and partner," made with you, but I won't lift another finger to assist in this filthy business. God knows what your true aim really is, but I'm through with it. And you!"

"I do not think so,"the man in the Hong Kong tailored suit answered coldly.

"Don't you?" Charlton Elliott laughed. "You've murdered my baby daughter. Do you really think that your threats hold any terrors for me?"

"Apparently you've forgotten what I mentioned earlier," and now the voice hardened as the small man stepped out of the shadows and snapped his fingers saying, "Ritchie?"

The younger Chinese man picked up the elegant French Art Deco phone off of the boardroom table and dialed a number.

There was a sound on the other end of the line and Ritchie spat a staccato burst of commands in Chinese and then with a cold smirk held out the receiver to Charlton Elliott.

He took it with shaking fingers and slowly said, "hello?"

Francis (Frankie) could hear the wailing cry emerge from the receiver all the way from the other end of the boardroom table.

"Oh my God," Charlton Elliott moaned, his pale face turning a chalk-dust white.

"Daddy!" answered the terrified voice. "Help me!"

CHAPTER 53

▼

Prides Crossing
North Shore
May 8th, 1968
11:48 a.m.

"Captain?" the powerful voice rumbled. The owner of the voice knows from decades of experience, that he never has to raise it. It had been heard in the halls of Congress, Senate chambers and Oval Office for almost half a century.

It was a voice that was used to being answered. And quickly.

There was only half a second's pause before the trim, uniformed figure standing in front of the enormous marble fireplace, spun around and snapped out, Sir!"

"Please Captain," the voice said with the same charm that had disarmed presidents and kings. "We can dispense with the chain of command. I haven't worn a uniform for over twenty-five years, and it even then I really wasn't one to ever stand on the trappings of rank."

"Yes sir," the feminine form responded, clasping her hands behind her in the classic 'at ease' posture and finishing with, "Mr. Director."

"Please captain," the voice responded with just a touch of ice, "no titles either."

"Yes sir. With your permission sir...Just how should I address you?"

The owner of the voice was silent for a moment and then added in an amused tone, "Just call me...Mr. Smith. Like, as in," Mr. Smith goes to...or comes from, Washington. "And he gave a cavernous, rumbling laugh.

"Yes sir...Mr. Smith then."

She didn't smile.

"And what shall I call you, Captain?" The still amused voice asked.

"Just…Captain sir" the feminine but flat, dead voice answered.

The large, imposing figure stared at the rigid female form in the well tailored, but severe uniform standing in front of him and sighed. "Very well, Captain, is he ready?"

"Yes sir…Mr. Smith," came the clipped reply.

"Well then, we best be going…" Captain."

Commonwealth Avenue
Allston, Mass
May 8th, 1968
1:51 a.m.

Danny pulled the 'borrowed', Camaro up behind a rusty old panel van on the other side of Commonwealth Avenue from Boomers apartment, where with any luck, it would be partially hidden from anyone coming out from the front door.

"Which one is it Holly?" Bridget whispered even though no one could hear them with the windows rolled up.

"That one," Holly whispered back, pointing to a gray stone, four story apartment building with a black Ford Fairlane parked illegally blocking a fire hydrant, in front of it.

"Jesus," Danny laughed from the front seat, what the hell are you two whispering for? I mean for Christ sakes, it's not like anyone can hear us for crying out loud."

"No," Bridget hissed from between clenched teeth. "Only anyone three parts senile and nine parts deaf who happens to be passing by between here and Kenmore Square. So kindly hush your bloody big mouth Mr. Daniel Peter McCarthy…If you please kind sir." And she gave Mick's cousin a half curtsy from the front seat. Danny grinned back and blew her a kiss which she responded to by sticking out her tongue in a flashback to her ten-year-old behavior.

Bridget and Holly looked at one another and broke out in tension-shattering giggles. Danny just shook his head and turned the radio back on in an attempt to find some Rolling Stones songs.

Suddenly Holly grabbed Bridget's hand and whispered, "look!"

Bridget followed Holly's pointing finger and she saw three men in badly fitting gray and brown suits emerge from the apartment building across the street.

Bridget looked and suddenly drew in a sharp breath. "I know two of those bastards. They're the very same ones who are arrested me and said they were from the INS!"

"What are they doing here?" Holly asked.

"I don't know but…" Bridget's voice froze in her throat. Because the door swung wide again and two white coated the EMT's rolled out a gurney that was topped with a black plastic bag. A body bag.

"Oh no," Holly breathed in a barely audible voice, "oh dear God, please no!"

She started to open the door, but Bridget held her by the shoulder, saying, "no Holly, not now. They'll be time enough for that later. I promise you. I know, I come from a country that knows how to grieve," she finished bitterly. "But right now we need to follow them. Because wherever they're going, I just know somehow, is going to be wherever Mick is. And that's where we're going to find the answers to all of this."

The two 'INS men', a big beefy plain clothes detective and another medium sized figure with a peaked hat and captain's bars, all climbed into the black Ford Fairlane and pulled away from the curb, down Commonwealth Avenue, heading towards downtown Boston.

"All right Danny," Bridget said grimly. "Drive."

Everything was quiet for a few minutes as the pale lights of the black Ford followed closely by a rounded ones of a red Camaro, blended into the traffic and faded from sight.

The large form sitting in the passenger's side front seat of a big Lincoln Continental, stuffed the 'slim Jim' sausage he was munching, back into his pocket and poked the skinny, snoring form hunched over the steering wheel.

"Ha…What the…?" the skinny figure with a harsh nasal voice sputtered awake.

"God damn it. I was trying to get some sleep. What the hell is going on, T…?"

"Just shut up and drive," the large lump grunted.

"Where?" The smaller of lump answered .

"You know where," the fat one said, "it's where he wanted all of them to wind up…In the end."

CHAPTER 54

▼

Cambridge, Mass
Memorial Drive
MIT—Reference Library #4 B.
May 8,1968
1:52 a.m.

Carlos Vasquez shuffled up to the time clock in the night watchman's station, inserted his round key and turned it one complete rotation.

"There," he sighed to himself, "now I can catch at least an hour's sleep before I have to be back here again." He stretched his arms over his head, rubbed his belly and ambled over to one of the overstuffed chairs next to the reference desk.

Being a night watchman wasn't a bad second job he reflected, it was just that it was so hard to stay awake after working a full eight hour shift in the Boston Globe's make-ready press room.

"Well," he sighed, "I'll just close my eyes for a few minutes and…"

He was snapped out of his light sleep by a thud and crash from somewhere at the end of the mezzanine floor of the cavernous, reference library.

Carlos came awake with a start, and stumbled to his feet and as he tried to rub the sleep from his eyes.

As he stood there shaking his head and trying to rid himself of the last vestiges of his rudely interrupted sweet dreams of Rosalie and home, he became aware of the sound of breaking glass and stealthy patter of feet.

He pulled the cheap single action .38 revolver that MIT security had issued him, and checked his load.

He then took a deep breath and warily began to climb the stairs to the mezzanine and the classified, heavily locked 'Technology/Bio Lab' reference room.

As he reached the top of the stairs, he heard a noise. He quickly thumbed on the flashlights powerful beam and seemed to see a portion of the darkness detach itself and quietly run down the hall.

"Halt," he yelled, feeling somewhat foolish, when nothing but silence answered him.

He moved carefully toward the locked door of the reference room, but stopped short when he saw the glass on the floor. The reference room door's pebble glass had been broken.

The door was open.

Carlos looked about nervously and wiped the sweat from his upper lip with the forefinger of his left hand.

"Who'd want to break in here he wondered." But someone, obviously had. And it was his job to investigate…And fill it out a very long report.

He sighed, pushed open the broken glass door and stepped inside.

The world exploded in his face.

"Whoa man, catch that!" the skinny, acne scar-faced figure called back to the silent, hulking lump slouched inside of the two-tone Lincoln Continental parked next to the Esplanade.

The porcine figure only grunted and said, "that's his signal. Get back in and drive."

"Where?" said the skinny half of the duo.

"You know where," the fat one mumbled and closed his eyes.

Downtown Boston
Harrison Avenue and Beech Street
Dragon Palace Restaurant
May 8th 1968
1:54 a.m.

"Jasmine Lilly!" The whip sharp voice rang out across the restaurants empty dining room.

The slight but voluptuously formed teenage girl paused from where she was a folding red napkins and placing them next to each plate.

She tapped her dainty little foot for a moment before turning around with an exasperated sigh and saying, "what Ma! For Christ sakes…What's your problem now!?"

"You know what my problem is, Jasmine Lilly. It is your attire and. .," she paused to glare at her youngest daughter and continued, "your disrespectful attitude."

Jasmine Lilly ('Jazzy' as she was known to her friends) just stood there and glared at her mother.

"Madam Wu," as she was known with deserved terror and trepidation, to the mostly illegal kitchen staff, crossed silently to her youngest daughter, and grabbing her by the elbow hissed, "do you remember what your cousin said the last time you came into the bar in this scandalous attire?"

Jasmine, who perhaps because she had lived fourteen of her seventeen years in the United States, wasn't impressed or intimidated.

"Let go Ma!" she yelled, twisting her arms out of her mother's grip, "I'll dress up like a 'Shanghai pleasure girl' in red silk when the dinner crowd comes in tomorrow. But until then my butt is gonna' rest in bellbottoms and beads!"

She threw down the rest of the napkins' onto the table and stamped out of the room.

Jasmines mother clenched her hands in a cold fury until she felt the presence of her eldest daughter behind her.

"Jade, what can we do with her?" She breathed.

Jade knew the real answer, but only sighed and said, "I'd do not know my mother. Perhaps all we can do is wait."

"Yes wait," came the cold reply. "But we will not have long to wait, will we Jade?"

There was a small intake of breath and then Jade answered, "and why is that my mother?"

The moments of silence stretched away into minutes and just when Jade was sure that her mother hadn't heard her and was steeling herself to repeat the question, the answer came in a low, silky monotone, "because everything…The Golden Bowl. The Paper Dragon. The wealth and power it will bring…And all of those who lust for it or who will be used by it…They are all converging here."

"Wealth and power mother?" Jade asked softly. "It is that what it will bring?"

"Oh yes, daughter," she answered, but then with a backward glance added, "but just like the universal truths of Ying and Yang…It will also bring something else."

"What is it that mother?"

Madam Wu paused for an instant before finishing, "for some…death and destruction."

Boston
China Town
Dragon Palace Restaurant
May 8th 1968
2:09 a.m.

"Stop the car Kev," Mick said quietly

"Why?" Kevin asked.

"Because we're here," Mick replied in a cold, flat voice. "This is where it all gets answered isn't it Dad." Mick said, never taking his eyes off of the sputtering red neon sign that flashed, 'Dragon Palace', while a stylized Chinese dragon crawled up the English and Mandarin characters in flashing red neon light.

"Mickey," Mike said heavily, "you and Kevy wait here for me."

"No way Dad," Mick answered shaking his head.

Mike turned around in seat and growled, "listen to me hot-shot, you're gettin' in way over your head here. I'm just beginning to figure out what's going on, and if it's as much as I think it is…It's twice as much as you can handle."

The minute the words left Mike's throat, he wished them back.

There was a minute of angry silence from the back seat before his son exploded, "you know, that's why the fuck I went to Viet Nam, God damn you! You always thought I was a prissy, little Prescott wimp who didn't have the guts or balls to get my hands dirty or be able to handle myself. Well screw you Dad! Where the hell were you when I got the crap kicked of me at the Ringe High dance. Or in the locker room at South Boston Army Base Annex! Were you there holding my little lily-white Prescott hand when I was leading my squad across the those stinking rice paddies in 'Nam?! No! My men were looking at me to get 'em out of there Dad…me."

Mike opened the car door and slowly got out and stood on the sidewalk. Mick sat in the backseat, drawing in deep ragged breaths and biting the inside of his lip to keep from…

"Mick."

He could barely make out the word he thought he heard his father call from the sidewalk. It sounded almost…Soft.

"Mick," and he heard a word that neither he nor anyone else for that matter, had ever heard from 'Big Mike' McCarthy…" Please."

Mick got out of the Mustang and slowly closed the door as Kevin concentrated on studying the reflections of the street lights through the rain streaked windshield.

Mick stood in front of his father's silent hulking form while the sullen drizzle coated their faces and pooled in their eye sockets like cold wet tears.

"Mickey," Mike began in a low rumble, "when your mother and I got divorced…Well, I didn't…I couldn't. I mean I tried…I wanted to…dammit Mick!" Mike mumbled hoarsely, "do you know how much I cared about you…And how…proud I always was of you?"

There was silence…

It seemed to stretch away into the wet night.

After his own personal eternity, Mick looked into his father's face, shook his head and said flatly, "no Dad…I never did. I still don't."

Mike stood still for a moment and then shook his head. "No," he said heavily, "I guess you wouldn't."

They looked at one another.

"Mick," Mike said quietly," will you come with me then, and watch my back?"

There was a slight pause and finally his son said with a half smile, "sure Pop, lead the way."

CHAPTER 55

▼

Boston
Harrison Avenue
Chinatown
May 8,1968
2:11AM

"Danny stop!" Bridget snapped.

"Why?" Danny asked half annoyed and half amused, and as he downshifted.

"Because you pea-brained spalpeen, you're gonna' run right into the back of your brother's car at the end of the block!"

Danny pushed the clutch in and popped the stick shift down into first gear and as he headed for the curb

"Look," Bridget whispered back to Holly, "see, there's Mick and his Dad and Kevin. They're going into that restaurant."

Danny leaned back in the seat and lit a cigarette with the dashboard lighter.

"Put it out," Bridget said.

"Hey, who died and made you Queen of the frigging universe, "Danny snorted as he took a deliberately deeper drag.

Bridget smiled, reached over and plucking the cigarette from his lips, tossed it out the window, answering "I did Luv."

Danny stared back at her for a moment, and then laughed. "okay, 'Queenie', what now?"

Bridget looked at Danny and then at Holly, and finally at the entrance to the restaurant.

Slowly she turned back towards Danny and said softly, never taking her eyes off of the door that Mick, his Dad and Kevin had disappeared into, "Danny-Boy, do you think that place might have a back entrance?"

From the alley on the other side of the street, two pairs of eyes watched the twenty-year old from Southie and two girls climb out of Camaro, to go searching for the back entrance to the Dragon Palace .

But they didn't move out of the car. Not yet .

They knew exactly where that backdoor was.

$$* \qquad * \qquad * \qquad *$$

Boston's Chinatown
Dragon Palace Restaurant
May 8th 1968
2;14 AM

Mike pushed open the red and gold painted doors of the Dragon Palace Restaurant, and motioned Mick and Kevin inside .

It was very quiet…And very dark .

"Hey, Uncle Mike," Kevin said in an unusually quiet voice, "is this place even open?"

Mick pulled the piece of paper out of the right hand pocket of his leather bomber jacket and looked at it again. "Yeah," he said uncertainly, "this is the right address…I think."

"It is." Mike said with a flat finality.

"How can you be so sure Dad?" Mick asked.

"Because," Mike said as he started walking towards the red lamp lit bar off to the right, "I've been here before."

Mike pushed through the beaded curtains that separated the bar from the main dining room and heard them click and rattle back as Mick and Kevin pushed through them and stepped to either side of Mike.

All three men stood there trying to let their eyes adjust to the surrealistic red gloom, when a voice from behind them made all three jump.

"Hey, are you guys lost or did you just drop in for a late night 'Moo Goo Gai Pan'."

Mick spun around, his hands going up in automatic combat reflex defensive posture, but it was Kevin who found his voice first.

"Jesus Christ! Hey you scared the piss out of me girly! God damn…Don't go sneaking up on people like that."

The cute little Chinese teenager in the skin tight bellbottoms and beads, put her hands up to her pretty red lipsticked mouth and giggled.

"Whoa…Take a chill man! Boy do you guys ever spook easily. Besides it's me who should be nervous, what with you guys showing up here at 2:00 AM in the frigging morning!"

"Yeah?" said Kevin, his cocky 'McCarthy grin' coming back. "Do I make you nervous?"

"In your dreams man?" She quipped with a half smile.

"That'll be good enough for me," he answered and took a half step forward.

"Hey, hold your horses Romeo," the dark eyed little vixen answered as she daintily spun on one tiny booted foot and slipped under the entrance panel to the bar.

"The place is actually closed," she said in a mock stage whisper, "but maybe if 'Mr. blue eyes' here," she gave Kevin a slow sensuous wink," will ask me real nice, I might be able to scare up a couple of beers or something."

Mike took out his silver flask of Bushmills Irish Whiskey and took a long pull.

"Sure," he said, "if you've got a chaser for this, I might be persuaded."

Mick looked at the flask and said quietly, "I think I may need one too Pop."

Mike just nodded and passed him the flask.

Kevin, now immensely enjoying himself, leaned across the bar and took her tiny hands saying, "why angel, I'll go down on one knee and sing, 'When Irish Eyes are Smiling' if you like. Or maybe you could just bring that beer around to this side of the bar and tell me how you got to be so damn cute."

The girl giggled again and grabbing three Budweiser's out of the cooler said, "you know, that sounds like the best offer I've had all night."

She slipped around the bar and opened the cap of Kevin's beer with a flourish saying, "now I forget, which you were gonna' do first. Was it sing, or go down on one knee?"

Kevin laughed and pulled her towards him. "How about you just sit on this knee, and then I'll sing 'Irish eyes', just for you."

"Okay," she said surprising even Kevin as she wiggled her shapely little butt onto his left knee. "Sing away canary."

Mike sighed and moved forward to tell his nephew in no uncertain terms, that this had gone quite far enough when…

"Jasmine Lilly!" Followed by three sharp claps, snapped out like a whip across the darkened bar.

The teenage girl stiffened but didn't move off of Kevin's knee.

A severe form, clad in a somber black high collared dress, glided silently across the floor.

She stopped directly in front of the girl, who defiantly and with slow deliberation, put both of her arms around Kevin's neck.

The elder woman hissed out a string of harsh invective in Chinese but the girl just glared back at her with angry determination, and wrapped her arms tighter around Kevin.

Finally the woman turned to Kevin and in a barely controlled but icy voice said, "it is far past my young daughters bedtime. So you will release her so that she may go to her bed and think about what is the proper way for a decent young girl to behave."

The teenage girls eyes glistened with suppressed tears of rage and she stared at her mother with a look of hatred so intense that it froze the entire room for an instant.

Kevin jumped up off the barstool and said, "whoa…hey, like sorry lady…Ma'am, I mean…I didn't know like she was your daughter and everything…uh, how old did you say she was?"

"Kevin!" Mike snapped.

"Yeah, sure, Uncle Mike," and turning to the girl, whose face was now contorted with rage and humiliation, said, "hey babe…Jeez, sorry. I mean, maybe you can give me a call or something in a couple of years."

She never even looked at Kevin, but stared at her mother and said something cold and sharp in Chinese and without turning back, stalked out of the room.

The older woman's carefully powdered and painted face looked shaken for a moment and then with some effort, she regained her composure. She turned back to the three men and finally said calmly and without expression, "you are expected, follow me please" and walked through another beaded curtain at the back of the bar without looking back.

Mike gave an uneasy look at his son and nephew and raised his eyebrows.

Mick just shook his head as if to say, "hey, I'm not backing out now."

Kevin merely shrugged his shoulders and grinned.

Mike sighed and thought to himself "are you two just brave or stupid or both!"

"Well," he grinned to himself, "I guess it all does run in our bloody family," and he parted the beaded curtains and walked into the back room.

What he saw there, made them all stop dead in their tracks.

The room was empty. Except for…

Dennis Bannon and the hulking, beetle-browed Morrison, standing behind him, the left side of his suit jacket pulled back to display his holstered Smith and Wesson.

"Where is she you son of a bitch!" Mike spat, crossing the space that separated the ornate lacquered black and gold desk from the door, in three angry strides.

"Where's who? Michael darlin'," Bannon smirked using the phony, mocking brogue that he knew from long experience, was calculated to get under 'Big Mike's' skin and cause 'errors in judgment.'…Big time.

Like right now.

Captain Dennis Bannon watched with satisfaction as Mike stopped in front of the ornate desk and reached out a scarred-knuckled hand for him.

"Look but don't touch, McCarthy," Morrison growled from behind Bannon as he drew out the Smith and Wesson and thumbed the hammer back.

Mike stared back Morrison and while never taking his eyes from the face of Bannon's pet 'junk yard dog', rumbled in a voice almost too low to hear, "I'm not going to ask you again you bastard, and unless the next words coming out of your mouth tell me that my daughter is here…well and unharmed," Mike shifted his gaze to Bannon's eyes, "I'm gonna' reach down your slimy, weasel throat and rip your lying tongue out."

Morrison raised his .38 and made a great show of sighting the barrel straight at Mike's forehead.

Captain Bannon smiled and leaned back in the desk chair saying, "put it away Johnnie…Michael's just blowing off steam aren't you Michael?"

"Answer the question Bannon," Mike said quietly never lowering his gaze.

Bannon shook his head and smiled, "patience Michael, she's here.. . And well. And she will stay that way, provided…"

"Provided what?" Mike leaned forward and locked onto the precinct captain's eyes.

"Provided that you brought what you were told to bring."

"Which was?" Mike asked, unable to focus on anything except getting his daughter back.

"What they think I have Dad." Mick supplied from behind him.

"And do you?" Bannon asked still locked in Mike's hard stare.

Mike held up his hand without turning around to Mick, "not another word 'til we see Bronwyn…Now!"

There was silence as the two former co-workers and long time adversaries stared at one another.

In the end, it was Bannon who dropped his eyes and slowly nodded his head. He reached under the lacquered desk, pushed a hidden button and a portion of the red wallpapered wall behind him slid back.

CHAPTER 56

▼

Boston—Chinatown
Behind the Dragon Palace Restaurant
2:38AM

"That's it!" Jasmine Lily exploded, punctuating her declaration by shattering an empty beer bottle against the brick alley wall behind the restaurant.

"Hey, chill out Jazzy," Amy Chen admonished her best friend.

"Here," she said holding out the damp end of a slowly smoldering joint, "take a hit of this."

"Yeah and then take a chill babe," said Peter Wong as he slid off the overturned trash can he'd been sitting on.

He walked over to Amy and put his arm around her. Then turning back to the still fuming Jasmine Lilly he said, "hey if your old lady is still hassling you that much, why don't you just split and come with us. We can all crash over at Tommy Lee's place."

"I can't," Jasmine said sullenly shaking her head.

"Why not Jazzy?" Amy asked, putting an arm around her friend.

"Because…Oh crap, it's too hard to explain. There's just all lot of weird shit going on with things that are happening here and in the old country and some kind of hold that my cousin has got on us. Especially my sister—and I just can't leave her stuck in…" she waved her hand at the back door to the restaurant,

"All of this."

"OK Jazzy," Amy Chen began, "I still don't understand why you can't just…"

"Cool it!" Her boyfriend interrupted.

Jasmine and Amy paused and followed Peter's pointing finger to the alley entrance.

Peter pulled them back into the shadows next to the brick wall and all three watched as another trio crept down the alley as if looking for a...

The tallest of the three, stopped in front of the restaurant back entrance. He motioned the other two shadows to join him, and as they moved into the weak light over the door, Jasmine and her friends saw that there were two girls and a tough looking red-haired Irish kid. He eased the door open, waved them inside, and closed it behind him with a click.

Amy, Peter and Jasmine waited for a minute before Jasmine sighed and said, "thanks for listening guys, but I'd better get back inside and see what the hell is going on now. I'd really like to..."

"Shush!" Peter hissed, covering her mouth with his hand, and then whispered in her ear..." Look!"

Jasmine Lilly followed his eyes down the alley again to where two more shadows materialized out of the darkness. As they watched silently, a fat and skinny shadow stepped into the tiny pool of light and opened the restaurant's back door.

Amy and Peter were momentarily startled when Jasmine drew a sharp intake of breath.

"What is it Jazzy?" Amy asked her friend.

Jasmine Lilly looked at her two friends, and then back at the door, her eyes growing cold and calculating as she slowly said, "I know those two. They've been here before...To meet with my cousin. And they were here with another man." Jasmine gave a small involuntary shudder but continued on in the same hard, calculating tone. "A man with cold, dead eyes. A man they called...Sloan."

∗   ∗   ∗   ∗

Boston
Chinatown
the dragon Palace restaurant
2:43 AM

"Welcome, Mr. Private Investigator McCarthy...and family," a well controlled voice with a slight lilting accent, spoke from the back of the room that was locked in shadows.

"Ling." McCarthy said without expression.

"Please—please, come in," the smiling man in the expensive Hong Kong tailored suit said, "and bring your nephew and your very...busy and 'inquisitive', son."

"Please…sit." Mr. Ling motioned.

Mike held out both arms and pushed them back against Mick and Danny's chests.

He shook his head and without taking his eyes off Ling said, "where is she?"

"Ah, your lovely daughter," he smiled.

"She'll be delivered when we have our 'package'. "Ling's smile remained fixed but his voice grew cold as he looked at Mick and said," you have brought it, yes young McCarthy?"

"What do you think, I'm an idiot?" Mick lied. "You produce Bronwyn and I'll tell you where it is."

Ling's eyes remained hard for a moment, and then relaxed slightly as he shrugged and called over his shoulder, "very well…Ritchie, 'produce' Bronwyn."

The large room that had been illuminated by only a single red shaded lamp next to Ling, suddenly glowed to life over his left shoulder.

All three McCarthy's gave a start forward, before they were stopped by the sounds of multiple pistol hammers being cocked as Bannon and Morrison drew their guns and Ling raised a Russian made automatic from his lap.

"Hasty actions, will certainly not help the lovely young Bronwyn, will they McCarthy's," Ling smiled pointing the automatic at Mike's chest.

"Isn't that right Ritchie?" He called over his left shoulder.

"Oh absolutely right," came the mocking response as the three McCarthy's watched in helpless, frustrated horror.

Ling had 'produced' Bronwyn all right, Mick thought, as he clenched and unclenched his fists. Except, she was trussed up like a Christmas turkey, tied to a chair that was balanced precariously on a three foot, round pedestal table. But what froze Mick, his father and cousin in their tracks, were not the three guns pointed at them, but the fact that Ritchie Feng's foot rested on the edge of the small table that he was gently rocking back and forth with the tip of his shiny black leather loafers. And every time he did, the rickety chair that Bronwyn was tied to, gave a protesting squeak and a tiny slip.

All three stood there. Frozen with a helpless dread as Bronwyn's eyes pleaded with them while her mouth worked frantically against the gag taped over it.

Ritchie laughed and gave the wobbling table another small nudge.

Mick clenched his fists so tight that he barely felt the blood start from underneath his fingernails.

All three pairs of McCarthy eyes focused in horror, on the thin red silk cord that stretched tautly from the overhead light fixture, to a tight loop around Bronwyn's slender white neck.

There was silence in the dark cavernous room, except for the sound of heavy breathing and shuffling feet.

Finally Mike spoke, "if anything happens to her Ling, I swear by all of the Saints in heaven, I'll hunt you down and rip out your heart."

Ling only smiled back and answered nonchalantly, "I'm afraid not, 'Mr. Private Investigator' McCarthy…Not unless you can get a visa to the glorious People's Republic of China. Which is something that I think we can both agree, you will find it impossible."

Mick shot back at Ling, "O.K. and conversely, how do you expect to get out of this country when we'll have every government agency combing every rat hole for you!"

"I'm glad you asked, young McCarthy," Ling answered, "s a matter of fact, I've retained the services of a very respected, old Boston law firm to arrange all of the paper work. Please correct me if I'm wrong, but I believe that you already know them." He pressed another hidden button and another light went on in the right hand corner of the room.

"Frankie!" Mick gasped.

"Michael, Dad!" Francis McCarthy Prescott called before a black glove hand holding a Browning automatic pulled him back into the shadows.

And, "Ling continued," while I have no doubt as to your esteemed brothers ability, just to insure complete success, I've also retained the wholehearted cooperation of the two senior members of the firm."

Ling barked a brief command in Chinese and Charlton Elliott and Preston Hayward stumbled into the light.

Mick looked at them and said in disbelief, "you're doing this for money?"

"Only the esteemed Mr. Hayward," Ling supplied to Mick's question. "Mr. Elliott has another reason. Somewhat similar to your own, young McCarthy."

He clapped his hands together twice and the light in the corner grew at a shade brighter, revealing another girl tied to a chair. Page Elliott!

She looked at Mick and then to her father with frantic, panicked eyes and tried to yell something but she was gagged like Bronwyn. But unlike Bronwyn, the chair that she was tied to, rested firmly on the floor.

"Yes," Ling answered Mick's unspoken question, "it was not necessary to subject Miss Elliott to the same form of restraint and threats as your rather uncooperative sister.

We found Miss Elliott to be far more...Sensible."

"And now," Ling said, "as pleasant as this little interlude has been, it is time that we concluded our business. You will bring me the sample of Golden Bowl that you stole from the MIT laboratory. We will release your sister, and all will be well."

Mick looked around stalling for time...Time to think of the way out of this.

"OK, but first one question. Since so many people have died for it, I'd like to know...just what the hell is Golden Bowl?"

Ling was silent for a moment and then shrugged his shoulders as if to say, 'why not?'.

"Very well," he began, "I'm sure you remember your part in locating a very extraordinary young student, deep in the jungles of Vietnam in June of 1966."

"June 15th," Mick whispered with a shudder.

"Exactly," beamed Ling, "well that young man had been developing very special strains of rice for the government of Vietnam. He succeeded admirably. Producing a genetically altered rice that had the potential to triple the output of rice production and end the specter of starvation in Southeast Asia forever. However, unknown to the Vietnamese government, but very well observed by our agents, the new altered strain of rice had another highly unique and potentially even more valuable side effect."

Ling paused and looked at Mick. "You are familiar I'm sure, with the drug that is now so popular with your spoiled younger contemporaries, Lysergic Dymethistd Acid?"

"L S D," Mick responded. "...Acid."

"Precisely," Ling nodded."

"Well, we found that when a fungus was cultured from this new rice and administered in even small doses, it had the most remarkable effect of turning a contrary, individualistic population, into docile but disciplined workers or soldiers. Ready to obey unquestioningly all commands of authority."

"So that's what this is all about?" Mick said shaking his head in disbelief, "trying to turn your poor starving peasants into mind numbed robots?"

"What do you mean, 'trying'?" Ling smiled without mirth.

"And do not be so glib about our poor starving peasants. They have already come to appreciate the 'Glorious Revolution' of the proletariat, and with the perfection of Golden Bowl, even the few still dissident voices, will be brought into line. No," he continued, "all our young people are already on the right path. It is the vain, spoiled selfish children if this country, that Golden Bowl is intended for."

"Yeah, well you're a friggin' moron," Kevin McCarthy yelled from the other side of Mike, "if you think that guys like me and Mick would take that crap and let some commie SOB like you, boss us around!"

"Oh but obstreperous McCarthy nephew, that is exactly what I think. And contrary to your loud protestations, it is been proven very successful...On your own cousin and his men in Vietnam."

"That night in the village," Mick whispered, feeling sick to his stomach.

"Yes, Ling smiled," thanks to the invaluable assistance of my esteemed comrade."

A black-gloved figure with dead white skin and coal-black, lifeless doll's eyes stepped out of the shadows.

Sloan.

Sloan stood there silently. Half of his bone white face in the light, the other half in the shadows.

"So you were behind that twisted 'special opp' and the massacre in the village," Mick said through gritted teeth.

"Yes,' Sloan replied in a low emotionless voice.

"And," Mick continued suddenly remembering what he just realized were the still lingering effects of the insidious drug, "it was your voice on the phone last week when...When..."

Mick felt his rage ready to boil over as he remembered the phone call and the commanding voice. And how he'd almost murdered the girl he loved.

"You bastard!" He exploded and took two steps forward.

"No!" Sloan's voice snapped out like a whip and was punctuated by a single shot from the Browning automatic.

Mick stopped short and looked at the smoking bullet hole in the wooden floor, just inches from the toe of his right cowboy boot.

"The next one goes through your knee," Sloan said quietly.

Mick strained to hold himself back. "Ok, let's stretch a point and pretend that I believe you. Who was it on the phone that night?"

Sloan's face twitched into something that might have been interpreted as a smile and said, "You already know the answer to that Sergeant. The same person that gave you the order that you obeyed in the jungle."

"Yeah," Mick breathed bitterly, "who else, the mother fuckin' colonel."

CHAPTER 57

▼

Boston
High Street
2:51 a.m.

"Take a left at the next light captain," the low voice rumbled.

"Yes sir," came the terse reply.

The sole occupant of the back seat said nothing.

"All right young McCarthy, we have answered your questions," Ling said, his voice becoming terse, "as much as we ever will and in more detail than is probably good for you. So now without any further delay, you will tell me where the sample is or. ." Ling looked at Ritchie over his left shoulder, "your pretty sister will have a tragic encounter with Newton's inescapable law of gravity."

Ritchie gave the small table a sharp push and Bronwyn's chair teetered precariously backwards on two legs. The silk cord cut into Bronwyn's neck and she gave a muffled scream as the chair started to tip over.

Before any of the three McCarthy's could react, Ling clapped his hands sharply once.

Ritchie reached out, caught the back of the chair and slowly pushed it upright.

"I will wait ten seconds. Then I will clap my hands again. This time Ritchie will not catch the chair."

Mick could feel the sweat ran down the back of his T-shirt, as his muscles clenched involuntarily against the bundled lump of the test tube inside of his jacket.

"It's back in Cambridge," he blurted out.

"I left it with Danny at the Oxford Alehouse tonight. Go and call your goons, I know they were following me. They'll tell you that I was there."

"That will not be necessary," Ling grinned without warmth, "you can ask them yourself."

Mick drew in a deep breath as Ling, still smiling his cat-like smile at Mick, called to the back of the room, "Mr. Tony?…Or should I say, 'Mr. Goon'" He gave a small chuckle. "Was young Mr. McCarthy at the Oxford Alehouse tonight?"

"Yeah," Mr. Ling, 'Fat Tony'answered stepping into the light, "the little prick sure was."

"And," Ling continued in a silky voice laced with menace, "did he leave something with his cousin and two female companions?"

"I don't know Mr. Ling. Why don't we take a look for ourselves."

"Oh Christ," Mick moaned to himself, "can it get any worse?"

It did.

He looked on helplessly as Danny, Holly and Bridget were pushed stumbling and blinking into the center of the room.

*   *   *   *

Boston
Dragon Palace Restaurant
May 8, 1968
3:07 a.m.

The red and gold painted door to the restaurant was locked, but that was no impediment to the man from Washington. He'd come up against locked doors before. Plenty of them.

In less than half a minute, he swung the heavy front door open and said, "Captain, after you."

He stepped aside as the captain and the other two officers who he'd instructed to meet them there, walked into the darkened front entrance.

The man from Washington followed close behind and then stopped as he heard the sound of voices coming from the cocktail lounge.

Putting his forefinger in front of his lips for silence, He motioned the captain and his charges to follow him towards the voices.

Slipping through the beaded curtains with surprising grace for such a large man, he produced a pocket flashlight and snapped it on to two young Chinese girls, conversing in low, rapid tones at one of the far tables.

"Ladies," he rumbled pleasantly, "I believe we have some business at a 'conference' currently under way in one of your back rooms."

The two girls looked panicked, but the man from Washington only smiled and said, "so we'd be much obliged if you could show us the way."

Something in the big man's eyes, made both girls reluctantly get up from the table and slowly walk towards the back of the lounge.

The man followed close behind and said with a soft chuckle, "and don't bother announcing us. We'll take care of that ourselves."

———————————

"And now young McCarthy, since Mr. Tony and Mr. Bingie have so thoughtfully delivered your three companions from your quaint 'Alehouse' tavern, you could help us conclude our business by instructing them to produce our property."

Ling's eye's bore into Mick's as he said, "I believe that you said you left it in the care of your other cousin…Danny is his name?"

He gestured to Bingie who poked a .380 automatic into Danny's ribs and snarled, "give it up punk."

Danny turned his head towards Bingie and snorted, "Fuck you."

Bingie's right hand traveled in a short savage arc as he backhanded Danny on the left side of his head with the heavy barrel of the big automatic. Danny staggered back and Bingie shoved the .380's muzzle under Danny's jaw and hissed, "try it again, asshole!"

Danny sucked the blood running down his cheek and spat it back into Bingies face. "I said, fuck you!"

He slammed the pistol into the back of Danny's head and Danny went down. Hard.

"Enough!" Ling snapped. "Mr. Tony, search them. And start with…" He looked at Mick and then gestured with his chin towards Bridget…"Her."

Tony gave Ling a nod, then turned to Bridget with leering grin and said, "come 'ere chickie."

Before Bridget could even react, Tony reached out with one meaty paw and ripped her blouse down the front.

Bridget screamed and tried to twist away but Tony just laughed and clamped a beefy arm around her throat as the other fondled her breast through the torn blouse.

"Let's see if you've got anything hidden in here," he laughed.

"God damn you!" Mick roared and took three rushing steps towards Tony before a shot rang out. Mick took another stumbling half step and looked down his right leg in disbelief. There was a small round hole just above his kneecap and a red blossom of blood was spreading down the right leg of his jeans.

"I warned you," Sloan said holding the smoking Browning automatic that was still trained on Mick.

"No!" Bridget screamed and tried to run to Mick.

Mick gave one last lurching step towards her before his leg gave way and he toppled to the floor.

"Please Mickey…Please," she sobbed still held fast in Tony's grip, "please, don't let them hurt you any more. Give them what ever it is they want."

"I'd advise you to listen to your young lady sergeant, because the next bullet is going to go right between her pretty green eyes."

"I don't think so Mr. Sloan," a low commanding voice, laced with steel, called from the other side of the large room.

Sloan's gun stayed fixed on Bridget but his eyes slowly move towards the sound of the voice.

"Stay out of this," he snapped back, "this isn't your operation."

"It isn't yours any more either Sloan, "the man from Washington said as he advanced into the lighted center of the room," you're under arrest for treason."

The room was silent for a moment and then Sloan grinned a death's-head grin, took two steps over to Bridget and put the Browning to the side of her head.

"The sample Sergeant," he said.

Mick looked at Bridget. Then at his blood, pooling on the floor underneath him.

He reached into his inside jacket pocket, pulled out the test tube, unwrapped it from the Kleenex and rolled across the floor to Sloan.

Ling quickly got up and scooped up the test tube.

He was just about to put it into his pocket when Sloan held out his hand and said, "no Ling. This is where it belongs."

"But we had agreement?" Ling said in disbelief. "Your inner circle and my government. One Supreme order to mark the rule of the proletariat."

Sloan just shook his head. "The bargain has been changed. We decided that we'd rather rule own proletariats by ourselves. You've got your 'proletariats' pretty well under control," he said sardonically, "but we've got a long way to go with ours, so let's just say that we need this more than you."

Ling shook his head and started to back away.

Sloan moved the barrel of the gun towards Ling and said, "put it in my hand...now, or the People's Republic will be decorating another hero...Posthumously."

Suddenly there was the unmistakable clank of the slide being drawn back on an old army model 1911 Colt .45 automatic pistol and a broken tortured voice croaked out, "no Sloan. It's over. This is where all ends. Finally."

Sloan turned and looked into the haunted eyes of the colonel

Sloan looked at the colonel and was shocked by what he saw. The man had the pallor and waxen features of a day old corpse. His face twitched uncontrollably and his eyes blazed with something that was close to madness. But the hand that held the enormous old Colt .45, was rock steady.

The shell of the former commander stared at Sloan and began to speak in a low tormented monotone. "You have destroyed and corrupted everything you've come in contact with. But I have only myself to blame for letting you seduce me with your lies about glory and power. I should have realized that you were an insane megalomaniac that first day you approached me with the details of operation 'Paper Dragon'. But I was ambitious. I was only a colonel and I wanted to be a general, so I deluded myself into believing your lies, instead of recognizing them for the treason that they were.

"As you've said before colonel, fortunes of war," Sloan said with contempt and added. "why don't you stop whining and try to act like the soldier that you never were."

The colonel's already deathlike pallor turned a chalky white.

"Yes," he rasped, "you're right. I should just suck it up and bear my inescapable guilt like a man. And I could do it, because as you say, I'm guilty too. But what I can't forget, or forgive either you or myself, is your crime and my eternal shame of letting you convince me to drag my daughter into this...this abomination. And for that," the colonel said his voice rising, "we both deserve to die. But," the colonel continued, pulling his lips back from his teeth in the parody of a grin, "you first Sloan."

He pulled the trigger .

In the same instant, Sloan whirled his gun towards the colonel, but when the Colonel had surprised him, Sloan had been caught with the barrel of his automatic pointing half way between Bridget and Ling. And now, before even his lightning fast reflexes could focus and fire, the heavy slug from the colonel's .45 caught him right in the chest. The blast lifted Sloan off his feet and he fell back inches from where Mick lay in a pool of his own blood .

The room erupted into chaos .

The colonel rotated the barrel of the .45 until it pointed underneath his right ear. Then he called softly to someone still hidden in the shadows of the back of the room. "Please forgive me. I am so, so sorry."

But before he could pull the trigger, Ling, sensing an advantage in the confusion, issued a staccato string of commands in Mandarin.

"Ritchie…Kill them all!"

"Madam Wu, bring your daughters and follow me…Now!"

Ling switched back to English and turned towards the door, shouting,

"Captain Bannon, we are leaving and…" His voice trailed off as he realized that Bannon and Morrison were gone.

In those few seconds, Ritchie had reached behind him and pulled an AK-47 from an open packing crate. He slapped the curved magazine into place and looked up at Bronwyn still tied to the chair, silken rope around her neck.

"So long sweet thing," he grinned, "too bad we never got to know one another better," and he kicked the table out from under the chair.

From ten feet away, Mike gave a bellow and with Kevin close behind him, charged Ritchie.

"OK, you next Pops," Ritchie spat with contempt and leveled the automatic weapon at Mike.

But before he could squeeze off a round, a tall cadaverous figure crossed the room and grabbed the AK-47's muzzle.

"Back off old man," Ritchie snarled and pulled the trigger.

A stream of bullets ripped through the colonel's abdomen, but his hand closed around the muzzle with a death grip and held on. At the same instant, Mike reached the toppling table and caught the chair and Bronwyn in a bear like grip. "Kevin, cut the rope," he gasped.

Kevin pulled out his pocketknife and slashed the cord in one swift movement, while Mike gently lowered his daughter to the floor.

At the same time, Ritchie was still trying to free the barrel of his gun from the dying colonels grip.

Suddenly another higher pitch shot rang out and the colonel staggered forwards, falling onto Ritchie.

Madam Wu walked to the center of the room and waved the still smoking small caliber Beretta .25 that she held in her right hand, at the rest of the room. She looked over Ritchie who had finally managed to free the barrel of the AK-47 from the dying colonel's grip and said, "Ritchie finish them. Jade...Jasmine!" She snapped, "come, we are leaving!"

The two girls began to follow her, but as she turned towards Ling and the door, she felt a numbing slap on her right hand and the small Beretta was twisted from her grip. She spun around and stared in disbelief as she looked straight into the muzzle of the .25 that was now held in the shaking hand of her eldest and most obedient daughter...Jade!

"What are you doing?" She hissed. "You must come with me. We will become high officials in the People's Republic. We will have power, and the wealth that such power brings."

"No, my mother," Jade said in a steady voice, "you will have power. We will be what we have always been...your servants. I have finally come to agree with my sister, that true freedom for us to become whatever is that we want to be, is here in this unruly and individualistic country. Not in a place of mind-numbed robots and slaves."

Madam Wu looked at her two rebellious daughters with hatred and her eye's sought Ritchie's. "Do as Ling says," she hissed, "finish them...And I mean, all of them."

But before Ritchie could even raise the AK-47, Jade whirled with the speed and determination that no one would've expected of her, and shot her cousin right through the center of his forehead.

Jade turned back to her mother and eyes bored into hers as she said, "my sister and I are leaving now mother. I do not think that we will ever see you again." They walked past their stunned mother and Ling and disappeared out through the door.

"Boys," the man from Washington called to Kevin and Danny, "if you wouldn't mind giving me hand, you could put these on a 'Mutt and Jeff here," and tossed two sets of handcuffs to Danny who had gotten up from the floor and was dusting himself off.

At the same moment, Bridget sank her pearly white, tiny, but very sharp teeth, into 'Fat Tony's' arm. He screamed with pain and let go, which was all Bridget needed. She spun around and with every ounce of strength and her five-foot-two inch form, kneed him squarely in the balls

Tony's yowl of pain rose to soprano pitch and he dropped to the floor clutching himself.

"That's fer me blouse, ya' dirty lump of lard," she said over her shoulder as she ran and kneeled beside Mick.

Her rage evaporated as she saw the blood on the floor and the pain in his wavering eyes.

"Oh my God darlin', what have they done to you?"

Mick tried to focus his eyes. Then Bridget saw that he was desperately trying to speak. Trying to tell her something.

"Hush darlin'," she soothed. "It's gonna' be all right, your dad's gonna' be calling an ambulance, and…"

"Bridge," Mick finally managed to croak pulling himself painfully half upright," behind you!"

Bridget swiveled her head from her kneeling posture and stared with horror into the muzzle of the Browning automatic pistol held in the blood drained, but still steady hand of Sloan.

Like a hard to kill cockroach, he raised himself up on his elbows and aimed the Browning squarely at Mick and Bridget.

Mick tried to pull Bridget behind him, to shield her.

He closed his eyes and a shot rang out.

He slowly opened them to find Bridget looking back at him.

They weren't dead.

Cautiously he raised his eyes up past the prone body of Sloan who was lying face down, the back of his head blown off.

Mick's bewildered eyes finally focused on the feminine figure in a captain's uniform standing behind Sloan, holding the still smoking army model 1911 Colt .45.

"That's for you Dad," she said quietly.

Mick could only stare in disbelief.

Starr!

EPILOGUE

▼

Cambridge—Mount Auburn Hospital
May 8, 1968
11:52 PM

"McCarthy," a voice rang out. "Report Sergeant!"

Mick felt panic. He didn't know what he was supposed to say. He couldn't remember the mission. What was it that he needed to do? He needed to save his men.

No, they were all dead.

Save First Lieutenant Steve Benson. Boomer.

No, he was dead too.

What the hell was he supposed to do?

He called for the Angel…Again.

And she came…again.

Mick looked up at her and asked for the millionth time since Vietnam, "what should I do? Where is the end?"

This time the Angel smiled and said, "you don't need me anymore Michael, the answer is standing right in front of you."

She kissed him on the forehead and said, "goodbye…Everything will be all right." And disappeared…Forever.

Mick opened his eyes and saw another angel standing in front of his hospital bed…Bridget.

. . . .

People's Republic of China
Beijing
People's Court Tribunal
May 10, 1968

"Comrade Ling!" The harsh voice of the People's Court advocate general rang out.

"You stand accused of treason and collaboration with the running dog capitalist pigs of the degenerate democracy of America. How do you plead?"

Ling wiped a bead of sweat from his upper lip and leaned forward into the cheap courtroom microphone, "please Mr. People's Advocate, I am a loyal comrade and follower of our illustrious chairman. Ask my partner and colleague, Madam Wu."

The chief judge advocate put his hand over the microphone and said something to the other party appointed judges. One by one, they nodded their heads. Finally the chief advocate turned back to the now profusely perspiring Ling and said, "there is no need, 'former comrade Ling'. We are all agreed. Both of your fates are fixed."

Young students wearing the armbands of Red Guard units, appeared on either side of them. They all filed out into the brick courtyard. There were a pair of shots and then...Silence.

*   *   *   *

Prides Crossing
Boston's North Shore
May 10, 1968
11:58 PM

The flames of the enormous open fireplace cast bizarre, twisted shadows on the cold marble floor of the big empty living room in the big empty house.

A solitary figure sat in the lone wingback chair in front of the sputtering logs and stared deep into the flickering flames.

She listened for a moment, but the house was silent. Everything there was dead and gone.

She idly fingered the silver and gold medal, that the man from Washington had placed around her neck two days ago.

She slipped the ribbon over her head and held the medal out in front of her for a moment. Then with a shake of her head and snort of disgust, she threw it into the fireplace.

She stared blankly as the medal's red, white and blue ribbon, smoldered and burst into flames.

She sat there staring into the flames for a long time, and then slowly got up and went into her lavishly appointed bedroom.

The minutes of the cold empty house ticked away, measured only by the unfeeling, grandfather clock in the walnut paneled hallway.

Finally she reappeared.

But she looked different.

She was dressed in skintight bellbottoms, a low cut macramé peasant blouse and long painted purple fingernails.

She sat down once again in the solitary wing-back chair in front of the dying fire.

She slipped a photograph of a smiling young man with short blond hair, from a silver frame.

She held it in front of her for a moment and gently kissed it.

"I'm so sorry baby," she said in a husky pain filled voice.

She picked up her only real legacy from her father. She put the Army Model 1911 Colt .45 to the side of her head, closed her eyes and pulled the trigger. There was a sharp crash.

Then the sea damp silence filled the sad gray house again.

*   *   *   *

Inman Square
Cambridge, Mass.
May 11th 1968
10:42 a.m.

"Wake up ya' lazy thing!" was the way that Mick's Wednesday began.

The command was followed immediately by a slap on his pajama clad rump as Bridget passed by the bed and let the shade up with a loud stuttering snap.

Mick blinked owlishly as he stared at her petite form silhouetted against the sunlit bedroom window of their third floor apartment.

"Well," Bridget asked putting one hand on her shapely little hip, "are you gonna' loll about in bed all day, just because you have one little bullet hole in your leg?"

She quickly crossed over to the bed and gently sat on the edge of the mattress, smoothing his hair back from his forehead.

"Does it still hurt much Luv?" She asked, her flashing green eyes turning soft.

"Not half as much as it's gonna' after I pull you down here beside me and make mad passionate love to you," he grinned wrapping his arm around her shoulders and pulling her sweet little pixie face next to his.

He drank in the sight of her high cheekbones, pale skin, strikingly offset by jet black hair and sparkling green eyes.

He kissed her gently at first, then a little harder on her soft responsive lips and felt her velvet soft cheek against the sandpaper stubble of his unshaven face.

"Mickey," she said, "we can't...I mean your leg won't be fully healed for another three weeks the doctor said, and..."

"Ha!" Mick interrupted, "you think I'm gonna' wait that long? Hell I'll go back to the hospital today and tell them to cut it off if that's gonna' be a problem!"

"Oh darling don't do that," Bridget said raising her eyebrows in mock horror. "They might get carried away and cut off the wrong thing. And then I'd have to find myself a new lover!"

"Have no fear in that department my dear," Mick laughed pulling her closer to him. "Come 'ere, let me show you!"

"Well it looks like someone is sure as hell feeling a whole lot better," Michael McCarthy's gravel voice rumbled from the bedroom doorway.

"I knocked but I guess you were...ah, busy," he said with an uncharacteristically gentle and amused smile.

Bridget jumped off the bed and began unconsciously smoothing the front of her skirt with small, embarrassed movements of her hands.

Mick didn't know whether to be mad or glad or both. He finally managed to squeak out..." Dad...ah, good to see you."

"Yeah, I'll bet," Mike answered cynically and then surprised Mick with a smile and a wink.

"I just came by to see how you were doing, but I guess you're doing just fine."

Bridget blushed and Mick propped himself on one elbow and pointedly changed the subject.

"What've you got there Dad?" He asked pointing to a bundle poking out of his father's hand.

"Oh," Mike said handing a large bundle of letters to his youngest son. "I brought up your mail. It was spilling out all over the floor."

"Yeah," Mick said, "I guess I've been kind of preoccupied lately."

His father smiled wryly and said, "yeah, I guess I'd call saving yer' sister's life and taking an 9 .mm slug in the leg, 'preoccupied'!"

"Hey Pop," I was just riding back-up for you that night." Mick protested.

"Balls," his father retorted and added with a grin, "remember, McCarthy's don't go in for false modesty."

"OK." Mick responded with a mirror image grin of his own, "I was a flaming hero!"

"Well you've got the flamin' part right anyway," Mike laughed back.

"You know," he added after a moments pause, "I always used to sort of wish that you'd be a little more like your brother Frankie. You know, a lawyer or some such thing. Now. . Well, I just want you to know Mick, how proud I am of you."

There was silence for a moment.

Finally Mick answered in a husky voice, "thanks Dad."

Mike looked down at the floor. Finally Mick cleared his throat and asked, "so speaking of Frankie, how is he, and what happened? I got bits and pieces of it in the ambulance, but it was all kind of confused."

"I shouldn't wonder," Mike said shaking his head. "Well before they gave any statements, Hayward made a call to city hall and it looks like Hayward, Elliott and Delbert's part in the whole sorry mess, is at least gonna' stay out of the papers. Your brothers gonna' stay working for them too, but I think he's got a little different perspective on corporate law then he did a week ago.

Oh, "Mike laughed," I almost forgot the best part. Remember that little blond slip of the girl that was hostage with Bronwyn that night? Elliott's daughter I think she was. She sat next to you at that birthday party of your mother's.

I think her name was…Peggy?"

"Paige." Bridget said in a cold flat voice.

Mick looked at the ceiling.

"That's right," Michael went on, unaware, "Paige. Well anyway, I spoke to your brother last night and he said he was taking her to dinner, so that they could 'comfort' one another. All I can say, is that I hope he's careful with his 'comfort'," Mike laughed.

Mick looked relieved and said, "I think they're gonna' make the perfect couple together." He looked up at Bridget's stony face and added, "don't you agree Bridge?"

He watched as her expression softened and she sat back down on the bed beside him and replied, "yes darlin', I do," and kissed him on the cheek.

Mick squeezed her shoulder and turned back to his father saying, "as long as we're tying up loose ends Dad, what happened to the 'ugly twins'?"

"Oh you mean the skinny and fat punks?" Mike responded with a snort.

"Well it seems that Sloan still had them on the army pay-role, so the 'Washington Man' had them court-martialed and they'll be doing 30 years hard labor in Leavenworth!"

"What about your old pals Pop. Bannon and Morrison?"

Mike shook his head.

"Ah, well the wheels of justice sometimes seem to turn a bit slowly, and that pair of weasels slipped out before the Boston P.D. boys showed up, so nothing could be proven conclusively. But...It seems as though that 'Washington Man' has some friends in pretty high places. So me and him had a nice little 'chat' while the Boston PD was mopping things up. And you'll never guess what interesting news I heard just this morning from one of my old friends down at Precinct Eight.

"What Pop?' Mick asked with a grin.

"Why it seems that these two old boyo's from the old neighborhood, have a pair of new assignments .

Dear old Dennis Bannon is gonna' be heading up a department of one as a sergeant in charge of Cambridge bicycle registrations and 'former' Detective Johnny Morrison is right now getting fitted for a new pair of walking shoes for his new assignment of school crossing guard, in Dorchester."

Mick, Bridget and Mike all looked at one another for a moment and broke into spasms of laughter .

"Oh man," Mick said wiping his eyes, "that's just too perfect. Right Bridge?"

But Bridget had stopped laughing. She had almost finished going through the stack of mail on the bed, when she came to a letter written with violet ink in a looping feminine hand. She also thought she could smell a faint whiff of perfume clinging to the envelope. And with that unerring female sixth sense, she remembered where she had smelled it last.

She dropped the letter into Mick's lap and said in a tone that grew frostier with each syllable, "it looks like you got a letter...From Holly."

Mick nervously opened the envelope and then let out a sigh of relief, which he quickly turned into the aggrieved sigh of a 'man wrongly accused'.

"Look Bridge," he pointed out with an almost injured tone, "it starts out, *'Dear Mick and Bridget!'"*

Bridget's stern expression wavered and then evaporated completely as they read together…" *So after everything that has happened, I called Mommy and Daddy and told them that I wanted to come home. I didn't know what I was going to do there until a man from the army came to see me this morning. He said that Steve had kept up his GI life insurance and named me as the beneficiary. I couldn't believe it when he handed me a check for $50,000! But what made me cry and feel so happy all at the same time, was the note that was attached to it. It was written by Steve, to me, six months ago when he started to feel that things were going wrong. He said that if anything should ever happen to him, he wanted me to use this money to fulfill my dreams.*

Suddenly I realized that I still did want to be close to home and close to Mom and Dad, but I also want to keep something of me and Steve and this whole big exciting city, alive too. So I'm going back to Iowa…And I'm going to be opening up Iowa's first folk music club. It's going to be called, 'Benson's Coffeehouse and Folk Club'!

I hope that you'll both come to see me play some time!

Thank you so much for everything,

Love,
Holly

Bridget grabbed a tissue from the box next to the bed and sniffed, "that is very sweet, isn't it Mick."

"Yeah, babe," he answered, "that it is."

Mike had watched the two of them throughout this exchange and thought to himself, "they almost act like an old married couple sometimes…But I won't push it. They'll come to that decision in their own time."

Instead, he reached into his pocket and took out a folded piece of paper.

"Now it's my turn to ask a question," he said.

"According to this report that an anonymous, 'friend' from Washington sent me, it seems that our Mr. Ling and his 'comrade', a Madam Wu, got a very stormy and very unexpected reception from the 'People's Revolutionary Council' when they got back to Beijing. As a matter of fact, instead of having their chest filled with, 'Heroes of the People' medals, their chest's wound up being filled with several ounces of lead, up against a wall."

"How come Pop?" Mick asked.

Mike gave his son a penetrating stare before he lowered his eyes to the report again

"It seems that the sample that Ling brought back was useless."

"Really?" Mick said raising his eyebrows.

"Yes," Mike said not looking up. "When they tested it, they founded been 'contaminated' by some foreign substance and that all the spores were dead."

"Foreign substance?" Mick asked innocently

"Yeah," Mike repeated and then paused before adding. "Alcohol…They think some kind of whiskey.

"Like Bushmills Irish whisky?" Mick grinned.

"Very well could be," Mike nodded.

He raised his eyebrows and looked at his son again.

"Do you remember when we got to the Dragon Palace?" Mick asked.

Mike nodded.

"And you remember when Kevin was flirting with that cute girl behind the bar?" Another nod.

"And she offered us a beer and you took a shot the way you always do whenever you have a beer. And then I asked for one too and you passed me the flask.

"So you…" Mike began.

"Yeah," Mick nodded, "I had just gotten some real bad vibes about 'Golden Bowl' and 'Paper Dragon' and I had this horrible feeling that we were walking into big trouble."

"So you…"

"That's right Pop. I decided to do a little 'East meets West' with 'Golden Bowl' and Mr. Bushmill. I guess things didn't work out between them," he grinned.

"No," Mike said shaking his head. "It worked out just fine."

"You know Mick." Michael Sr. said, "I know you'd never agree, but you'd make a great cop."

"Dad we've been over this before. I told you that I don't want to…"

Mike held up his hand.

"I understand and I'm not even sure as how I'd want you to take all that on. But you know, these last few weeks have started me thinking, and maybe I've come up with something that could be the best of both worlds."

He pulled a small box out of his left hand coat pocket and handed it to his son.

"Open it," he said

Mick opened the box and took out one of the simple black lettered business cards. He passed it to Bridget and she looked at it for a moment, then squeezed his hand and smiled. The card read; 'McCarthy and Son, Private Investigations'.

Mick looked up at his father's weather-beaten but hopeful face, and said in his best 'Bogey' imitation, "you know what Dad? I think that this is the beginning of a beautiful friendship."

Mick slipped his arm around Bridget's waist and said, "what do you think?"

Bridget looked at Mick's father, and then back at Mick and whispered…

"I think you're right Luv."

And kissed him, full on the lips.

THE END

*   *   *   *

Don't miss the next exciting' McCarthy Family Mystery"!...Newport Blues.
And watch for more 'McCarthy Family Mysteries' in these upcoming books;
"Cape Cod Girls", "Lay Down Your Weary Tune" and "Long Time Coming...Long Time Gone".

*   *   *   *

The novel 'Newport Blues', set in the turbulent but exciting year of 1968, is the second in the 'McCarthy Family Mystery' series.

In the first novel, 'Acid Test', we met the somewhat dysfunctional, usually eclectic and always interesting, McCarthy clan.

Michael McCarthy Senior, trying his 'Bull-in-a-China-Shop' best to look out for his headstrong offspring, is a former Boston beat cop, and now through forced retirement, a private detective operating out of a small office in Harvard Square Cambridge Massachusetts.

Michael Sr. has located his office there to be near his ex-wife (sort of) and three kids. Francis (Frankie) a young corporate lawyer, his only daughter Bronwyn, a freshman at Radcliffe College and Michael Jr. (Mickey) a Harvard dropout (now reinstated...sort of) and Vietnam Vet working through (sometimes successfully) the baggage and ghosts that followed him back from the jungles of Vietnam.

At the conclusion of the first novel, Acid Test, against all odds and expectations, Michael Sr. and Jr. reconciled their longstanding differences and formed 'McCarthy and Son Private Investigations'.

Now as the second novel of the series opens, Mick gets a phone call from an old Army buddy, who saved Mick's ass and his sanity in 'Nam.

It seems that the beautiful, pampered, pseudo-hippie daughter of a wealthy socialite family, summering in Newport Road Island, has turned up murdered and the last person to be seen with her...alive, is the cousin of Mick's old Army buddy, Smitty.

Mick owes Smitty 'a big one', so he offers to do what he can. He always does. But this time, his girlfriend and love of his life, Bridget, isn't going to let him do it alone.

Mick tries halfheartedly to persuade her to stay home in Cambridge. But he knows he's lost the war before the battle has even begun. You see, Bridget Ann Connelly, although attending a Radcliffe, one of the Ivy League's 'seven sisters', on a full academic scholarship, is both daughter and sister to an IRA father and son hit team.

And she doesn't ever take 'no' for an answer.

So backed by the last few bucks in the till of 'McCarthy and Son Private Investigations', Mick and Bridget fire up Mick's 750 BSA motorcycle and head off to Newport, to track down the real killer of the murdered girl, Blair Prentiss Vanderwall.

During the course of backtracking while trying to separate truth from innuendo and candor from jealousy, Mick and Bridget retrace the last few weeks of Blair's life from the marble mansions' of Newport to the free-flowing, free-love hippie crash pads of Falmouth Cape Cod.

But instead of presenting Mick and Bridget with a clear-cut picture of Blair Prentiss Vanderwall, each clue they uncover and person they interview, only seems to further muddy the water.

And as they prowl the vibrant, evolving pop/rock music scene in the smoke-filled bars of college kids on the Cape, to the folk and blues backstage at the 1968 Newport folk Festival, the mystery seems to grow deeper and darker.

Because rather than narrowing down the list of suspects until they're left with the one who killed the enigmatic girl, it seems that with every person they meet who knew Blair, the list of those who would have loved to wring her pretty little neck, continues to grow longer and longer.

Until, the question finally becomes not who would want to kill Blair Prentiss Vanderwall...But who wouldn't!

FROM "NEWPORT BLUES"

Chapter One
Falmouth Massachusetts
Cape Cod
'Father's Jazz and Folk Club'
July 25, 1968
10:13 p.m.

The smoke from hundreds of smoldering cigarettes and at least that many joints, swirled around the sweating, black folk\blues singer rasping out a hard version of 'Cocaine Blues'. It gave his dark craggy features a decidedly Mephistophelian look, Blair Prentiss Vanderwall mused and the thought gave her a delightful little shiver of well-concealed wicked speculation.

"What are you smirking about Blair?" asked her friend Valerie from across the tiny wine-wet table.

Blair didn't answer. She just took a deep languid drag from the innocuous looking Salem cigarette dangling between her left index and forefinger. She held the smoke in her lungs for a moment and let the mellow Acapulco Gold that they had replaced the tobacco with before they come to the club, free her mind to drift still a few more planes closer to her own personal nirvana.

The third girl at the table, Jackie (Jacqueline) Trainor, looked at Blair watching the stage and giggled to Valerie, "she's wondering what it would be like to make love to a…Black man."

The last two words were whispered, but they still would have made Valerie blush if she wasn't so concerned with losing her newly acquired "hippie cool".

The words had no such effect on Blair Vanderwall. In fact they only served to heighten her amusement…And excitement.

She loved the smoke and the smell of pot. The noise, the wine, the excitement…and the thrill of danger.

Blair Vanderwall especially loved the thought of "dangerous boys", and as she shifted her gaze to the long bar at the right of the stage, she saw pair of reckless and dangerous eyes staring back at her.

She drew another deep drag of the pot \ tobacco Salem cigarette and let the smoke slide out through her nostrils where it hung around her honey blonde hair like a wavering halo crowning one of Hell's cutest little angels.

The tall lanky guy at the bar pushed his sweat stained leather cowboy hat back on to his forehead and smiled at her.

Blair took the Salem out of her mouth and with the innocent/erotic look that she had perfected so well, slowly licked the outside of her upper lip.

She watched with the satisfaction of impending conquest as the denim shirt and faded-jeans guy, pushed his elbows off the bar, picked up his beer and walked towards their table.

Blair allowed herself a small smile while she looked into his smoky blue eyes as he closed the distance to her table.

They held the promise of new thrills, excitement…And danger!

*   *   *   *

Newport Neck Tennis and Beach Club
July 26, 1968
9:06 a.m.

"Come on Davy," four year-old Timmy Perkins whined at his older brother, "let me see."

"No," David answered back with a scowl. "Go back over to the sand castle and I'll be there in a minute."

As the 'Big Brother', David's Mom had drilled into him, he was expected to take charge, set an example…and above all, keep Timmy out of trouble.

And this, seven year-old Davy Perkins thought to himself, most definitely looked like trouble. Big trouble.

As David stared at the big pile of seaweed…and something else, Timmy began inching closer and reached out with his right hand to pull aside the long strands of green and brown seaweed that were almost covering something.

Something that was…

"Damn it Timmy!" Davy yelled, "I told you to go back over to the sand castle. Now get out of here!"

Timmy looked at his older brother for a moment and then his face crumpled and he let out a wail. "Mom! Mom!" He yelled running up the beach to where his mother had just finished lathering herself up with Johnson's Baby Oil, and was now comfortably settled into a beach chair with the latest Harold Robbins' novel.

Therefore, at the first familiar cry of, "Mom!" she only glanced up long enough to make sure that her youngest wasn't drowning and let her eyes drop back to the pages of her book.

But she should've known better. After the third insistent, "mom-my!" blasted at a four year-old eardrum splitting screech, she reluctantly put a finger between the pages of her paperback and looked up.

"What is it now Timmy?" she sighed.

"Davy's not being fair Mom!" Timmy gasped out stamping his foot.

"He said we should go look for seashells for the sand castle. And I did, but I didn't find any. "Timmy stopped only long enough to draw a breath and went on in a rush," and Davy found a whole big, giant, humongous, super-big pile of shells and all this seaweed and then when I came over to get some he told me to get away and go back to the sand castle and…and, "Timmy paused once more and then added triumphantly, "and he swore!"

His mother sighed again and shielding her eyes from the glare of the morning sun, looked down the beach at her oldest boy who was poking a big pile of seaweed with a stick.

Timmy followed his mother's gaze and said, "see, he's got a whole big pile of shells and stuff and he's hogging them all for himself ."

Timmy's mother looked at him again wondering if she was really going to have to leave this comfortable chair and Harold Robbins to deal with this.

Timmy sensed the indecision and with the tactician's skill, added the coup de gras, "Mom…He's not sharing."

That did it.

With the long-suffering sigh of beleaguered mothers everywhere, Mrs. Donald Perkins got up from a chair and still holding the paperback, walked down the beach to the harmony-shattering pile of seaweed.

"Really David," she called the she approached her eldest son. "I don't see why you can't let Timmy play with the silly seaweed too!"

She was starting to get annoyed. It always happens, she thought angrily, no sooner do I get a chance to sit down and read when one of them has some sort of a problem.

She looked down at the paperback novel and her hand and sighed to herself, "I was just getting to the good part too. That guy had just gone into that girl's apartment in Hollywood and found her sprawled on the bed and she was dea.. ."

She let the thought trail off as she watched her youngest son gleefully pulling shells out of the seaweed pile.

"Hey Davy," Timmy asked, his hurt appeased with the achievement of his goal, "what's this?"

"I told you Timmy," his brother answered with a worried frown, "leave it alone!"

Timmy suddenly stopped and ran to his mother.

Davy looked up at her, his eyes filled with seven year-old seriousness.

"Mom, I think there's something bad here."

His mother took two steps closer, bent down and picked up the stick. She hesitantly pushed two long strands of seaweed back from something…White.

"Oh no," she murmured, was this a dead sea gull? No, it was too big. A seal? No, it was too white. Good heavens, she shivered to herself, you don't suppose it was a shark?

"No," she mumbled peeling back a few more strands of seaweed, it was too thin to be a shark. It was thin and pale white and it had dozens strands of thick black fishing line wound tightly around it. She moved the stick a little higher and pushed away another clump of seaweed. She froze and the Harold Robbins novel dropped unnoticed from her fingers as life once again chose to imitate art.

She clapped her hand, still sticky with Johnson's Baby Oil and sand, over her mouth. But it still couldn't stifle the scream when she saw what the thin, slender white thing wrapped in dozens of strands of black fishing line, was attached to.

A slim neck. A bone white face, framed by blond, seaweed tangled hair and a pair of cold blue eyes that stared lifelessly back at her.

0-595-32982-9

CPSIA information can be obtained at www.ICGtesting.com
Printed in the USA
BVOW08s0907121115

426608BV00005B/37/P